PLAYING THE GHOST

PLAYING
THE
GHOST

A NOVEL

JOHANNA CRAVEN

AUSTRALIA, 1857

CHAPTER ONE

An accident, they say. Some poor fool trying to blast his way to glory by digging with black powder instead of a shovel. But we can all hear the whispers beneath. Those whispers that poor old Fred Buckley did this to himself. Tossed the explosives into his mining claim and leapt in there after them. Another failed attempt at fortune on the goldfields.

And now here we all are in the graveyard, gathered around the small wooden box containing all that's left of the man. I haven't seen inside myself, of course, but word is it contains a few brass buttons and a boot that was miraculously blown clear of the explosion.

I only met Buckley once or twice, but my husband Tom knew him well, their claims not far from each other's on the western edge of the Forest Creek gold diggings. The morning of Buckley's death, Tom said, he was heading out to start work when the explosion ripped through the air and made the ground move like sea.

The vicar murmurs a prayer, and down that sorry little

box goes into the ground. Buckley had no wife or children, so there are no tears at his grave, just curiosity, and a fairly ceaseless torrent of murmuring.

We traipse back down the hill after the burial, clouds of dust blooming beneath our boots.

"Well," says Leo Evans, "if you're going to do away with yourself, that's a damn spectacular way to do it."

"Aye," Ollie Cooper agrees. "Something with a bit of drama to it."

"Let's go to Martha's," says a leather-faced digger who's just introduced himself to us as Clyde. "Was poor old Fred's favourite place for a drink."

Martha's is a canvas-walled grog shop on the edge of the diggings, a remnant of the days when this place was nothing but a few holes in the ground, and outlawed drink was sold in the shadows. These days, the town's made of more solid stuff than canvas, but Martha's hasn't lost its pull over the locals.

"Lucy?" Tom asks me. "Do you want to go home?"

"No." I can't bear the thought of another stilted night in our cottage, where Tom and I make strained small talk before falling asleep with our backs to each other. "You knew Mr Buckley well. We ought to drink to him."

We pile into the carts and traps waiting outside the cemetery and rattle back towards Forest Creek. The sun is lying low over the hills, bathing the scarred landscape in shadow. Trees have been cut away in the scramble for gold, and the earth is a bleak forest of windlasses and tents. The evening shriek of birdsong is beginning in the sparse bushland that remains beyond the diggings. A silhouette of parrots swoops past the wagon.

Tom offers me a hand to help me out of the cart. I haven't been to the tent village on the edge of the diggings since we moved into town a few months ago. But one glance at the place, one inhalation of that earth-and-ash scent brings back memory after memory: cooking bread in coals out the front of our tent, walls flapping like sails in the night. The constant rattle of mining cradles, of shovels, of footsteps, of men. Knuckles and fingernails thick with dirt. And the flies, the flies, the flies.

When Tom hands me a tin cup filled with Martha's most vicious moonshine, I gulp it down quickly. I don't want these memories lingering.

The grog shop tent is crowded and noisy, pipe smoke rising into the pitched roof and making the hot air near unbreathable. Men spill into the street, a few patched-skirted women among them. Most of the diggers who didn't attend the burial have finished work for the evening, and the crowd is growing. Conversation turns to who found takings today, before circling back to Fred Buckley.

"It was no suicide," announces Arthur Wallace, who always knows everything about everything. "I heard he just sold five pounds' worth." He brings a fat cigar to his lips. "Why would the man have done away with himself if he'd just found a haul?"

"A haul isn't everything," I say to my cup. I feel Tom's eyes on me, but he doesn't speak.

"Maybe he didn't do away with himself then," says Leo, ignoring my comment. "Maybe someone done it for him."

A fresh murmur ripples through the crowd, more drink-laden thrill than horror at the thought of there being a murderer among us.

"If someone did take him out, you could hardly blame them." Martha, the landlady, speaks up from behind the barrels and wood planks that serve as the bar. "He were fond of swinging his fists, that Fred Buckley. Maybe he had a go at someone who didn't half appreciate it."

"Let's ask him," Clyde booms suddenly, waving his hand with the drink in it and spilling ale over his round belly. "You know, like them girls in America done, with the knocking on the walls. Talked to the dead and all, they did. Asked them all sorts of questions. Knock once for no, knock twice for yes, and all that."

I rush another gulp of liquor. I suppose it was only a matter of time until we got here. Because ask any man on the street and they'll tell you the dead are all around us. There's something about this land, they say, as they toss back ales and speak in whispers. If you listen real hard and the wind blows the right way, you can hear the ghosts of the blackfellas drumming away, keeping watch over the mountains and creeks and the rusty open plains. These are the spirits, they say, that were here long before our ships arrived; those that carved the hills and rivers, and make this land seem to ripple in the dark. And then there are the ghosts we brought out on the ships with us: the banshees and the will-o'-the wisps, and that headless horseman that turned out to be a dressmaker's mannequin someone pinched from the dust yard. The infamous Green Lady who walks Barker Street, despite there being no castle within ten thousand miles. Holding on to these stories makes home feel not quite so far away.

I don't believe in spooks. Never have. Before me and Tom came out from England, I spent five years scrubbing dishes at Hartwell Manor in Horley, a place so full of creaks and groans and ghost stories it was a wonder anyone ever got a wink of sleep. But while the other girls loved working themselves into a frenzy at every screech of the floorboards, I found the draughts and the shadows and the tricks of the light. I couldn't see the fun in having the dead living alongside you.

"What's he going to knock with?" demands Leo. "His hands got blown off."

"A ghost don't need hands," Clyde says matter-of-factly. "They knock with their soul."

I snort into my cup, earning a sideways glance from Tom.

"So what do we do then?" Leo scratches his matted beard. "Go back to his grave and just ask him some questions?"

"No point going to his grave," says Clyde. "He ain't there, is he. Just a few buttons and a shoe. Best off going to his claim. Where he died."

He heads for the door, causing a string of other men to follow.

"Let's go home," says Tom, tossing back the last of his liquor.

"No, I want to watch." There's something oddly enthralling about all this. While I didn't go in for ghost stories at Hartwell Manor, it feels strangely appealing to go along with them now. As though it might take me away from the bleakness of what my day-to-day life has become. Juxtaposed against all that deadness, maybe I'll remember what it is to feel alive.

I can practically see the indecision move across Tom's face. Stupidity, yes, but lately he agrees to anything that falls into the category of *making Lucy happy*. With an enormous sigh so there can be no doubt he's doing this under duress, he nods. Takes a firm grip on my arm and joins the procession across the diggings.

"Do you think there's really a chance Buckley was murdered?" I ask as we weave through the claims. Holes yawn in the earth, signposted by tents at their edges. Smoke curls up from the campfires and disappears into the stars.

I try to keep my voice light. If Tom knew the men's talk has worked its way beneath my skin, he'd be whisking me back home before you could say *knock twice for yes*.

"It was an accident, Luce," he says. "That's all. Black powder's bloody unpredictable. Why do you think the most of us stay away from the stuff?"

But it is not a huge stretch to imagine we might be living beside a murderer. After all, the fact that we're among thieves cannot be denied.

In a place where greed and desperation are this rife, petty thieving is a part of life. Gold nuggets and coins stolen from tents while men sleep. Pockets picked. Goods taken from shop shelves by men with light fingers. Barely a day goes by without a robbery being reported. The troopers have made a few half-hearted arrests – Chinamen and Irish usually – but none of them ever stick.

"Well," says Tom, when I remind him of this, "petty thieving is one thing. Murder is something else. And I promise you there's nothing to worry about."

"I'm not worried," I say. But I'm not sure if that's true. My emotions feel clouded these days, as though I can't quite catch hold of them long enough to read them.

We reach Fred Buckley's claim. Or rather, what's left of it. One by one, we climb over the rope set up by the police to mark the site of the incident. The side of the pit has been blown out in the blast, mounds of earth now filling the shaft. Blackened pieces of the windlass lie not far from the hole. It's only a matter of time before some brassy sods are down there prospecting. If they haven't been already.

We cluster around the ragged edge of the claim, Leo and Clyde shoving their way to the front. I realise I'm the only woman who's bothered making the trek out here.

"Fred!" Clyde bellows. "Can you hear me? Who done this to you? Did you do away with yourself? Knock once for no, twice for yes."

"On the windlass, Fred," Leo adds. "Knock on the windlass."

Everyone falls silent. Waiting. Even I can't pull my eyes from the broken windlass lying by Clyde's feet.

Nothing.

"Were you murdered, Fred?" calls Leo, his face furrowed with such seriousness I'd laugh if I wasn't standing where some poor bastard was just blasted to pieces.

Still no knocking. In the forest behind us, an owl shrieks.

"Fred? You there, man?"

"This is madness." Tom's hand wrenches around my arm, and we're marching away suddenly from Buckley's claim.

"Tom. You're hurting me."

"Sorry." He lets his hand fall. "Watch yourself. The—"

"The claims are hard to see in the dark. Yes, I know."

We walk back towards our cottage in near silence, the newly erected streetlamps throwing yellow light onto the road. Trees tower on either side of us, their white trunks ghostly in the semi-darkness.

"Madness," Tom says again. And then, "Poor Fred. How could those bastards be so disrespectful?"

I give a short smile. "I think Fred's past caring if he's disrespected."

"You think?"

I don't answer. We fall back into our usual silence until we reach the cottage. It sits lightless on the corner of a new row of houses, close to where the town of Castlemaine gives way to the bush. Tom slides the key into the lock.

And then, *crack, crack, crack* – the emptying of the guns, in perfect synchronicity with the turning of the key. Every night this comes; this sudden violent outburst from the diggings that hem the town. And every night it manages to scare me. Nothing to be afraid of, Tom has assured me. Guns emptied in the night to prevent the ammunition becoming damp. There are those who say the emptying of the guns is not a measure of maintenance but a warning to would-be thieves. Stay away from my tent. Hear what I've got in store for you if you try and cross me.

To me, hundreds of weapons roaring together each night is a reminder of how fragile this life is. How easily it could be any one of us lying in the earth, with Clyde trying to get us to knock on the damn windlass. A reminder of how many ways there are to die here.

The last echoes of gunfire are swallowed by the night, the burn of powder faint on the air. And just as I do every evening when the pistols are emptied into this eternal sky, I imagine myself screaming.

CHAPTER TWO

*"To those of my own sex who desire to emigrate to Australia, I say do
by all means, if you can go under suitable protection, possess good
health, are not fastidious or 'fine-ladylike,' can milk cows, churn
butter, cook a good damper, and mix a pudding. … But to those who
cannot wait upon themselves, and whose fair fingers are unused to the
exertion of doing anything useful, my advice is, for your own sakes
remain at home."*

Ellen Clacy
A Lady's Visit to the Gold Diggings of Australia
1852

I'm up at dawn, boiling pots of tea and porridge before
Tom heads out to the diggings. The kitchen is sweltering with
firelight and steam, and carries the faint stale smell of the
laundry I've to do today. Our little stone cottage is neatly
divided in two; one half the bedroom, the other, the living
quarters. The kitchen is crammed with a fireplace and dining

table; shelves lined with cups and plates, and pots hanging along the walls.

I take the pot of porridge from the hook above the fire and fill two bowls, kicking muddy boots out from under my feet.

Tom comes in from the bedroom, his shirt half untucked and his vest hanging open. His fair hair is in dire need of a brush. The lines in his forehead always look more pronounced in the mornings.

He lifts the teapot from the middle of the table and fills a cup, sleepy-eyed. "I think I dreamt about Fred Buckley."

I give him a short smile. After the long trudge home from Forest Creek, I fell into far too deep a sleep to dream.

With the cooking done, I toss a bowl of water into the fireplace to put out the flames. Open the window to let the steam curl out of it. Hot summer air blows in in its place.

Tom takes a gulp of tea. "I got a good feeling today, Luce. This might be the one." His smile looks as forced as his enthusiasm. I don't answer. I've run out of appropriate responses.

When Tom bought his mining license three years ago and was given his first claim, it seemed like such a glamorous thing. Here he was in charge of this little piece of the colony of Victoria – never mind that it was just a few feet across. We went to stand on it together, smiling at each other as our boots sank into the mud. I imagined all the gold hidden beneath our feet, ready to be brought up into the light. That little piece of earth, we were both so certain, would see us live a life of luxury until the day we died.

And down into the earth Tom went, sure it would only be a matter of time before he brought up things that glittered.

And yes, he brought gold back to that lopsided tent we called home; tiny fragments wrapped in handkerchiefs, tucked into his pockets. In those early days, when they first divided up the land, the earth practically shone. They said if you walked Moonlight Flat with grease on your boots, the gold would stick to the soles.

The first time Tom came home with that tiny suggestion of treasure, we sat at the table and stared at the flecks shimmering in his handkerchief. It felt like a beginning; the start of a golden future in which we would rise above our station and be something we could never have dreamt of being in England. We'd have wealth and luxury, and a life of sipping tea on some grand balcony; me and Tom and the child inside me, conceived in that tiny ship's cabin, with nothing around us but sea.

But there was never more than specks and scraps. And while the men in the surrounding claims pulled nuggets the size of walnuts from the mud of Forest Creek, my husband's land never gave up more than gold dust. He worked from first light until sunset or even later, digging and cradling by lamplight. But finding gold, we both came to realise, was as much about luck as it was about skill and dedication.

Now, almost three years after our arrival in Australia, Tom is working a claim with Leo, a Cornishman he met at Murphy's Hotel. This time, he says, things will be different. No more scraps. Just nuggets the size of walnuts.

With Leo's tin mining expertise, they shored the walls of the claim and burrowed far deeper into the earth than Tom went the first time. Constructed a windlass from a felled tree to bring loads up from the shaft.

But I've stopped waiting for Tom to bring home that

nugget. Have come to the conclusion that this is not how our lives are supposed to go. When will he come to the same realisation? Perhaps he already has.

Tom is out the door with the rising sun. I take the breakfast dishes to the trough to wash them, then check on the laundry fluttering on the line at the back of the cottage. It's dried slightly stiff in the hot wind. I pull each shirt, each sheet, each nightshirt from the line and place them in neatly marked bundles, ready to be collected by their owners.

Far too many men on the diggings, I learnt early on, have no thought of how to use a washboard. And in the absence of their wives, their mothers, their housekeepers, a woman can make a good penny washing clothes.

One, two, three bundles of clothing collected and paid for as the day wears on. I pull out the small wooden box hidden beneath our bed. It's empty apart from a few tiny gold pieces, barely enough to make a single sovereign. I toss in the coins, ready for banking later in the week, then tuck the box back under the mattress. I grab my bonnet and head to the Sunday School building for my theatre rehearsal.

The theatre troupe, well that was Tom's idea. A means of distraction. A way to make new friends and move past my grief. I wasn't sure my grief was something I was supposed to move past. But when the young and dashing Will Browning strutted into Castlemaine in his top hat and announced the opening of his new amateur theatre troupe, Tom was adamant I attend.

"You love the theatre," he insisted, though my only experience of such a thing was a church Christmas play when I was nine. Dressed in my most beatific white nightgown, I'd dithered behind the other angels and said my one line – *"Fear not, for we bring you tidings of great joy"* – in such an inaudible voice that one of the other girls had to repeat it.

Nevertheless, I trudged along to the first meeting of Mr Browning's little troupe, determined to despise it.

Somewhat infuriatingly, I did not despise it. For two hours, I sat through a bungled reading of *Macbeth* and prompted the actors with their lines, and had more fun than I'd had in what felt like forever. I came home and offered Tom a begrudging smile. Couldn't help but admit there *was* something I rather loved about the theatre, even though the thought of actually stepping onto stage terrified me.

The ridiculousness of that is not lost on me.

The group had its first performance last month – a half-baked pantomime, performed in the middle of Barker Street and attended mostly by people who wandered out of the tavern and accidentally found themselves in the audience. I stood in the front row and hissed out forgotten lines to those few actors who weren't performing open-book. Did a stellar job of packing the costumes away afterwards.

Beside the hastily constructed Sunday School building, the half-built church emerges from the earth like rock stacks rising from the ocean. Rough wooden scaffolding hides much of the construction, but I see the beginnings of a spire straining towards the sky.

I let myself into the Sunday School, a box of a building with desks crammed in rows and the perpetual smell of chalk and children. Most of the group is already here. They've pulled chairs up around the larger table at the front of the room and are chattering loudly. I weave through the rows of desks and shuffle a chair onto the corner of the table. Edith Markham, with her steel-grey hair and matching face, sets a glass of lukewarm lemonade in front of me.

There are five or six of us who usually turn up to rehearsals, the number swelling or dwindling depending on what play we're reading, and if it's raining too hard to go to the diggings. Edith and I are staunch regulars, and so is the painfully dazzling Clara Snow, the only one of the group with any theatre experience whatsoever.

Well, unless you count my one line in the Christmas play. Which I don't.

Today, Ollie Cooper is here, as is the prime know-it-all, Arthur Wallace. Ollie is a good friend of Tom's, and I know he only comes here for a laugh, while Mr Wallace seems to harbour secret dreams of being the next William Don. Wallace is a wealthy Londoner who pushes papers in the Gold Commissioner's camp; Ollie among the mass of Irishmen come out to escape the Great Hunger.

"Hear about them fossickers last night?" he asks no one in particular. "Out on Moonlight Flat. Some lads come out of their tents and seen lamplight in their claims. Thieves were out of there before they could catch them."

Hardly surprising, given half the settlement was knee deep in moonshine last night, trying to hear Fred Buckley's ghost bashing away on the windlass. There were likely more than a few unguarded claims around the diggings.

"It's those damn Chinese," Mr Wallace snorts, crossing one leg over the other. "Can't be trusted."

"A little predictable, don't you think?" Clara Snow swans into the room, letting the door thump closed behind her. "Anything goes wrong in this place and it's poor old Johnny Chinaman to blame." She takes a chair from behind one of the desks and carries it to the table, lemon perfume wafting in her wake. I shuffle over to make room for her.

Wallace's cheeks turn red in annoyance. "And with good reason. Thieving's been twice as bad since they turned up."

Clara takes off her bonnet and settles into her chair. She pours herself a glass from the jug of lemonade on the table. "Why would they go to the trouble of stealing from the white man? They find more in a day than the most of you find in a week. They must be far more methodical than you lot who just going around swinging your shovels."

Wallace gives her a thin smile. "I must say, Miss Snow, you have quite an opinion on the matter for a woman of your inclination."

Clara's eyes flash, but whatever fierce words she's about to fling out are cut off as Will Browning charges through the door, apologising for his lateness. In his neat frock coat and silver cravat, he somehow manages to look impossibly dashing, despite being so pink and flustered I suspect he may have run here. He slides his armful of bound booklets onto the table ceremoniously. I feel myself straighten in my chair.

Today, well, what an important day it is in the life of the Castlemaine Amateur Theatre Group. The unveiling of Will Browning's new play. An original work written just for us. The ridiculousness of that is not lost on me either.

According to Clara, Mr Browning was a semi-professional dramatist in London, bursting onto the theatre scene at the age of just eighteen, with a play that was wildly successful. Almost a decade has passed since, and judging by the calibre of actor he is now writing for, I can only assume his career has taken something of a wrong turn. Nonetheless, it's a thrill to have been written a piece by a man who once walked the London stage.

As I discover when Mr Browning passes the booklets around the table for us to read, it's not just the men at Fred Buckley's claim who have their heads firmly lodged in the land of the dead.

"*The Lady of Fyvie,*" Clara reads.

"Ah, the Green Lady of Fyvie Castle, I presume." Mr Wallace chuckles as he turns the pages, his animosity at Clara momentarily forgotten. "My dear old granny used to tell me ghost stories about her when I was a lad. Used to scare me half to death."

Clara flicks Mr Browning a smile. "You've certainly managed to find a topic that's all the rage."

I've heard this story too; this folktale he's based his new play on. The woman murdered by her husband in a Scottish castle, who somewhat predictably proceeded to haunt the place for all eternity.

"Been listening in on a few conversations at the tavern, have you, Will?" Ollie chuckles. "There's been talk of sightings of the Green Lady for months now."

Mr Browning sits in the chair left empty for him at the head of the table. He takes off his top hat and sets it beside him. "Indeed." His brown eyes shine boyishly. "I believe one sighting even made it into the papers."

Edith clucks as she turns the pages. "What's this world coming to?"

I open my copy of the script, a small smile on my lips. I think of stealing my older brother's Penny Bloods and hiding in the wardrobe to read them.

We've brought our myths and legends with us to this place; stories to remind us of home, to keep us linked to what we know. The Green Lady walking the streets of Castlemaine is a fragile thread tying us back to our homeland.

I skim through the first few pages. The play has all the mystery and horror of a Penny Blood; Lord Fyvie and his new bride haunted to near madness by the ghostly Green Lady, the vengeful spirit of the Lord's first wife.

The role of Lady Fyvie will obviously go to Clara, the only one of us with anything even resembling the ability to act. The story goes that she was sent over as a convict; spent a few years sewing shirts at the female factory in Hobart before dazzling her overseer into submission and winning her ticket of leave. I have no idea if that's true and am far too terrified of the woman to ask her. The story also goes that in England, Clara was a burlesque performer, thrilling audiences around London with ballad operas and breeches roles. Though I'm simultaneously fascinated and repulsed by the idea, I'm far too scared to ask about that too. I can't imagine what a woman like her is doing in Castlemaine.

The role of Lady Fyvie in Will Browning's new play is hardly Drury Lane, but when he invites Clara to take the lead, she gives him a suitably coy smile and says, "I'd be honoured."

He turns to me. "Mrs Earnshaw, I thought perhaps you might like to read the role of the Green Lady."

My stomach loops. I don't *read* anything. That's not why I'm here. The horror is unthinkable.

"Oh no," I say quickly. "I couldn't. I—"

Mr Browning falters. "You do have your letters, don't you? I'm sorry, I thought—"

"Yes," I say, then wish I hadn't. I've just blown the perfect way out. "But I…"

"Just a reading," he assures me. "You'd be helping me

get a sense of the character. Determine whether her lines need work."

I chew my lip. It's mortifying. I'm not here to perform. I'm the line-prompter. The floor-sweeper. The tea-refiller. But I can see the stupidity of joining a theatre troupe and refusing to even read out a few lines. And so, I nod. Besides, the Green Lady is dead. How many lines can she possibly have?

Mr Browning flashes me a bright smile. "Wonderful." He assigns the rest of the parts before opening his manuscript to the first page.

Clara hurls herself into the read as though she were back in the theatre in London, while I tiptoe through my lines in a miniscule voice.

"A little louder, please, Mrs Earnshaw," says Browning, "if you wouldn't mind."

"Well done, Lucy," Edith Markham says dutifully as we make our way out of the Sunday School two hours later. A pleasantly cool breeze rustles the trees, cicadas wailing somewhere in the half-built church. "Shall I see you home?" she asks, tucking a worn carpet bag into the crook of her arm.

The two of us have the kind of friendship that comes from there being few better options. Edith and her husband came out from Manchester, long before Hargraves found those first flecks of gold and the place went madder than a sack of badgers. They'd been full of the same dreams of a new life Tom and I once shared — a life of adventure and success and enough money to bathe in. Twenty years later, Edith is a widow to smallpox, and her sense of adventure seems to have been thoroughly trampled out of her. Nonetheless, when the world flocked to Victoria to dig treasures from the earth, she carted a few of her children down here and opened a general store in her eldest son's name. Now she's a necessity for all the new arrivals; her shelves lined with shovels and gold pans, billies and bed rolls, ropes and coats and pistols and shot.

Edith is stiff and achingly sensible, a trait she claims has allowed her to get so far in such a challenging place. And yes, a trait I have to admire. But it is not a trait that allows for a close friendship.

"I can see myself home," I tell her. "I've to stop at the market on the way."

We make neat goodbyes and I turn in the direction of the grocer. The sound of footsteps stops me. Will Browning is striding from the school, a copy of the script held against his chest and his frock coat open casually. How different he is to so many of the other men here; wool and silk in place of stained corduroy; clean shaven, with not a grimy, earth-caked fingernail in sight. So polished he almost looks out of place. I can count on one hand the number of times we've spoken directly to each other. Usually it ends with me garbling out a flustered response, and then agonising over it for hours afterwards.

He jogs to catch up to me, making my heart quicken inexplicably. "Thank you for coming, Mrs Earnshaw. And thank you for your reading."

I nod mutely.

"What did you think of the play?" he asks, with something oddly resembling shyness.

"I enjoyed it," I say, finding my voice. "Very much." The play is well written – at least it seems that way to my untrained eye – and the story is thrilling. I enjoyed reading the Green

Lady's part far more than I expected I would.

Mr Browning's face lights. I'm surprised by it. I imagined him far too self-assured to be bothered by the opinion of some dough-faced washerwoman.

"You created a haunting atmosphere," I tell him solemnly.

A haunting atmosphere? I curse myself. Just when did I become so afternoonified?

"I'm glad to hear that. It was something I was striving for."

I carry on. And on. "Well, you certainly managed it. Like that part when we learn how the Green Lady died. And when the Lord and Lady see her for the first time, well I thought I was going to jump right out of my skin. I really did, even though I was reading the part myself and I…"

Stop talking, Lucy.

My cheeks get hot.

He gives me a kind smile. "Good. I hope it will have the same effect on the audience."

I pause, mercifully, for a breath. "The people here will love it, I'm sure."

"Do you think so?"

"Oh yes. Last night they were out at the claim of Fred Buckley, who blew himself up. Trying to speak to his ghost, if you can believe it."

Mr Browning digs his free hand into the pocket of his coat. "Yes, I heard about that poor fellow. Bloody awful, wasn't it."

I nod.

"Did they do it?" he asks suddenly.

I blink. "Pardon?"

"Those men who went to Buckley's claim. Did they speak to his ghost?"

"Oh." I give a short laugh. "No, of course not."

"I see." He holds my gaze for a moment with his rich coffee eyes. "Thank you for your kind words, Mrs Earnshaw. It means a lot. And thank you again for the reading."

And I wander dazedly off to the market in entirely the wrong direction.

CHAPTER THREE

"The Chinese here, who have lately arrived in crowds still continue their national costume in a great measure, and their national custom of carrying everything on their necks on a long pole. … At the end of [the] pole they suspend weights, astonishing considering their slight physical structure. … They go for scores of miles with ponderous burdens … their very legs seeming to stagger and their bodies to waver under their loads."

William Howitt
Ballarat
16th May 1854

"Have you heard about these latest thefts?" I ask Tom at supper that night.

He takes an enormous bite of bread and dusts the crumbs from his beard. "There was some night fossicking out on Moonlight Flat. Gold dug directly from the claims." He is still wearing the shirt he was digging in today. I can smell him from across the table.

"You and Leo had any trouble?"

"No. Do you not think I would tell you if I had?"

I hold back a snort. Tom rarely tells me anything that happens on the diggings. Most gossip I hear from Edith, or the men in the theatre group. "I know you don't like to worry me."

He tears off another piece of bread and dunks it in his mutton stew. "Well. We've had no trouble, in any case."

I've decided I'm not worried. Merely asked out of curiosity. The thefts feel like a distant thing. A thing that's always in the background; something that has little bearing on my life. So many things feel like that these days. Like I'm standing on the outside looking in. Observing life from the wrong side of the curtain.

We eat in silence for several minutes, our wooden spoons tapping against the sides of the bowls. The lamp hisses steadily.

"How was the theatre?" Tom asks eventually.

"Mr Browning has finished his new play," I say. "I read one of the parts."

Tom's face lights. "That's wonderful."

"Just a reading. I'm not actually going to perform it."

"Why not?"

"The stage, Tom?" I say. "Women like me don't go on stage."

"Women like you? What do you mean, women like you?"

I look down, embarrassed. Women who hate being looked at. Women who hate opening their mouths in case something stupid falls out, like *you created a haunting atmosphere.* I know Tom doesn't need me to explain. I'm irritated by his question.

"I think you should consider it," he says around another mouthful. "I really do. It would be good for you."

His words grate inside me. So often, he tells me what I ought to do, what would be good for me. I've come to resent it. It feels as though Tom knows the way through this grief and I don't. It doesn't feel fair that he has navigated a way out, while I'm still foundering.

"Well," I say, sharper than I intended, "I've not been offered the role in any case. So it's neither here nor there, is it."

A knock at the door interrupts. I look at Tom. "Are you expecting someone?"

"It's Leo and Ollie, here for a drink. Remember?"

"No. I don't remember."

Tom shovels down the last of his stew. "I told you yesterday they were coming."

"You didn't," I say stiffly.

He gets to his feet, tossing the dirty bowl into the trough. "Well. They're here now. You've a cottage now, Luce. You ought to expect a few guests."

We're among the few people I know who live within solid walls. This is not a place of solidity. People come and people go; diggers usually, but sometimes the shopkeepers or even the troopers, going wherever the trail of new gold leads them. I heard that when those first nuggets were found in the valleys, all but three police officers abandoned Melbourne for the diggings.

But my husband promised me some kind of permanence here; at least more stability than those mud-caked miners who move on to the newest diggings the moment the reports come in. It was part of his spiel when he first presented the idea of Australia to me. Back then, I didn't need much convincing. I would have gone working on the railroads if Tom had suggested it.

We met on the grounds of Hartwell Manor, that sprawling estate in Horley, a three-hour ride from London. Tom was one of an endless battalion of farmhands, and there was me in the kitchen. Every day at noon I'd trot out to the fields with lunch for the workers, hoping for a smile from the burly blond-haired farmer whose cheeks were always pink with sun. For months we exchanged nervous pleasantries, thought up, at least on my part, hours in advance.

Tom, at thirty-five, was almost fifteen years my senior, and the other girls in the kitchen tried to nudge me in other directions. *Billy Harper ain't married yet, you know;* or, *That new coachman is real handsome.* There had to be something wrong with Tom Earnshaw, they argued, for him to have got to such an age without finding himself a wife.

"Too soft spoken if you ask me," said the scullery maid.

And from the other kitchen hand: "I heard he's got no money."

But to me, Tom was perfect. He was hardworking, never got mad with drink, and knew the names of all the horses. Each afternoon, when I'd hand him his sandwiches, he'd give me a smile that made me feel like the only soul on the planet.

We spent most of the estate's May Day celebration in each other's company, hiding under trees to shelter from the drizzle, and passing a bottle of mead between us. Our small talk about the manor evolved into discussions about our lives, our hopes, our fears, and our dreams – of which, I realised, I had few. Tom spoke of a longing to see the world, to earn his fortune and be his own man. But my life felt too narrow and fenced in to dream.

And then, because my cheeks were hot with alcohol and the mead was swirling around in my brain, I asked, "Why've you not married yet, Tom Earnshaw?"

Beneath his sandy beard, his lips parted in surprise, but his smile was warm. "Well," he said, "what point is there in marrying until you've found the right person?" And that look that said a thousand words warmed me at my core. That was how it always was with Tom; so many things went unspoken.

Our courtship gathered speed, as though we were making up for all the time we'd wasted nattering about the weather over bread rolls and cheese. Barely a month after May Day, Tom sat me down in the manor garden and spoke of his plans. A meagre inheritance left by his father. Enough for passage on the seas to the colony named for our queen. A small house on our arrival.

"Gold's just been discovered there," he told me. "They say it's right there for the taking. If we get in quick, we'll make a bloody fortune."

And well, I knew nothing of gold mining, or the colony of Victoria, at the bottom of that vast land we'd stuffed with our prisoners. But I knew I loved Tom Earnshaw. I would follow him wherever he led me.

We gave our notice at the manor that afternoon. Two weeks later, there was a wedding ring on my finger, and we were tucked onto a migrant ship, with England dissolving into a wall of cloud. Unsteadying as it felt to be leaving all I knew, there was no sense of sadness. My life in England had been punctuated by loss; my parents within weeks of each other some four years earlier, and my brother the previous

Easter. For years, my life had revolved around washing dishes for Lord and Lady Hartwell. Now the manor was a memory and Tom was my everything.

Even on the days when we were tossed by the ocean and could do nothing but cling to the raised edges of our bunk, I felt secure with his arms around me. The days of the voyage blurred, and I remember little but the sensations. Rough hands tracing every inch of me; his coarse beard against my skin, whispering, sighing, and the groaning of the ship. Tom and I discovering each other in the half light of our cabin, tasting sea spray on each other's skin. I felt utterly consumed by him, existing only in the present moment. The land we were journeying to was completely unknown to me, so how could I even begin to imagine the life that lay ahead? All I had to go on was Tom's vision for our future.

I trusted every word of that vision until our first night on the Castlemaine diggings. Beneath a flimsy sheet of canvas, we curled up on a damp sleeping mat and listened to the miners empty their weapons into the sky. Rain pattered steadily into the puddle forming in the doorway, the mud creeping towards our bed like a living creature. What kind of barbaric place was this? Was this really where we would raise our child?

My stomach rolled and rolled; whether with dread or impending motherhood, I couldn't be certain — at that moment, they felt one and the same. This was the gravest of mistakes; I sensed it then with such weight I could hardly breathe.

"This is just for now," Tom promised, breath warm against my nose. "We'll have a real place to live soon. A cottage of our own. Build it just the way we like." He shuffled across the sleeping mat, pulling me into his arms. We were still wrapped in our coats to keep out the damp. He held his lips to mine. And in that kiss, I could sense his own fears, his own uncertainty. "We're going to be real happy here, just you wait. You, me and the little one." I heard his voice waver.

Tom put his name to a plot of land not long after they went up for sale. The tents of the diggings were slowly turning into the town of Castlemaine. It was land we could barely afford, but always one to keep his promises, he scraped together the pennies and set about giving us that life of permanence.

But before the cottage was more than a hole in the ground, camp fever swept through the diggings, taking our daughter Elsie just weeks after her first birthday.

Now we have our permanence. Our walls that don't blow in the night. A locked door to keep out the thieves. The cottage feels far more solid than the foundations my life is teetering on.

I drop my spoon into my half-eaten bowl of stew. "We can't have guests. Just look at the place." I wave at the unwashed stew pot and the flour I've managed to coat the kitchen in. "It's a right mess."

Tom chuckles. "Ollie and Leo won't even notice. You ought to see the tent Leo's living in. Wouldn't keep a pig in it."

I drop my bowl into the trough. "It's near enough to a pigsty in here. And you don't smell much better than one."

Tom peels off his shirt as he goes to the bedroom for fresh clothes. "Calm down, Luce. What does it matter if the place is tidy?"

"It matters to me." I scrub angrily at the plates, water

splattering down the front of my skirts.

But Tom is out of the bedroom, tugging on a fresh shirt and throwing open the door. Leo and Ollie waltz into the cottage while I bluster around the kitchen, trying to deal with the flour. I untie my apron and turn to greet the two men.

"I'm sorry about the mess," I say.

Leo flaps a hand in response. He's made half-hearted attempt to wash himself, gems of clean skin visible between the grime of the diggings and a storm cloud of a beard. He thrusts a bottle into Tom's hands. "Here. Gin from the homeland. A stock of it just came in at the Cumberland."

The men settle themselves at the kitchen table, while I try to surreptitiously wipe a glob of stew from beside Ollie's elbow.

I take a long breath, determined not to let my guests see my annoyance. There were two things my mother taught me about being a wife before she passed. The first was to always put on an agreeable face. The second was to clean the damn house before guests showed up. For not the first time, I wish Leo or Ollie had a wife with them. Someone I could relate to a little. But here on the diggings, the men outnumber the women five to one. We're a novelty – I know that's part of why I cling to Edith like a limpet.

Tom yanks the cork from the bottle and fills a cup for each of us. I perch on the edge of a chair, folding my hands tightly in my lap.

"Lovely to see you both," I say, in an acting display Will Browning would be proud of.

Ollie turns to Leo. "How goes things with the Tipperary boys?" He winks. "They still calling you out for the cheating bastard you are?"

The feud between the Irish and the Cornish has been going on the entire time Tom and I have been on the goldfields. Ask any Irishman and they'll tell you the Cornish use their tin mining skills to drive deep into the earth and dig beneath other men's claims. While Ollie's banter is friendly, I know Leo has had more than one bitter run-in with the Tipperary boys who work the top end of Forest Creek.

He chuckles. "Still talking out their arses. The bastards are just jealous that some of us know how to dig a real shaft."

My eyes dart between the men. I've never had any doubt about Leo's honesty. After all, if he and Tom were driving into other claims, surely they'd have more to show for it than a cradle full of mud.

"Come on now," says Tom, "let's not talk business around Lucy." He gives me a strained smile. "Tell us more about your theatre rehearsal, sweetheart. Tell us how bloody awful Ollie was."

Ollie chuckles, tossing fair hair from his eyes with feigned indignance. "You bastards'll be blown away by my talent. Won't never have seen nothing like it. Lord of Fyvie Castle, I am. Got lines and everything." He nudges me. "Go on, tell them how gifted I am."

I can't help a laugh.

"You want to hear about the mining, don't you, Mrs Earnshaw?" Leo cuts in before I can speak. "That's where all your riches is going to come from. As long as we can keep the thieves out."

"The money in this place is in feeding the masses, not sifting through the ground like badgers," says Ollie, who makes his living at his butcher's shack on the edge of Forest Creek.

"Bull," says Leo. "A good day in the claim and you'll make more than you'd earn in a lifetime hacking up sheep carcasses."

"Least until you end up blown to pieces like poor old Fred Buckley." Ollie leans forward, grey eyes shining. "So what d'you think? He do away with himself? Or someone do it for him?"

"He wasn't murdered," says Tom. "That's enough of that talk."

Leo refills his glass. "I say if we want to put an end to these thefts, we just have the coppers wait outside Johnny Chinaman's camp for a few nights. I bet they'd see a few things."

The men mumble between themselves, evidently all in agreement.

"Where else is all their gold coming from?" Leo continues, though no one is arguing otherwise. "We was mining that land at Moonlight Flat for years before they showed up. Took everything out. Now they turn up, mine the same land and find more? Tell me what's going on there."

"They say they have more luck because they work more methodically," I venture.

Tom's glance pulls towards me, annoyance in his eyes.

"Who says that?" Leo demands.

I don't reply. I ought to have known the wisdom of Clara Snow would not be well received in this circle. I look down, sorry to have spoken.

"I don't know why you're on their side," Ollie says to me. "You know they're making money doing people's washing. Some lad at the tavern last night said he took his laundry up to their camp cos they was only charging him sixpence." He jabs a meaty finger in my direction. "You'll be out of a job soon, just you watch."

I turn my cup around in my hands. I didn't mean to take anyone's side.

I was as rattled as anyone when the Chinese appeared a few months after our arrival. They marched into town in single file, long black hair in queues down to their waists, pointed hats upon their heads. They looked like no one and nothing I had ever seen before. All I could do was stare.

I was glad when they set up their camp on Clinkers Hill, away from the main settlement. Glad when they kept to themselves. The thought of sharing the town with people so unfamiliar was terrifying. Because what is more unsettling than the unknown? Isn't that what fear is made of?

Back in Horley, there was no one that was not entirely like ourselves. We were a uniform mass of pale skin and colourless hair; stories of the same people and the same places told in the same neat version of English. No one who wasn't born and bred in Surrey, except for the occasional traveller seeking London, who wandered into town and left as quickly as they came.

But this place, it's so different. Men pour into the diggings from places I've never even heard of, bringing with them their cultures, their languages, their greed, and desperation. Walk down the main street of Castlemaine and you hear a chaos of accents, of stories, beliefs. Selkies in the seas, and knockers in mines; trolls and dwarves that hide in the woods.

"They're digging round mines," Leo continues. "To keep the spirits out. Damn unnatural if you ask me."

I rub my eyes. This from the man who tried to coax Fred

Buckley's ghost into conversation.

"Government ought to hike up that tax they're charging them," says Ollie. "That'll keep the bastards out."

I stand abruptly. "Excuse me. I'm not feeling well. I think I'll go to bed."

Tom's eyes meet mine. But he doesn't speak. Doesn't argue. Doesn't insist I stay. I can't tell if I'm annoyed or relieved.

On my way home from the market later that week, I pass the vast expanse of Castlemaine Hall. With its high, pitched roof and grand stone façade, the building always draws my attention. Its owner, Councillor Hitchcock, built it to house his auctioneering business, and now rents it out for everything from public meetings to performances by the professional troupes that tour the goldfields – using the slightly hopeful name of Castlemaine's Theatre Royal.

"Good evening, Mrs Earnshaw." I whirl around at the familiar voice. Will Browning is striding out from the back of the hall, dressed in a dark frock coat and top hat. His smile is warm. "What brings you here?"

"Oh." My cheeks flush. "Nothing, I was just… passing." I shift my basket from one arm to the other.

He nods towards the theatre. "I've just come from a meeting with Mr Hitchcock. He's agreed to us using the hall for the performance and rehearsals."

"Really? How wonderful." I'd expected we'd be prancing around in the street outside the tavern again.

Mr Browning glances over his shoulder, then looks back

at me. "May I walk you home?"

A pink dusk has fallen suddenly, shadows lying long over the street. Time for the Green Lady to emerge. Or for the thieves who roam the diggings to emerge, in any case.

"I'd like that," I say. "Thank you."

"Your husband won't mind?"

I pause. In all honesty, I spoke without the thought of Tom entering my mind. "He won't," I say. "He doesn't like me walking the streets alone at night. I didn't mean to be out so late." I don't know if I'm speaking the truth. Don't know what Tom's reaction would be if he saw me alone with Will Browning. And truly, I don't wish to find out.

We begin to walk, Mr Browning with his hands dug into the pockets of his frock coat, and me with my basket hugged to my chest. Cockatoos bawl as they swoop through the dusk.

Browning nods to the street behind Murphy's Hotel. "Apparently the Green Lady was seen over there on two separate occasions."

I nod. I've heard people speak of the ghost sightings, of course. Like any good piece of gossip, one flows into the next.

"Interesting that that's just behind the tavern," I say.

Mr Browning chuckles. "You're a non-believer."

I don't answer at once. It's true, I suppose, though the label feels cold. "And you?" I ask. "Are you one of these so-called spiritualists?"

His smile is tinged with embarrassment. "I confess I may have spent a night or two in a London séance parlour."

"And? What did you see?"

"Some trickery, I'm sure. Theatrics for the sake of making a little coin. Nonetheless, I do believe it would be foolish to close our minds off entirely to the possibility of communicating with the dead."

Foolish, perhaps. But I've learnt that a person can't just squeeze their beliefs to fit their desires. I could wish with all my heart that stepping inside a séance parlour might deliver me a message from my lost daughter. But that doesn't mean I believe it will happen.

I raise my eyebrows. "You think these men really saw the Green Lady behind the tavern? And do you think this is the same Green Lady that's come all the way from Fyvie Castle?"

Mr Browning laughs. "Of course not. On both accounts. But I do think there's much we can take from these supposed sightings. They tell us much more about the living than the dead."

"People are homesick," I say. "Seeing these familiar ghosts here is a link back to where we come from."

"Yes!" His eyes light. "Indeed. And I believe ghosts represent that which is yet to be understood. The things we fear because we cannot make sense of them. So is it any wonder that in a place as unfamiliar as this, we might see such manifestations of our collective terror? After all, this land can be downright frightening at times."

I blink, feeling suddenly overwhelmed. No one has ever discussed anything so intellectual with me before. Up until Will Browning, my life was all, *wash those pans, would you, Lucy; and mind where that horse has dropped one...*

He's right – there is something frightening about this land; the way it stretches and stretches and seems to disappear into the sky. The way the clouds feel so impossibly high, and the dark so impenetrable it could hide the devil himself.

I choose my words carefully, afraid of upturning the intellect and revealing myself as a grand idiot. "This place is so raw and confronting. It's not an easy life. Sometimes people need to escape to another world for a time."

He looks at me with interest. "They do. Certainly."

I offer him a shy smile. "Maybe your play will help them do that."

"I hope so."

I glance sideways at him as we walk. A sudden seriousness seems to have fallen over him, giving his brown eyes an almost sombre expression. In this moment, he looks flawed and human, and I don't feel quite so overawed by him.

"Why are you here?" I blurt. I feel my face flush, grand idiot style. "I mean, what could possibly have drawn a man like you to a place like this?"

He walks for several paces with his eyes down. Watching your feet is a habit you learn quick here, or you'll topple headfirst into someone's claim.

"Well," he says finally, "I'm here for the same reason as so many others. I'm hoping to find a little success. Although in my case, it's success in the theatres, rather than on the diggings."

I nod, urging him to continue.

"I came to realise I was not going to have the career I hoped for in London."

"I heard your first play was extremely successful."

"Well, yes, it was. But with that came enormous expectations. From both myself and the public. Expectations I'm afraid I was unable to live up to. After a number of failures, I began to suspect my reputation had suffered irreparable damage. And they say this is the place to come for a new start, whether you're a prospector or not. I thought perhaps I'd start small here on the goldfields. Provide some much-needed entertainment. Gain a few reviews and something of a following before I try my luck in Melbourne."

"I see." I'm surprised at his openness. At his willingness to share such things with someone like me.

He smiles, his solemnity evaporating. "I enjoyed your reading very much. Perhaps you might consider performing the role?"

My chest jolts. Oh no, there is not a chance. No way in hell am I getting on that stage.

"I couldn't," I say.

"Why not?"

I falter. *Why not?* My usual line of self-critical thought has tangled with Will Browning's eyes on me.

"Won't there be auditions?" I ask, clawing desperately at the prospect. "Surely there's got to be auditions?"

Mr Browning chuckles gently. "And who do you imagine might audition? Truth be told, I wrote the part for you. I rather hoped it might convince you to take the stage. I can tell just from the way you prompt the actors that you have something of a talent."

The thumping in my chest intensifies. What in hell am I to say to that? And even more horrifying, how can I possibly turn the part down now? I feel frustratingly cornered, though oddly, I'm far more flattered than angry. And in a flustered mix of delight and dread, I find myself agreeing.

He smiles; a gentle, warming thing that seems to reach deep inside me. "Excellent." We walk in silence for several paces, my heart knocking hard. "Do you know the Commercial Hotel?" Mr Browning asks suddenly.

"Of course."

Everyone knows the Commercial. It was one of the first

public houses to emerge in this place that was made of brick, rather than the liquor-filled tents that surround the diggings and operate as sly grog shops. But in the two and half years since the hotel's doors opened, I've never done more than peek through the window. The Commercial is a place for gentlemen and merchants, and miners who have found that elusive fortune. It's not a place for people like me.

"I gather there on Friday evenings with friends," says Mr Browning. "Likeminded friends. I'd very much like you to meet them. I think you might enjoy their views on the world." He buries his hands in his pockets. "You ought to bring your husband, of course."

I smile wryly to myself. The only thing more out of place than me at the Commercial would be Tom at the Commercial. He's a grog shop man, a back table at Murphy's Hotel. I can't imagine him sitting among men like Will Browning and discussing the manifestations of the colony's collective terrors.

He shakes his head. "I'm sorry. It was out of place of me to ask."

"No," I say hurriedly. "It wasn't. I just… I'm not sure it's my husband's scene." I'm caught off guard by how much I don't want to talk about Tom.

"Well," says Mr Browning after a moment, "you could always come alone. If you wish."

My mouth opens and then closes again, without any words coming out. "You wouldn't be offended?" I ask, colour flooding my cheeks. I can hardly believe I'm considering something so indecent.

Mr Browning just gives a cool smile, his eyes meeting mine. "Of course not. After all, rules are made to be broken.

You'd be very welcome. With your husband or without."

CHAPTER FOUR

"It appears that some individuals … have laid a wager with a mischievous and foolhardy companion … that he durst not take upon himself the task of visiting many of the villages near London in the three different disguises of a ghost, a bear, and a devil; and moreover, that he will not dare to enter gentlemen's gardens for the purpose of alarming the inmates of the house. The wager has, however, been accepted, and the unmanly villain has succeeded in depriving seven ladies of their senses."

The Morning Chronicle
London
9th January 1838

I step into the Commercial Hotel, my heart thundering.

I told Tom I was going to a rehearsal. He was so pleased I've agreed to perform that he didn't even question my going out alone in the evening.

Word will get back to him eventually, I suppose. Though I don't see anyone I recognise inside the hotel, I'm sure there are a few familiar faces I've missed. Familiar faces with a love for gossip who might tell my husband I've been gallivanting about the place like a wild thing.

But I'm too exhilarated to care. I need more of that kind of conversation I had with Will Browning the night he walked me home. Conversation that sparked my thoughts like they've never been before. I want to be taken to new places; places that aren't quite so bleak and suffocating as the life I've stumbled into.

The Commercial is richly decorated with dark wooden panelling, gold trim lining the bar and balustrades. Lamps are dotted along the walls, casting a warm glow over the place. The men and women sitting at the tables are dressed in bright, lavish colours, a distant cry from the mud-coloured mutedness of the prospectors I usually associate with. The place is a chaos of laughter and voices, and the constant clinking of glasses.

I'm not sure I've ever been more nervous. The day I stepped off England's shore and felt the ship quake beneath me, perhaps. But this is certainly a close second.

In the sixteen months since Elsie died, my days have felt interminably empty. Time seems to stretch out around me, vast and unfillable. I can't seem to remember how I passed my days before I became a mother.

This week though, as I've lost myself in Fyvie Castle and the Green Lady, the emptiness has not felt quite so deep. Mr Browning's belief in me has given me a scrap of belief in myself, and my initial horror at taking the part in the play has given way to something bordering on enthusiasm. I finished the laundry and housework in record time this morning and spent the rest of the day learning my lines.

Beyond the nerves, as I make my way further into the hotel, is a long-ago feeling I recognise as excitement. I am wearing my blue wool visiting dress with all three of my petticoats beneath it, and the ribbon-trimmed bonnet I usually save for church. I shuffled out of the cottage with my hands pressed to my sides, so Tom wouldn't notice the extra flounce of my skirts. Even so, when I pass two men dressed in fine embroidered waistcoats, I feel like I've crawled out from under a bridge.

A sign on the wall coaxes me towards the room for unaccompanied ladies. Through the doorway, I glimpse a sea of feathers and coloured skirts, hear a peal of high laughter. I keep walking.

Rules are made to be broken.

I glance around, sure it will only be moments before someone bundles me back out to the street. Or into the unaccompanied ladies' room at the very least. The barkeep catches my eye for a second and I feel my cheeks heat.

What am I doing here? I'm not this person.

Flustered, I turn on my heel, ready to jot this down as a mistake. And then I hear someone call my name.

Will Browning sits facing the door, several people around him at the table. He waves me over enthusiastically. I try to swallow, my mouth ridiculously dry.

"I'm so pleased you could make it." He pulls out the chair beside him and gestures for me to sit.

I realise, with no small amount of relief, that I'm not the only woman Mr Browning has invited to this… whatever this is. Not the only woman who's dared to shun the unaccompanied ladies' room. Sitting between Browning and two young men I don't recognise, is Clara Snow. She is dressed in striking mauve taffeta, with a black trim at her waist and collar. Her dark curls are piled high on her head, several loose pieces falling onto her shoulders. Shadow on her eyelids and scarlet salve on her lips. She is head-turningly bold, and almost painfully beautiful.

"Clara," I say, giving her a shy smile.

There is a flicker of recognition in her eyes. "Oh yes. You're from the theatre group…" She hesitates, then glances up at Browning for assistance.

"Lucy," I supply. "Lucy Earnshaw."

"Of course. Yes. Lucy."

Mr Browning gestures to the two young men beside him; one tall and slender, the other with round glasses and thinning hair. The three men are dressed so similarly they may as well be in costume – a fashion plate of silk shirt sleeves and bright, double-breasted waistcoats. "These are my dear friends Charles and Matthew. Visiting us from Melbourne for a few weeks. They're keen to see what all the fuss is about. Gentlemen; Mrs Lucy Earnshaw."

I hold out my hand to the men and murmur a greeting, dazed by Browning's introduction. Am I really to call them by their given names? My mother would be horrified.

Mr Browning lifts the wine bottle from the centre of the table and fills the glass that has clearly been put there for me. I breathe in the heady smell of cigar smoke and allow a little of the tension in my shoulders to dissolve. For a strange, dizzying moment, anything feels possible.

"You're a Castlemaine resident then, Mrs Earnshaw?" asks Charles, the taller of Browning's two friends. He leans back in his chair and brings a cigar to his mouth. "Tell me, what do you think of the place?"

No, I don't want to speak of myself, or of this dirt-encrusted town. I want to hear the stories of these people and their lives and their travels; want some glimpse of the outside world to take back to the cottage and cradle.

I garble some flat response about the diggings that makes it clear I have little of interest to say. "And you?" I ask. "Have you been in Australia long?"

"Barely a fortnight," Charles tells me. "Came over with that mad sea captain who says he can make the journey in two months."

"Captain 'Hell or Melbourne Forbes'," Matthew puts in with a chuckle. "Sixty days to the colonies – or die trying!"

I sip my wine. "And did he do it?"

"In fifty-eight days." Matthew pushes his glasses higher up his nose. "Though I don't think my nerves will ever be the same again. Or my insides, for that matter."

My mind goes fleetingly to my own journey on the oceans. Though the days melted into one another, I know we were at sea for far longer than two months. Not that I minded much, intertwined with my new husband. Those days feel impossibly distant.

"Charles and Matthew attended a séance in Melbourne," Mr Browning tells me, with a glimmer in his eyes that, I've noticed, appears whenever our conversation heads in the direction of the supernatural. "The great Madame Moulin. She has quite a following in London. It seems spiritualism is beginning to find its way across the seas."

"Only a matter of time, wasn't it," says Matthew. "Where England goes, the colonies follow close behind."

A smile flickers on Clara's red lips. "What did you think of the great Madame? Do you believe she's able to speak with the dead?"

Charles blows a line of smoke into the faint cloud above the table. "I believe in the great art of deception. Praying on women in widow's weeds and calling up dead Johns and Marys. I hear the crazy old bat hollowed out the walls in her parlour and hid people behind the wallpaper to make ghostly noises."

Matthew laughs. "She's making, what, five, ten pounds a night? Nothing crazy about her."

"That's how they do it?" I ask. "They hide people in the walls?"

"Among other things," says Browning. "Hidden wires and the like."

"It's all electricity," Charles cuts in.

"Electricity?"

He nods. "All those bells ringing mysteriously, and words appearing on slates, they're simply the result of a natural force. One we don't yet fully understand."

Mr Browning smiles at me conspiratorially. "I hope we haven't destroyed the illusion."

"Not at all." Because as I sit here immersed in spiritualism's scams, I feel a spark of old enchantment. For a second, I'm a girl hiding in the wardrobe, scared and thrilled by her brother's Penny Bloods, with her life stretching out in front of her, full of possibilities. And that requires more than just a small amount of magic. "It's fascinating," I say. And dizzyingly refreshing to be speaking about something other than Tom and Leo's empty claim.

"Mrs Earnshaw had some interesting insights into the

sightings of the Green Lady," Browning tells the table. "A symptom of homesickness." He turns to me with an encouraging smile. "Tell them."

I take a gulp of wine for courage. "Well, yes. The ghost sightings, they remind us of the home we've left behind. One we'll likely never return to. People convince themselves they're seeing these spirits because they want a little of the familiar."

I'm relieved by the murmurs of agreement.

"You're right, I'm sure," says Matthew, refilling his glass. "Why else would people claim to have seen the Green Lady all the way out here?"

What a strange thing that people like this might be sitting here among their wine bottles, nodding along to something that came from me. And for a second, amid all this talk of ghosts and trickery, and amid these voices of strangers, I see outside the shell my life has become. And I'm peering into a world in which it might be possible to live again, instead of just survive.

I feel myself smile. Feel myself sit a little straighter in my chair. Feel a long-forgotten shine behind my eyes.

I'm suddenly aware of Will Browning's gaze on me. A passing, sideways glance, but one that simmers against my skin. Clara sips her wine, peering between us over the rim of the glass.

"Speaking of the Green Lady," she says, "will you be performing with us, Lucy?"

"Yes," I say, clinging to that hint of boldness I've just managed to unearth. "Yes, I'm looking forward to it." I realise it's the truth.

Clara gives an approving nod.

"Can we expect a bit of ghost hoaxing then, Will?" asks Matthew. "To stir up a bit of publicity for the new play?"

Browning smiles crookedly. "In a place as small as this? I wouldn't dare."

"Ghost hoaxing?" I repeat. "What do you mean?"

Matthew grinds his cigar into the ashtray in the middle of the table. "Will here has been known to play the ghost," he tells me. "He calls it an act of publicity." He chuckles. "I call it being a public nuisance."

I frown. "Play the ghost? You mean dressing the part and scaring passers-by?"

"Like Springheeled Jack himself," says Matthew.

I know of Springheeled Jack, of course, the devilish ghost that leapt from the darkness across England to terrify those who crossed his path. These days, we all know he was nothing more than a string of different flesh-and-blood men donning a costume and creeping about the night, to satisfy their need to create havoc.

"I thought ghost hoaxers were all troublemakers." The words fall out before I can stop them, bringing a round of gentle laughter from the table.

"He's a troublemaker, all right," says Charles. "The dreaded Phantom of Fitzrovia." He adopts a theatrical voice. "Come out from the shadows to terrorise the living."

Clara laughs loudly.

I look at Mr Browning with a surprised smile. I imagined him far too put together to do such a thing. But the thought intrigues me. "The Phantom of Fitzrovia?" I repeat on a laugh.

He chuckles. "To be fair, that name was not my doing."

"Why did you do it?" I ask.

He turns the stem of his wine glass around between his fingers, and stares into the crimson liquid. "Well," he begins after a moment, "as you know, I enjoy writing about the supernatural. And I hoped talk of the sightings would heighten enthusiasm for the play I was working on. But it was also for the exhilaration. For the thrill of being someone you're not. Escaping your reality for a time." He sips his wine and gives an unenthused chuckle. "It all sounds rather mad when I say it out loud."

"That's Will for you," laughs Charles. "The public nuisance with the greater goal of fostering interest in the arts."

Mr Browning laughs too, a thin sound, with little humour. His brown eyes lock onto mine. "Haven't you ever wanted to be a troublemaker, Mrs Earnshaw? Even for a night?"

I allow myself a small smile. But speaking is too dangerous. My heart is speeding, and it feels as though anything might escape my lips.

"In any case," Browning's voice levels as he turns back to Matthew, "there'll be no hoaxing here. In a small settlement like this it's far too dangerous. Anyone could recognise you."

"Not if you do it well enough," says Matthew.

"It would be quite something, Will," Clara puts in. "People have been wandering out of Murphy's in their cups for months and telling stories of seeing the Green Lady. Imagine if there was actually a sighting. By someone who wasn't half-shot."

"Quite something indeed." But I can tell he's unconvinced.

I look around the table, feeling a smile. It's as though I'm part of a delicious secret. Us against the world.

Mr Browning catches my eye and smiles. I notice the faintest hint of a dimple in his cheek.

Clara stands abruptly. "I'm going to the retiring room, Lucy," she declares, and it takes me far too long to realise it's an invitation to join her.

I stand beside Clara while she peers into the mirror and dabs scarlet salve against her lips. I look at my reflection. Look into my own eyes. Into the grief and the worry and the tiredness that has been there for so long I can barely remember being without it. I look closer to Tom's age than my own.

Clara holds the pot of lip salve out to me. I've not gone near makeup since the queen pronounced it the domain of actresses and whores. But I feel violently plain standing next to Clara, with her red lips and felonious curls. My hair is neatly parted and pulled back within an inch of its life, trying so hard to be blonde, but only managing something like the colour of half-cooked toast.

I reach for a miniscule dob of lip salve. I'm an actress now, after all. The queen would approve. Even if my husband wouldn't.

"Will is quite taken with you," Clara says, as casually as if we were discussing the weather. "I can tell."

A blaze goes through me. "I'm married," I say.

Clara slips the lip salve back into her reticule. "Yes."

I peer sideways at her, trying to find the meaning behind her response. What in hell am I to do with this information? I know what I ought to do, of course – tuck it away into some forgotten part of my brain, never to be thought of again. But I also know how little chance there is of that happening.

"Don't look so terrified," says Clara. "Will's a good man. And he knows you've a husband. He'd never do anything untoward. I can just tell he enjoys your company."

I hover by the mirror, suddenly afraid to return to the table. And perhaps even more afraid to stay in the parlour with Clara. I feel as though I've just leapt inadvertently off a cliff and am tumbling towards something I can't quite make out the shape of.

CHAPTER FIVE

'It was a sight! Mounds of earth lying beside holes presented the dismal appearance of a graveyard, [men] washing dirt in tubs, carrying its colour on their skin, hair, hats, trousers, and boots, miserable-looking low tents their places of refuge. … The whole scene to a new chum was one of unspeakable squalor…'

James Robertson
New arrival on the goldfields
1852

I kneel over the washtub on the square of grass behind the cottage, scrubbing sweat stains from the shirt of a stranger.

With my hands pruning in the washtub and ants crawling up my ankle, it feels as though the previous night never happened. At least it would feel that way if it weren't for the remnants of the wine still thumping around in my brain.

I arrived home close to midnight to find Tom sprawled across the bed and snoring. When I woke, sun was blazing through the curtains and my husband was gone. The first morning in almost four years of marriage I was not awake to see him off.

I hang up the shirts, then follow the aroma of baking bread into the kitchen. I pull the loaf from the oven and set it on the table beside an unwashed pan of bacon grease.

When the loaf has cooled a little, I hack off a couple of slices and wrap them in a cloth, setting out towards Tom's claim.

I can't stop thinking about playing the ghost. About how it might feel to be utterly unrecognisable; to hide from the world in plain sight. I've always been a hider. Always one to avoid attention, and yet is it possible that some part of me also craves it? Longs to be seen, to be heard, to be more than I am?

To find that momentary escape from reality.

Hollow walls and ringing bells and electrical currents making shapes of ghosts. My thoughts are circling around and around the idea and refuse to let it go.

The moment I get to the diggings, I can tell something isn't right. Men are charging between each other's claims, locked in red-faced conversation. The eternal rattle of mining cradles has been replaced by angry voices.

Bunching my skirts into my fists, I make my way through the maze of pits. Some are neatly dug, walls shored firmly with a windlass above. Others are little more than holes in the ground. In the hot morning, dust rises from the claims in clouds, the river a thread through parched brown earth. The sky is fiercely blue.

I find Tom hunched over the windlass, winding the handle with his sleeves rolled to his elbows. His sweat-soaked shirt clings to his back and shoulders. He unhooks the bucket of earth and gives me a strained smile.

"Has something happened?" I ask. "Everyone seems worked up."

"The thieves came out to Forest Creek last night," he tells me. "At least three people reckon their claims have been dug into." He tips the bucket of earth into the cradle.

Leo's grimy head emerges from the depths of the claim. He leaps up the ladder and squints in the sunlight. "This is the worst possible time for this to happen. We're close to a big find. I can feel it."

Tom nods.

I wave a wild hand, battling away an onslaught of flies. How much time do Tom and Leo spend convincing each other that today is the day?

A murmur ripples through the diggings as two policemen appear, the Gold Commissioner on horseback beside them.

"Here we go." Leo takes off his straw hat and uses his wrist to wipe his forehead. "About bloody time. For all the good these bastards are likely to do. What's a place coming to when we're trusting lags to uphold the law?"

It's no secret that Constable Stone, the taller, stockier of the troopers, was sent out here as a convict. Though his sentence is behind him, so they say, the convict stain follows a man for life. Everyone knows who came out by choice, and who was sent here at Her Majesty's pleasure.

Stone nods at Tom as he passes. The two met in the boxing ring last month and I can still see hints of Tom's right hook on the side of the trooper's jaw. He tips his hat at me.

"Mrs Earnshaw."

Following my husband's lead, I turn away in silence.

Stone and the other policeman go to a claim a few hundred yards away that I guess belongs to the fellow who sent for them.

The thieves must have come close to Tom and Leo's claim last night. Why does that make me so uncomfortable? It's not like they would have found anything.

I suddenly remember the bread. "Here." I hold it out to Tom. "It's still warm."

He smiles; a true smile this time. "Thank you. I'm starved." He unwraps the cloth and takes a bite. Hands the other piece to Leo. "You were late last night," he says to me, his mouth still half full. "Was it a good rehearsal?"

Remorse twists my stomach, and I can do little more than nod. "I'm sorry I wasn't awake to make you breakfast."

"I can find my way around a kitchen when I need to. You know I'm glad you're doing this little show." Tom glances at the troopers, then back at me. "You ought to get back to town. There's no need for you to get involved in all this mess."

Three days later, I venture onto the stage beneath the beamed roof of the Theatre Royal. Last year, Lola Montez danced right here with her legs on display, twirling her skirts in her infamous Spider Dance. Left half the colony cheering and the other half in fits of outrage. Had men throwing gold nuggets at her feet. There's something oddly thrilling about performing on the same stage.

Edith, who's requested only a small part in the play, watches from the front row, ready to prompt us with forgotten lines. The rest of us flit around the stage at Browning's prompting; Ollie Cooper and Clara as the Lord and Lady, and Arthur Wallace as their footman. And then, of course, there's the ghost.

I am acutely aware of Browning. Acutely aware of the way his eyes follow me around the stage. I'm being foolish, of course. What kind of half-baked dramatist would he be if he wasn't watching his actresses closely? But I am painfully deliberate in not looking his way. Allowing myself to believe what Clara said – that Will Browning might be taken with me – is a thing I cannot go near.

Nonetheless, I'm excited about my role in the play. Excited to be more than just a shadow, hidden at the back of the theatre with a teacup in my hand. I have only a handful of lines in the opening scenes, my role largely involving hiding in the shadows and looking suitably terrifying. But I've spent hours this week memorising everything up to the end of Act One. Reading the script has become something of an addiction. Losing myself in the world of the play, I've discovered, makes the oppressive walls of the cottage retract, and the silence around our supper table feel far less hollow.

Arthur Wallace charges onto stage and announces Lord Fyvie's arrival in a display of overacting that makes Ollie snort with laughter.

Clara rolls her eyes.

"Perhaps a little less gusto, Arthur," says Browning. "After all, Lady Fyvie is expecting her husband's return. There's no need to announce it as one would the outbreak of war. Let's take the scene from the top, if you please. Mrs

Earnshaw, perhaps we might try it with you standing stage left so the footman passes you when he arrives."

I hurry across the stage with my head down.

We stumble through the Lord's arrival again, Ollie squinting at his script in an attempt to find his place.

"You have your back to the audience," Clara tells Mr Wallace as he prances through his next lines. "They'll not hear a word you're saying."

Wallace ignores her.

"Did you not hear me?" Clara demands. "Or are you just pretending not to?"

"I heard you, Miss Snow," says Wallace. "But I don't remember you being in charge of this production."

Browning clears his throat and hurriedly calls a break. Ollie tosses his script on the floor and heads for the tray of Edith's biscuits, while I fling myself between Wallace and Clara in an attempt to diffuse the tension. "Some tea?" I ask, whisking her off the stage before she has a chance to protest.

Mr Wallace paces back and forth repeating, "'My Lady, your husband has returned.'" Clara looks over her shoulder and gives him a glare I'm surprised doesn't turn him to ash.

I fill two teacups from the pot Edith has set up on a small table beside the stage, leaving Clara to stew in the front row of seating.

"We've two rather strong personalities to contend with, don't we," Mr Browning murmurs, appearing at my side.

My heart jolts at his sudden closeness. I stir the tea with exceptional vigour. "We do," I manage. "Yes."

Arthur Wallace was one of the men who made a scene over Lola Montez's Spider Dance, though I suspect he secretly enjoyed it. No doubt he has a similar disdain for a former burlesque star like Clara.

"See if you can't calm her down a little," says Browning, filling a cup of his own. "I'll take care of Arthur." He gives me a conspiratorial smile that I struggle to return. "Hopefully we can make it through the performance without blood being spilled."

I nod hurriedly and disappear with the two cups in hand. I pass one to Clara, taking a seat beside her. "Don't let Mr Wallace bother you," I say. "I suspect he just doesn't like being told what to do by a woman."

"No," she says icily. "I don't suppose he does."

I give her a sympathetic smile. "This must feel like quite some come-down after performing on stage in London."

She nods at Ollie, whose mouth is rammed with biscuits. "What's someone like him doing here anyway? This is all a joke to him."

"You're right," I say. "He's a friend of my husband's. I know he's only here for a laugh."

She gives a wry smile. "Never would have guessed."

"Why not try and find paid work on the stage?" I ask. "There's all sorts of acts touring the goldfields now. And think how many people were here to see Lola Montez perform."

Clara gives an unenthused chuckle. "Can you imagine how the men in this town would react if they saw me doing the Spider Dance? Arthur Wallace would chase me into the bush with a pitchfork." She sips her tea. "I tried finding work on the stage when I first got here. But the theatre world's too small. Everyone knows everyone. No one wants to hire a lag." She gives a wry smile. "Especially a woman past thirty whose career's been somewhat… interrupted."

I've never heard her speak of her transportation before, and it catches me by surprise. A part of me believed it a myth, made up by men like Arthur Wallace in an attempt to shame her. Clara Snow, with her taffeta gowns and red lips, is not what I imagined an ex-convict to look like.

I realise with horror that my eyes have drifted to Mr Browning as he chats with Wallace – presumably telling him not to speak with his back to the audience. I focus intently on the contents of my teacup.

"It was good of you to join us on Friday," Clara says.

"It was?" I'd not imagined my presence, or lack of it, would have any bearing whatsoever on the life of Clara Snow. She looks at me quizzically and I scramble to redeem myself. "It was a very interesting night," I say, feeling the thump of my heart strike up again. Before Clara can speak of other Will Browning-related things, I add, "I enjoyed hearing about the ghost hoaxing."

Her lips tilt upwards. "The hoaxing. Yes. It wouldn't be the worst idea. It'd certainty stir up interest in this play if we got people talking about seeing the Green Lady." She smiles wryly. "Although after this rehearsal, I'm not so sure stirring up interest in the play is such a good idea."

I laugh a little. Although I do think she may be right.

"Of course, you ought to be the one to do it," she continues, "given you're playing the Green Lady."

"Me? No, I couldn't…" I trail off. Because isn't this what a part of me has wanted since I first heard Browning speak of playing the ghost? Isn't this what I've been angling for? However subtly and unconsciously.

Perhaps I do want to be a troublemaker.

"Maybe you should tell that to Mr Browning," I say,

stunning myself with my boldness.

"Maybe you should be the one to tell him. Might have a little more bearing." She sips her tea. "I asked him about you, you know. He thinks you're rather lovely. And that you have a lot of interesting things to say about the supernatural." She chuckles. "The surest way to a man's heart."

My fingers tighten around my teacup. "Why are you telling me this?"

She shrugs. "Just thought you might like to know." After a moment, she looks sideways at me. "Sorry. I know you're a married woman."

Yes, I am a married woman. One who has never questioned her love for her husband. But this new world of theatre and magic that Will Browning is pulling me towards is far too alluring to turn away from.

When we flounder to the end of the first act, Browning claps his hands together. "Thank you, everyone. That's enough for today."

Clara plants her hand on her hip. "You can't leave things there. That was a complete disaster."

"Sorry love," Ollie sings. "It's four o'clock and the tavern waits for no man."

Clara snorts. "Get out of here and learn your lines then." She drops her voice. "Or learn to read at least." She watches him leave, then turns to Browning. "Get rid of him, Will. He's not taking it seriously."

"Yes, well. I'm afraid this is not the professional outfit you're used to, Clara." Browning gathers up his notes from the table and slides them inside his script. "We'll go over the last few scenes again on Saturday."

Clara huffs dramatically and strides from the stage. As I make to follow her, Mr Browning calls my name. I look back, heart thumping. He steps towards me.

"You seem rather distant today," he says, voice low. His forehead is crumpled with concern. "Did I say something to offend you on Friday night? If I did, I apologise."

"No," I rush. "Not at all. I suppose I'm just…" I dare to look up at him, and the intensity of his gaze steals my breath. "A little uncertain about all of this."

His face lightens, and I'm surprised at his palpable relief. If he's sensed the hidden meaning beneath my words, he doesn't show it.

"You've a talent," he says. "Truly. There's no need to be nervous. All you need is confidence." A little of the tension in my shoulders eases. His words warm me like wine.

Unbidden, something flickers inside me. Something distant, almost forgotten; something I dimly remember from the early days of my marriage. That feeling of being drawn to a man; of wanting skin against skin, the warmth of another's breath. And – perhaps I'm imagining it – that feeling of a man's eyes drinking me in. I'm mistaken, surely. Clara is mistaken. What single thing is there about me that might make Will Browning look at me in such a way?

"Thank you," I say, and it's a weighted phrase. Because it's not just his kind words I'm thankful for, it's this world of newness he's leading me into, and everything forgotten he's waking within me.

As if sensing the gravity of my words, he gives a faint, wordless nod, a tiny smile attached. I'm rushing off the stage before either of us can speak again.

Clara is waiting for me outside the hall. "You have

somewhere to be?" she asks.

"No." I tie my bonnet beneath my chin, trying to steady myself.

"Good. We need to keep rehearsing. Come on."

She grabs my arm, and before I know what's happening, I'm being swept out into the street in her wake.

"Can we rehearse at your house?" she asks.

"My house?" I think of the hastily painted sign on the fence, advertising my laundry services. If Clara Snow sees it, I might just die of shame. But I don't want to turn her down either. I nod. "This way."

"Bloody Browning," she says as we walk. The road has just been watered to keep down the dust and the wet earth sighs beneath our boots. "He's too soft. How's he expect to make something of himself if he's letting people like Ollie Cooper make a joke of everything he's worked for?"

"Did you know him?" I ask curiously. "In London?"

"A little. We moved in the same circles. I worked on one of his early plays at the Haymarket before I got hauled out here. Could hardly believe it when I saw him strutting around the Commercial."

"What was he like?"

"Passionate," she says. "And talented. But he could never quite live up to the success of his first play. They had him pegged as one of the great playwrights of the nineteenth century. Expected everything that came from him to be gold. But his second and third plays were lacking. It was as though he couldn't quite find the magic of his first piece. The reviewers tore him to pieces. Said his first play was just a stroke of luck. Some even went so far as to suggest the work hadn't been his own."

"That's awful."

Clara shrugs. "That's the theatre for you."

"What about the ghost hoaxing?" I ask. "Were you involved in that?"

"The hoaxing? No. Will got into all that after I was gone."

I watch my feet as I walk. "It's so interesting," I say. "The way no one knew it was him."

Clara smiles crookedly. "I suppose shock can blind us to what's right in front of us."

I herd her quickly past the laundry sign and unlock the front door. Realise with horror that I've forgotten to clean the bacon pan. The smell of cold grease turns the air. I charge past Clara and grab the pan, tossing it into the trough. "Sorry about the mess," I babble. "I'll just do a quick wash—"

Clara takes my arm as I blunder past with the bucket. "Lucy. It's no matter." She holds my script out to me. "Scene six."

I put down the bucket and take the script. Force myself to concentrate. Though this is just an amateur play, I want to do a good job. I want something I can be proud of. And perhaps there's a part of me that wants Will Browning to be proud of me too.

I toss the script on the table and act through the scene from memory.

"You're good, Lucy," says Clara, after we've run it several more times. "There's no need to be so nervous." She takes a seat at the table. Her eyes drift around the kitchen, taking in the blackened bricks above the fireplace, the faded gingham curtains pulled back from the windows. "Why did you come out here?" she asks curiously.

I sit opposite, turning the pages of the script without reading. "My husband said he was going to find our fortune." An all-too-common tale. I'm almost embarrassed to tell it.

"And you're still waiting?"

I find a wry smile. I know our ash-streaked cottage speaks for itself.

"Well. I'm making my own luck," says Clara. "Going to make my own fortune. I've got myself land on Hargraves Street. I'm going to open a dressmaker's parlour."

"That's why you came to Castlemaine? To start your own business?"

She nods. "I've been working as a seamstress since I came up from Hobart. Small, private jobs and the like. Thought I could make a go of running my own place. The land's a little cheaper here than in Melbourne. And there's plenty of folks on the goldfields ready to spend their new fortune before they ride off into the sunset."

I smile. I like the idea of making your own luck, instead of hoping blindly for the earth to give up its secrets.

"Some of the men have been making trouble for me though," she says. "Men like Arthur Wallace. They don't like to see my kind have success. Not an outspoken woman with the convict stain. I think this place is too upside down for their liking. Anyone can make something of themselves, even if they've got a prison sentence behind them. Men like Wallace, who are used to being on top, it makes them nervous. Makes them question how powerful they really are."

I frown, playing with the corner of my script. "What are they doing to you?"

"Nothing I can't handle. Little comments when I pass them in the street. That sort of thing. Someone even tried to oppose my purchase of the land. Don't know for sure that it was Wallace, but I know he's capable of it." She snorts. "Have you seen the way he struts around with the Commissioner like he has a pole up his arse?"

"Maybe that's why his acting's so bad."

Clara laughs. "Do you want to see some of the pieces I made?" she asks suddenly. "I'd be interested in what you think of them."

"Of course."

She gets to her feet, and soon I'm trailing her across town again. She stops outside the boarding house on the edge of the settlement. I look up at the narrow, wood-panelled building in surprise. Edith once told me the place was full of no-good dollymops, and since then I've gone out of my way to avoid it.

"You live here?" I ask.

"For now. I'll move to the room behind the shop as soon as it's finished." She looks at me pointedly. "Is there a problem?"

"No," I garble. "Of course not."

I follow her inside, and onto a creaking wooden staircase. Soft laughter floats up from a room below. A young woman passes us on the stairs, dressed in threadbare brown skirts. Her lips are painted red, her eyes dark with lampblack. I smell a fog of liquor on her skin. I find myself stepping away from her instinctively. Does someone as glamorous as Clara really live in such a place? I imagined her in a suite at the Commercial Hotel, where I know Browning lives.

She pushes open a door off the corridor. Five or six narrow beds are lined up across the room, an older woman dozing on one of them. The room smells of bodies and woodsmoke that lingers in the walls. Though the building can be no more than a few years old, the light blue paint around the doorframe is already beginning to peel, the washstand in the corner chipped and discoloured.

Clara goes to the bed in the centre of the room and drags a small wooden chest out from under it. She fishes a key out from inside her stays and unlocks the trunk. She reaches in and lifts out the bodice of a steel-grey day dress. Hands it to me. "What do you think?"

I hold it out to inspect it. Fine embroidered flowers decorate the collar in silver thread, a row of tiny white buttons down the centre. The stitching is tiny and impeccably neat. "You made this?"

She nods. "Ready-to-wear pieces are all the rage these days. And if people see things they like in my window, they're more likely to come to me with commissions."

"It's beautiful," I say. "Really."

"Learned a few skills when they had me locked up at the female factory. Turns out I'm quite something with a needle and thread in my hand." She chuckles to herself. "Who knew?"

I try to imagine Clara in convict slops, her dark curls tied back and her lips free of salve. The image doesn't seem to fit.

She laughs a little. "Thieving," she says.

I blink. "What?"

"You wanted to ask me what I did to get sent over. I could tell."

"Oh." I feel my cheeks turn pink. "I…"

"Had a gentleman caller who tried to take more than I was willing to give. So I pinched his pocket watch when he got too close. An act of revenge I didn't think through so well. Coppers came to the theatre and arrested me before a show one night."

"That's dreadful," I say. "I'm sorry."

She shrugs. "Wasn't my finest hour."

The woman on the bed sighs loudly, making a show of flinging herself onto her side and pulling her pillow over her ears.

I run a finger over the neat stitching on the hem of the bodice. "Is it true you charmed your overseer into giving you your ticket of leave?"

Clara raises her eyebrows, a smile on the edge of her lips. "Is that what people are saying? Why not? Makes a good story." She kneels beside the trunk and pulls out a gown, smoothing its violet skirts over her knees. "My overseer at the female factory was a flat-faced matron with a temper like a hurricane. Believe me, no one was charming her. I served my time. Nothing more dazzling than that. Now I'm a free woman. And I plan to make the most of it."

The woman on the bed lets out another dramatic sigh and gets up, shooting us a glare as she tromps towards the door. I watch after her as she disappears down the hall.

"The women here," I begin, "do they… I mean, are they…"

"Whores?" Clara says brusquely. "Yes, some of them. Do you have a problem with that?" Sharpness in her words, and I see it then. See that, for a woman stripped of everything and transported to the colonies, mere sewing jobs would not be enough to afford a shopfront on Hargraves Street. When I look closely, and glimpse beneath her polished surface, I see the tarring on her boots, the criss-crossed mending on her skirts. And I see what Clara was forced to do to make her own way in the world.

I'm suddenly ashamed of the revulsion I felt when I walked past the woman in the stairwell. Ashamed of looking down on her. Ashamed of the self-righteous glances I threw the working girls who strutted through the diggings at night. Because what choice did any of them have?

I realise then how utterly tiny my life is. What a strange thing that my world might feel so small and sheltered when I've crossed oceans and traversed the globe. Even on the other side of the planet, I'm still the same righteous woman who feels the need to scrub her parlour before visitors arrive. Sometimes that woman is so rigid and dreary she makes me want to scream.

"Of course I've no problem with it," I say quickly. "I'm sure it wasn't a matter of choice."

"No." Clara takes the bodice from my hand and folds it, before setting it back in the trunk. She locks the lid and slides the chest back beneath the bed without speaking again. Have I offended her?

"I'd best go," I say stiltedly. "I've got supper to make."

Clara flashes me a smile and I feel my shoulders sink in relief. "I'll walk you back. Maybe I can show you the shop on the way."

"Here she is," Tom calls as I let myself into the cottage. "My little star."

I find him sitting in the kitchen, his long legs stretched out in front of him. An open bottle of liquor is on the table, a half-empty glass beside it.

"You're not usually one to drink alone." I take off my bonnet and hang it beside the door.

"Just something to take the edge off the day."

"Have there been more thefts?" I ask.

"No thefts. Just a long day is all." He smiles up at me. "But enough of that. Tell me about your play."

I realise with a bolt of panic that I left my script on the kitchen table when I went to the boarding house with Clara. Has Tom peeked inside it? The thought makes me oddly uncomfortable. As though I don't want him prying into this world he isn't a part of.

"It's a good play," I say. "Mr Browning is very talented. I think everyone will enjoy it."

Tom takes my hand. The gesture feels oddly foreign, and I feel my body stiffen. "And you? Are you enjoying it?"

"I am," I say. "Much more than I expected."

"Good. I'm proud of you, Luce. I know it was a difficult thing for you to agree to."

I looked down at our intertwined fingers. "Sometimes I can barely believe I'm doing such a thing. I hate people looking at me." Our conversation feels oddly pleasant, oddly easy. And that in itself stirs up wariness within me. Pleasant and easy is not something we do.

Tom reaches up and tucks a stray strand of hair behind my ear. "I don't know why," he says. "You're a beauty."

"Don't be mad. I'm no such thing." I turn away, suddenly embarrassed.

He wraps his arm around my waist, finding the curve of my hips. "I'm not being mad." His familiar scent surrounds me; whisky and earth and the carbolic soap we keep in the washbin. His closeness fills me with both comfort and dread.

I can barely remember the last time Tom and I were together. Since Elsie's death, there has been an invisible barrier between us in the bed.

In the first days and weeks, we held each other in the night – those long, silent nights not broken by the wails of a baby. Slowly, we reached an unspoken agreement that neither of us could handle the pain of losing another child. And so we would not take the chance of bringing another child into the world.

But in the past year, that unspoken agreement has become something deeper. These days, our conversations rarely do more than scratch the surface. Our reluctance to talk about our daughter has become a reluctance to talk about anything of meaning. I'm left to constantly guess what Tom is thinking, feeling. Left to wonder if there are traces of Elsie in his thoughts, or if his hunt for gold consumes all else. A part of me desperately wants for us to speak of our child; to remember the good times, and shoulder each other's sadness. But there's a fear in me of these conversations. A fear that it will be too painful, that I might say things I regret, that somehow it's easier to keep Elsie tucked away in my memory than to speak of the anger and grief that's festering inside me. And though I'm certain Tom will never speak unprompted about our daughter, there's a still a part of me that's fearful whenever he opens his mouth. These days, when I'm in my husband's presence, there's a knot in my stomach I can't find a way to unravel.

I swallow heavily, shifting my weight. "I ought to make supper."

"Supper can wait." Tom keeps his arm tight around me. His other hand slides over the side of my ribcage and squeezes against my corset.

"Tom," I murmur. "You're drunk."

"Drunk? Hardly. I've had one glass."

And I see it then – the liquor was not to ease the stresses of the day. It was to give him the courage to lie with his wife.

Emboldened by the whisky, Tom is persistent, a hand working beneath my skirts to squeeze my thigh. A sharp exhalation escapes me, and I stumble backwards involuntarily. Tom lets his hand fall.

"I'm sorry," I hear myself say.

Tom gets to his feet, grabbing his glass and tossing back the last of the liquor. Then he strides into the bedroom without speaking.

For several moments, I don't move. Just stare into the lamp, watching a draught catch hold of the flame. Tears prick my eyes, blurring the orange light. I blink them away quickly. I've had far too many tears. I don't want to cry any more.

Instead, I sit at the table and open my script. A slight tremor in my hands, I turn the pages to the scene Clara and I were rehearsing this afternoon.

I read through the lines several times. A confrontation between Lady Fyvie and the ghost.

"'I have been here longer than you know,'" I murmur. My voice sounds hollow in the empty kitchen. Out of place. What a strange thing, I think distantly, that my voice might sound so displaced in my own damn house. But it's not my voice, is it. It's the voice of the Green Lady; this watery tone I've adopted to play a part. A voice full of someone else's pain.

I repeat the line, louder this time. More confident. It seems to heighten the silence.

And: "'Beware of the man you married,'" I say, well aware of the irony. The poor devoted Green Lady, betrayed by the husband she loved so dearly. Starved to death in the charter room of Fyvie Castle for failing to provide an heir.

Here I am reading her lines with my half of the marriage bed cold and my thoughts swirling around another man. I feel the guilt twist violently inside me as I read, "'He is a cold and heartless beast.'"

CHAPTER SIX

"There are distinct signs that ghosts, which we thought were laughed out of existence by the robust common sense of the eighteenth century, are creeping back into the world, revisiting again the glimpses of the moon, in these rather sickly times of the moribund nineteenth century."

The Argus
Melbourne
March 1884

"I thought we might go to the ball tomorrow night," says Tom. He's standing with his back up against the wall of the cottage while I crouch over the tub of laundry on the grass behind the house.

"We don't have to do that. I know you don't like dancing."

"I want to go," he says. "Everyone will be there. And it's about time we attended one."

His words sting. We've missed both the annual goldfields balls in our time in Castlemaine, buried in grief as we were last year, and tied up with a newborn the year before. There's something brutal about being able to attend this one.

I pull a shirt from the washtub and feed it through the wringer.

Tom stands watching patiently, waiting for me to speak. I sling the shirt over the washing line, then gather the courage to face him.

We've barely said two words to each other in the days since he attempted to take me to bed. Sometimes, like right now, I miss my husband intensely. How is that possible, I wonder, when he's standing not a yard away? The loneliness feels painfully deep.

I nod. "All right. Let's go to the ball."

"Good." He gives me a smile that doesn't reach his eyes, then turns and disappears back inside the cottage.

The following night, I'm sitting in front of the mirror on my side table, trying to wrangle my hair into something other than its usual lifeless bun. I tell myself the extra effort is because it's the first goldfields ball Tom and I will have made it to, and definitely not because Will Browning is going to be there. I squint at my reflection. My cheeks are turning golden brown, after having caught the sun. I wish I had a little powder to cover them.

The floor creaks loudly and Tom appears behind me in the mirror. He's dressed in a clean shirt and waistcoat, a neckcloth knotted at his throat. Clean-shaven for the first time in what feels like a decade. He looks younger without his scruffy beard. I feel a sudden urge to touch his smooth cheek.

But something holds me back.

"You look lovely, Lucy."

He puts tentative hands to my shoulders, as though his thick fingers are trying to remember the shape of me. The feel of him makes sudden tears gather in my throat. Tears of happiness or sadness, I can't tell.

There are moments of this. Moments where there is no past or future, there is just him and me, existing. But they've become so rare, so fleeting. Him, fixated on a future in which he finds the gold he craves. Me, stuck in the past, wondering if there was something I might have done differently to keep Elsie with us. Things that have become much too painful to talk about. Silence and small talk are far easier.

I stand up, turning to face him. I grip the hem of his waistcoat, as though I might prevent the moment from slipping away. "Do you really want to go tonight? You hate dancing."

He chuckles lightly. "I do. But I just want—"

"Me to be happy," I finish. "I know." I let my hands fall, that familiar tug of unease returning. What is so wrong with sadness? Isn't that the right thing for a woman to feel after she's buried her child?

Except I realise then, with a quake that goes through my whole body, that it isn't sadness I'm feeling. The grief that has pressed down on me every bleak, lightless day since Elsie's death, I've stopped feeling that with such bone-breaking intensity. Somehow, in the wake of the play, and my night at the Commercial, and yes, in the wake of Will Browning, my pain has eased enough for me to breathe.

I swallow a gasp at the realisation. I am a horrible person.

Tom frowns. "Have you changed your mind about

going?"

I hesitate. It would be safer, of course, to stay home. Far less temptation.

But I can't bear another stilted, silent night in the cottage with our unspoken grief hanging so thick in the air.

I force a smile. "No," I say. "We should go. Can't have you shaving for nothing."

As we make our way to Castlemaine Hall, I glance out towards the glow of campfires that mark the edge of the diggings.

"Are you not worried about the night fossickers?" I ask. "With so many people away at the ball, it seems like a fine time for thieves to strike."

Tom doesn't answer at once. "Maybe it is. But how often do I get the chance to take my wife dancing? Besides, we've barely found more than gold dust in weeks." He chuckles humourlessly. "If fossickers find anything down there, good luck to them."

My chest squeezes. It's the first time I've heard anything but optimism come out of Tom's mouth, at least as far as the diggings are concerned. Is he starting to lose hope? Maybe it's best that he does. At least then we could acknowledge this adventure as a failure and move on to the next part of our lives.

Admitting he had failed on the diggings would crush him. When we first came out here, he didn't for a second consider the possibility of failure. That he'd dig his way to wealth and success was just a given.

I slip my hand around his elbow and give it a gentle squeeze. It's a pitying gesture, but what does that matter?

These days, anything that makes me feel close to my husband is precious. I can barely remember the last time I wanted to be near him. But maybe we really can find a way to move forward. Find a way back to each other.

The wail of bagpipes tumbles out into the street, and we follow the sound into the hall. I'm pleasantly surprised at what I find. The walls are hung with blue and white calico, which looks in the lamplight to ripple like water. Chairs and small wooden tables dot the edges of the hall, a bunch of bright yellow flowers in the centre of each. The stage where I walk as the Green Lady is tonight filled with fiddlers and pipers and everyone else who thought to throw an instrument in their luggage. People mill by the edges of the room; others leap around wildly to the music. Men are clustered around the handful of women, vying for a chance to dance with them. Those who know they have no hope dance with rolled-up swags instead. One look at their clothing tells you who's found success, and who's still slumming it in tents the calibre of pigsties.

Leo and Ollie wave us over. They're sitting at a table close to the door, tin cups in front of them.

"Give me a dance, Mrs Earnshaw," Ollie demands, on his feet before I've even made it to the table. "I've been waiting an hour for the company of a lady."

Tom slides an arm around my waist. "Will you at least let her sit down first?"

"Johnny Chinaman's having a party tonight too," Ollie says, as Tom pulls out a chair for me. "Sold half my meat to them this morning. Saw their camp all lit up on my way past tonight too. They was thrashing away on drums and everything."

"Good," says Leo. "It'll keep them away from here."

Tom goes to sit, but I press a hand to his arm to stop him. "Fetch us a drink?"

"Oh. Yes. Of course. Ale?"

"Stronger."

Off he goes to the bar, leaving Ollie and Leo to harp on about the Chinese. When he returns with a cup of gin for me, I swallow it down quickly. Feel a satisfying buzz in my brain.

My eyes drift to the other side of the hall, where Will Browning is sitting with Charles, Matthew and Clara. A burst of laughter rises from their table.

Mr Browning looks across the room and catches my eye. I turn away quickly. I can't let myself so much as look at him, not when my husband feels closer than he has in months.

I turn to Tom. "Will you dance with me?"

"In a while. You know me. Need a few drinks to work up the courage."

I smile stiffly. Tom has never been one for parties, and I can tell he's uncomfortable. Still, he was the one who insisted we come. I hoped he might make a little more of an effort.

"Coppers've showed up," Leo reports, nodding towards the bar. Constable Stone and two of the officers are standing in the corner, drinks in hand.

Tom takes another gulp of ale.

Leo snorts. "Little wonder they've no idea who's robbing us blind if they're spending their nights gallivanting around the ballroom."

The band bursts into a frantic jig and Ollie leaps from his chair. "You gonna dance with her or not, Tom?"

Tom glances at me, then gestures for Ollie to take me out to the dancefloor.

"Miserable old bastard, aren't he," Ollie chuckles, as he takes my hands in his. "One of the few lads who's got a lady with him and he won't even dance with her."

"Tom's not much of a dancer," I say.

"So I hear," Ollie replies, though he's not exactly setting the boards alight himself.

After the jig with Ollie and a reluctant set with Clyde, I excuse myself and head back to the table. "Now?" I ask Tom. My legs are getting tired, and I want at least one dance with my own husband before I'm farmed off to entertain all the other single men.

Tom glances up at me fleetingly. "In a minute, Luce." He turns back to Leo. "But it's all a matter of progress. They want to find more gold, then they…"

I grit my teeth and head for the bar, dumping enough coins on the table for a fresh cup of gin.

Clara sashays towards me in her shimmering violet-black skirts. She nods towards the side of the stage, where Arthur Wallace is in conversation with a group of other men. His thick grey brows are furrowed as he nods along to the speaker.

"Did you hear? Arthur's pulled out of the play. Will's going to take his part."

"Really? Why?"

"Says he doesn't have the time. But I think we all know that's bull. He just doesn't like being told how to act by a government woman. Especially one who's seen him with all his bits out."

I choke on my drink. "You and Wallace… I mean, he was your…?"

"My punter," says Clara. "It's all right, Lucy. I don't mind if you speak about it."

My cheeks heat at her directness and I swallow an ocean of gin.

"Was a cheap bastard too. Used his tent at the Commissioner's camp instead of paying for a room." She shrugs airily. "Mind you, I suppose I can't blame him. It just doesn't make good sense to rent a room for the night if one only needs it for two minutes."

A laugh escapes me and my eyes drift to Mr Wallace. Suddenly his animosity towards Clara makes much more sense.

"Made me promise him my silence every time I left too," she says. "I doubt he'd have bothered if he knew how many men here were doing the same thing."

"No wonder he doesn't like you telling him how to act."

Clara waves to the barkeep and orders a glass of wine. She turns to look back at Wallace as she brings it to her lips. "I learned a lot about men like him when I was working the streets. They just want things to be how they were in England. Everyone in their place, their class. They don't like that a lag can make something of themselves. When they see noblemen digging alongside ex-convicts, their poor little brains just implode. They can't make sense of it."

I nod.

"I think Wallace saw me as some creature of the night who ceased to exist in the daylight. Couldn't handle it when he realised we were to live in the same society." She presses her shoulders back. "Anyway. Wallace and the others of his kind will be mad as hops when their wives are coming to me to have their dresses made. Just think of the stories I could tell them."

I grin. "You wouldn't."

"Course not. But they don't know that, do they."

"Come on then, Luce," Tom bellows suddenly, lurching towards me and grabbing my hand. "Let's have a dance." I can smell the ale on his breath.

I wrangle him onto the dancefloor, desperate to get him away from Clara. I don't want these two parts of my life to become entangled. And maybe I'm a little embarrassed of the lumbering boor I'm married to.

Tom slides his fingers through mine. Looks me in the eyes and smiles. For a moment, I see him; the man I fell in love with. That gentle farmhand with dreams not tarnished by the goldfields. Something tightens in my chest and I let him pull me close. But before we can negotiate the steps of the Gallopede, Leo comes charging up to us.

"Clyde says he's just seen the Green Lady. Out behind Murphy's."

I look to the doorway. Clyde's telling a story to a gathering crowd, waving his arms animatedly. I dart a glance to Browning's table. I half expect one of them to be missing, dressed up outside Murphy's in a ghost hoaxer's costume. But Browning, along with Charles and Matthew, is at their table watching Clyde with amused eyes. Clara is still at the bar with her wine glass in hand.

Tom and Leo head for the door. With little else to do, I follow, and am swept up in the crowd. The Gallopede loses momentum as half the fiddlers climb off the stage to see what all the fuss is about. Clyde leads the throng of people towards the alley behind the tavern.

A part of me understands. If you can't catch a thief, why not catch a ghost?

"She was right over there by the window," Clyde's saying, a stumble in his step. "I swear it."

The men charge into the alley, peering behind bins, shouting '*Where are you, woman?*' and other phrases similarly unhelpful for catching a ghost.

Bitterness sears through me as I watch Tom among the men, chasing after shadows. I know I didn't imagine that precious closeness between us. But it's gone all too quickly.

As I look to the half-lit window at the back of the tavern, I see it. That pale sheath of curtain trapped beneath the window frame. With lamplight behind it, it seems in motion, almost breathing.

The Green Lady.

Do the men not see it? Or are they just choosing not to? Perhaps it's more fun to indulge in fantasy for a time, than to face the harshness of this life we've chosen.

"A manifestation of collective terrors," says a voice from behind me.

I turn to look over my shoulder, flashing Browning a quick smile.

"You see it, don't you?" he asks.

"The curtain? It's so obvious I'm surprised everyone doesn't see it."

I think of what Clara said: *Shock can blind us to what's right in front of us.* This colony, these men, they're so ready to be fooled.

From deep in the alley, Tom glances over his shoulder at me, as though ensuring I haven't been spirited off into the otherworld.

"Forgive me," says Browning. "I ought to leave you. I—"

I grab his wrist to prevent him stepping away. See the flash of surprise in his eyes at the contact. And I say, "I want to play the ghost."

CHAPTER SEVEN

"Residents of the quiet township of Rosaville … have been startled during the past week by the nightly appearance of a ghost. The nocturnal visitor assumed the form of a young girl, draped in what appeared to be a white shroud. … [One resident] of a more practical turn of mind looked upon the matter as a hoax. … He therefore laid in wait, and when the nocturnal visitant appeared … his arms encircled the form of a young girl who was enveloped in a sheet, instead of a disembodied spirit. The practical joker was conveyed home and cautioned against repeating her folly."

The Express and Telegraph
Adelaide
19th August 1880

I let my hand fall from Mr Browning's wrist. "I want to play the ghost," I say again, softer. "Look." I gesture at the men, who are hammering on the back windows of Murphy's

Hotel. "They're longing to see the Green Lady. So why not give them what they want?" My thoughts begin to catch up to my outburst. "Just think of how much interest it would create in your play. Get people talking about the Green Lady and they'll be lining up to see the show."

But it's not about the play. Not really. Yes, I want Mr Browning to have success, but this is something I long to do for myself.

My entire life I have followed the rules. And where has that got me? I want to do the unthinkable. Be someone else.

I want to be a troublemaker.

Mr Browning's face is creased with a frown. I can tell he was not expecting this from me. And why would he? I was barely expecting it from myself. He shakes his head. "I really don't think…" He looks up as Clara makes her way towards us, without having relinquished her wine glass. "Ah, Clara. Tell Mrs Earnshaw that playing the ghost is a terrible idea."

Clara's eyes shine. "Playing the ghost? I think that's a wonderful idea. This town is desperate to see the Green Lady. Let's give them what they want." She winks at me. "You can wear the costume I'm making for the play." She drains her wine, then turns to Browning. "I'll promise I'll make her look simply dazzling."

He swallows visibly and I feel my cheeks heat.

"Don't pretend you're not excited at the prospect," Clara says, pointing a long finger in his direction. "Phantom of Fitzrovia."

I hide a smile.

"That was different." He turns to me. "Once they see you on stage, they'll know you were the one behind the hoaxing."

"Good." My response is thoughtless, but I realise at once that I'm speaking the truth. Because I'm coming to see I don't want to be hidden anymore. Don't want to be so silent and submissive. There is so much grief and anger and frustration in me that I need to let a little of it out. Otherwise it might swallow me whole.

"We can do it with or without him, Lucy," Clara says easily. "I've nearly finished your costume. And he'll be ever so grateful when the masses are lining up to see his play."

I eye Mr Browning, hoping for a smile of agreement. But he shakes his head, arms folded across his chest. "It's a bad idea."

I hold his gaze challengingly. His lips part, but he says nothing.

"What's going on here, Luce?" I whirl around to see Tom marching towards us.

"Oh," I rush, "these are… from the theatre group…" My mouth feels too dry. "Mr Browning and Miss Snow."

Tom's eyes move between them warily.

"A pleasure to meet you, Mr Earnshaw," says Browning, shaking Tom's hand with a cool smile. He looks at the men outside Murphy's, then back at my husband. "Did you find the Green Lady?"

Tom gives a strained chuckle. Rubs his square jaw. "No, I uh… I'm not quite sure I believe in all that." His hand curls protectively around the back of my neck. "It's getting late, Lucy. Let's go home." His voice leaves no room for debate.

I nod obediently, murmuring hurried goodbyes.

"I wouldn't rush to be so sceptical, Mr Earnshaw," Clara calls as we make our way out of the alley, Tom holding tight to my arm. "Perhaps the Green Lady will show herself again soon."

Three nights after the ball, and I've arranged to meet Clara at the Commercial to deceive the superstitious people of Castlemaine. I plan to rattle out my well-worn lie – tell Tom I'm going to a theatre rehearsal. Not entirely untrue, I reason. After all, I'm about to play the Green Lady.

When Tom returns to the cottage late in the evening, he's flustered and angry. He paces back and forth across the kitchen as I serve up the stew that's been congealing on the hook since dusk.

More night fossicking at Forest Creek, he tells me. More claims robbed while people slept.

"Coppers have any word of who's responsible?" I ask, battering away the flies that have arrived in droves through the open window. The heat in the kitchen is thick and heavy.

Tom slides a chair up to the table. "We don't need to speak of it."

"You can talk to me about this," I say, tugging irritably at my stays. "I'm not going to fall to pieces at the slightest sign of trouble."

He hesitates, stirring and stirring his stew. Finally, he says, "There's been no arrests. Coppers are a pack of useless bastards. Talk among the men is it may be bolters. Bushrangers."

The muscles in my neck tighten. I've heard of the bushrangers, of course. Escaped convicts who hide in the Black Forest between Castlemaine and Melbourne, terrorising the coaches on their way to and from the goldfields. I don't like the thought of them straying into our settlement.

"Bushrangers?" I try to keep my voice from rattling. "Do you think maybe they were responsible for… what happened to Fred Buckley?"

"What happened to Fred Buckley was an accident," Tom says firmly. He puts his spoon down. "Listen to me, Lucy. Whoever's behind these thefts, it's gold they're after. Nothing more. They'd have had no need to take out poor old Buckley. Much as I don't want to speak ill of the dead, he shouldn't have been messing round with black powder."

I nod. Tom's explanation is the most likely, I suppose, no matter what my racing imagination tries to tell me. "There were no thefts the night of the ball, were there?" I ask. "Even though half the claims must have been unguarded."

Tom shakes his head. "Not that I know of."

"Do you think that just a coincidence?"

"I don't know," he admits. "Maybe not. All I know is I don't want them in my claim. I know what I said about them being welcome to whatever they could find there, but…"

"I know," I say. "You didn't mean it."

"I've worked too hard, Luce. I'm not about to let anyone get their hands to whatever's down there." He meets my eyes. "Leo and I have decided we need to take turns sleeping out there. Keep an eye on things. I told him I'd go out there tonight. I'm sorry."

"Don't be sorry."

"Of course. You'll be off galivanting around the stage anyway." He stirs his stew. "You're friends with that Clara Snow woman now are you?" It sounds like an accusation.

"Do you have a problem with that?"

"Leo says she used to work the streets."

I hold his gaze. "Yes. To earn money to open her dressmaking parlour."

Tom blinks at my directness. "I'm sure you can find more suitable people to be friends with. Why don't you pay Meg a visit?"

Meg was my closest friend when we lived at Forest Creek. But after an agonising spring in which we both buried children, the friendship became too tainted to hold on to. We've not spoken in almost a year.

"Tom," I say, sharper than I intended, "you were the one who pushed me to join the theatre group. You were the one who pushed me to perform. And now you don't want me to be friends with these people?"

Tom sticks his spoon in his mouth. I've laid out far too logical an argument for him to dismantle. After a moment, he nods resignedly. "Mrs Markham will see you back?"

I can't meet his eyes, my self-righteousness dying in the wake of my lies. "I'll be sure not to walk home alone."

I'm a jittery mess as I make my way towards the hotel. Though the population of Castlemaine is swelling by the day, there are still far too many familiar faces for me to disappear into anonymity. But the thudding of my heart makes me feel alive. Excited. And this is not a feeling I'm willing to give up.

The main bar is busy, the air thick with pipe smoke and jumbled conversation. I hear Clara call my name. Turn to see her sitting alone at a table by the window, a glass of clear liquid in front of her. She has not even bothered to sit in the ladies' area. A table of men sits opposite her, shooting her glares and murmuring between themselves. She gestures to me to join her. Emboldened by her presence, I march past the men and up to her table.

"Do you have the dress?" I ask.

"Upstairs in Will's room."

My heart quickens. "In Will's room? I thought he didn't want to be involved."

She flaps a hand dismissively. "He'll come around. He was the one who told me to use his room. Said it was safer than using the retiring parlour. Less chance of getting caught." She tosses back the last of her drink and slides from her chair, looping her arm through mine. She flashes the men a defiant smile – "Gentlemen" – then we sweep through the bar and up the staircase that leads to the lodgings.

We reach a narrow, lamplit corridor with doors on either side. The noise of the bar has become a muffled chatter. Clara knocks on what I assume is Mr Browning's door, and I feel a fresh flicker of nerves.

He answers at once. Leans against the doorframe as his eyes bore into me. "You're really going to do this then?"

I swallow. "I am. Yes."

"Very well." He takes his frock coat from the hook beside the door and slides it on. "The room is yours." He looks at Clara. "I'll be downstairs. Let me know when you're done."

He is off down the hall without another word, and I find myself staring after him. Feel a tug between my ribs at the brusqueness of his words.

Clara puts a hand to my shoulder, ushering me inside, clearly unfazed by his coldness. Browning's room is small and neat, with curtains drawn across a large window and a canopied bed in the centre. His rosewater scent infuses the space with his presence. I can picture him hunched over that little table in the corner, scrawling down the words to the play, ink splattering over the page and his dark hair spilling across his eye.

"Do you think he's angry?" I ask.

Clara pulls an array of salves and powders from her reticule and sets them on the table. "Don't worry yourself over it. He'll be thanking you when he fills the Theatre Royal."

I feel a knot in my stomach. As much as I want the thrill of playing the ghost, Browning's resistance cuts me. I can't make sense of why he's so against it. I'm only doing something he himself has done before.

Clara points to the dress lying across the bed. "What do you think?"

I take a step closer to inspect it. Its wide skirts and sleeves shimmer in the lamplight, a single line of beading along the neckline. I run a tentative finger along it. "It's stunning."

"I'm pleased with how it turned out," she says. "As far as history tells us, it's quite close to what Lilias Drummond, Lord Fyvie's first wife, would have worn when she was alive." She smiles crookedly. "And afterwards too, if you believe the stories."

She gestures for me to sit in the chair beside the dressing table. I feel like a blank canvas, ready to be done with whatever she pleases.

I close my eyes. Feel brushes and powder glide over my cheeks. Lampblack swept over my eyelids.

"Did you learn this from your time in the theatre?" I ask.

"I did. It's been a while. But it seems I remember more than I thought." She works in silence for several minutes, then takes a step back. I open my eyes. Clara tilts her head to inspect her work. "Perfect."

"Can I see?"

"Not yet." She presses the lids back onto the powders and slips them into her reticule. "Take off your dress. The Green Lady's gown laces at the back. I'll help you get into it."

I unbutton my bodice and step out of my skirts, letting them settle on the floor around me. The green gown sighs like sea as Clara sweeps it from the bed. She lifts it over my head and it falls cloudlike over my body. After the cloying weight of my pleated calico skirts, the silky gown makes me feel almost weightless. Clara guides the narrow ribbons through their eyelets on the back of the dress. My breath roars in my ears, heart fast with anticipation. With the Green Lady's gown flowing against my body, the excitement in me is building. Pushing out whatever doubts Mr Browning's coldness dredged up.

"Can I look now?" I ask.

"You can."

I turn to face the mirror above the dressing table. The face staring back at me steals my breath. Clara has turned my skin pale and otherworldly, highlighting my eyes in deep lampblack shadows. Against the whiteness of my skin, my mousy hair looks almost raven dark, lips the palest pink. The Green Lady has just enough realism to make men stop and question. Enough ghost about her to keep them awake at night. Beneath her wraithlike pallor, she is beautiful.

It cannot be Lucy Earnshaw, because Lucy Earnshaw would never do a thing like this, never in a thousand lifetimes. Tonight, I am someone else. Some*thing* else. I am utterly unrecognisable, even to myself. And how liberating that is.

"And now?" I ask, surprised when my own voice comes out of those unfamiliar lips.

Clara grins. "Now you play the ghost." She opens the door and peers out into the corridor. Gestures to me to follow. "We'll take the back way," she says. "It comes out beside the stables. From there you can—" The stairs creak loudly. "Inside." She shoves me back in the direction of the room.

Before I can get anywhere close to the door, a figure appears at the top of the staircase. Will Browning. He stops in surprise at the sight of me.

"Lucy. You look… unrecognisable."

Clara plants a hand on her hip. "Thought you wanted nothing to do with all this."

"Well." His eyes meet mine, before he looks back at Clara. "I thought if Lucy was determined to go out there tonight, I ought to be the one to go with her." He scratches his neck. "For safety and all."

Clara gives a snort of laughter. "Safety. I see."

Browning ignores her. "What do you say?" he asks me. The intensity of his gaze makes something heat in my chest. And when, I think with an ache, was the last time I felt that way while looking into my husband's eyes?

I push the thought of Tom away. Tonight, I am the Green Lady. And I can put Lucy's troubles aside.

"I'd like that," I manage. I glance at Clara. "For safety and all."

"Good." Before Clara can respond, Will has scooped up my arm and is leading me down the passage. Flames dance within the lamps and make the walls seem alive.

After several paces of stilted silence, he gives me a

begrudging half-smile. "Two weeks ago, I practically had to beg you to perform the Green Lady. Now look at you."

The staircase creaks beneath our feet. "You're not angry?"

"That would be rather hypocritical of me, don't you think?"

I don't answer. Don't want to upset the delicate truce we're balancing on.

He guides me to the back entrance of the Commercial and holds open the door for me. I peek out to check the alley is empty. The earthy smell of horses and hay floats out from the stables beside us. Though it's less than an hour from midnight, the wind is still warm, carrying the steady wail of cicadas. At the end of the lane, a wider street unfolds. A carriage rattles past, making a dog bark loudly. I draw in a breath and press myself against the wall of the hotel.

Will's eyes move over me. "I must admit, you do look rather otherwordly. And rather beautiful."

I swallow, heart knocking hard. And I realise at once that I have no thought of what I'm doing. How on earth do you go about playing the ghost?

"What do I do?" I blurt. The moment the words are out, I regret them. Because I'm sure Will is looking for any excuse to bundle me back upstairs and get me away from this madness. But he says:

"That's up to you. Although I've found it works best to be discreet. A fleeting glimpse can be the most powerful thing of all. It's often what most sends our imaginations racing."

"And it works?" I ask hesitantly. "I'll not be recognised?"

"It works," says Will. "Because people want it to work. They want to see ghosts. They want that bit of magic in their lives."

I smile faintly. I want that too. I remind myself that I barely recognised my own reflection. A fleeting glimpse of the Green Lady and no one will know who she truly is.

I see a small smile on Will's lips too. He understands, I realise. He understands this need to be someone new. To make trouble. To seek magic.

"Will you wait here?" I ask.

"Of course."

"For safety."

He grins, the dimple appearing in his cheek. "For safety."

I take slow, steady steps towards the main street, my heart pounding in my ears. I will hover at the end of the alleyway, I decide. Tempt passers-by with a peep at the Green Lady before she disappears, leaving them with more questions than answers. Mysterious. Fleeting. Appearing in shadows, like Springheeled Jack.

I peer out at the street beyond me. There is the bank, the dispensary, the cobbler's. A street I must have walked a hundred times or more. And yet tonight it feels different. Feels as though I'm seeing it through someone else's eyes.

I stand with one shoulder pressed to the wall of the alley, letting the wind breathe into the folds of my dress. Streetlamps flicker, making the shadows move.

For a long time, no one notices me. A well-dressed couple strides past with their heads down; a man rides by on horseback. Others howl with laughter as they stumble from the tavern, with not so much as a glance in my direction. I'm too hidden. Always, I'm too hidden.

I feel as though I truly am a ghost; like I'm balanced on the edge of existence, viewing the world without taking part in it. The sensation is suddenly unmooring. Because isn't that how I've lived my life since my daughter died? As though I'm existing without really living? As though I'm doing nothing more than waiting for my own death?

I don't want that anymore. Can't bear another day of it. This is not what playing the ghost was supposed to be about.

I step out of the alley.

Several yards away, a young woman stops walking. I feel my heart quicken. The woman is a stranger, and yet I'm suddenly terrified I will be seen for what I am; a living, breathing human.

What does it matter that I'm wearing this old-fashioned gown, that my face is made up beyond recognition? Surely people will just see a misguided woman standing in the shadows, trying to escape reality.

I fight the urge to turn and run. To call the whole thing a mistake.

I think of the curtain shifting in the back of the tavern; enough to convince Clyde he saw the Green Lady. I think of the men at Buckley's claim, desperate to speak with his ghost. And I hold my ground. Because perhaps it's our curiosity, or our desperate need for proof that death isn't the end, but there's just something about us that makes us want to see a ghost.

I continue to stare. To watch. Motionless.

The woman's eyes widen.

Yes, these people want to see spirits. Perhaps this generation's obsession with the other side has begun to twist our thinking. And instead of rationality, our minds leap straight to the fantastical.

Two knocks for yes; well of course that's a spirit trying

to speak.

And an eerie figure in a Renaissance dress? No question that she's a ghost, brought out on our ships to terrorise the living.

I look past the young woman with a vacant, dead stare. I am burning with curiosity, with impatience, waiting to see what she does next. How does one behave when they see the walking dead?

There is no screaming, no running, just an almost imperceptible intake of breath. She edges backwards, as though afraid I might give chase.

But no, the Green Lady does not chase. The Green Lady does not engage. This motionless, unblinking stare, I know instinctively, will be the most unnerving. Most likely to have the woman racing home to tell this story in a breathless, half-whisper.

She turns and hurries away, leaving me to slip back into the alley. "Did you see her?" I hear her say to people I cannot see. "Tell me you saw her."

But no one else is to see the Green Lady tonight. Let them wonder, let them talk. I glide back to the hotel where Browning is waiting.

"Well?" His eyes catch the shine of the lanterns above the stables.

Without a thought, I throw my arms around him. Exhilarated. Alive. Realising at once the indecency of what I've done, I pull back. His hands linger against the side of my ribs for a moment before releasing me.

I can't hold back an enormous smile, well aware of how foolish my grin must look, dressed as the dead. "There'll be talk, I'm sure," I say. "A woman saw me. Just for a second.

Enough to give her a good scare."

He gives a short chuckle. "Well done." He's standing close to me; too close, yes I know that. But I'm hovering on the border of another world, and I can't find the need to step away. Right now, I'm someone else, and my guilt will not find me.

Somewhere distant, the diggers' guns are emptied into the sky. Tonight, I barely react as the gunfire splits the night. Tonight, it feels like nothing more than an echo.

Browning is the one who finally shifts, putting a little more space between us. He clears his throat, hands in his pockets. "Well. I'm glad you got that out of your system."

And though I say nothing to upturn the fragile peace between us, I know this won't be the last time the Green Lady walks the streets of Castlemaine.

CHAPTER EIGHT

*Dysentery... [is] now stalking abroad through the diggings. ... Death
follows death in quick succession."*

The Argus
Melbourne
March 1852

It's morning and Tom's side of the bed is empty. No
doubt he's still out guarding the claim. I'm glad of it. Glad I
didn't wake up eye to sin-filled eye with him.

I crossed no line, I tell myself. Kept Will Browning at a
safe distance. Mostly. But at the back of my mind, I know the
truth – he was the one mindful of keeping his distance. And
that distance was anything but safe.

I think of Tom camped out by the claim, sleeping under
an impossibly vast sky, with nothing but a sleeping mat and
his old worn coat. The thought of his discomfort, his anxiety,

make my guilt come to life. He was out protecting our land last night, while I was busy creating a public nuisance, and fawning over some dashing young playwright. There is fear for Tom there too – are there truly bushrangers in the forest outside Castlemaine? Sneaking onto the diggings at night and rifling through the claims? I hate the thought of Tom being in their line of fire. Can't shake off that irrational dread that Fred Buckley's death was not an accident – and that perhaps my husband might meet the same fate. I know if Tom caught someone robbing his claim, he would confront them. Finding success means too much to him not to do so.

I climb out of bed and splash my face at the washbin, collecting up the cloth I used last night to wipe away the remnants of the Green Lady. Straight into the laundry it will go, so I might scrub away my secrets. But I find myself squeezing it between my fingers. Find my eyes closing and my thoughts gliding back to Will Browning. The feel of his fingers grazing my ribs. His gaze burning into mine. I open my eyes hurriedly, trying to anchor myself in reality.

I dress and hurry out to the kitchen, flinging the cloth into a bag of laundry.

I fry up some bacon and slap it between two pieces of yesterday's bread, then trudge out to Forest Creek.

When I arrive at the claim, I find Leo at the windlass, Tom's sleeping mat rolled up on the side of the hole. Leo unhooks the bucket and nods in greeting, hollering down into the shaft to announce my arrival.

I tense as Tom's mud-streaked face appears over the edge of the claim. I feel as though everything I've done is visible in my eyes. He climbs the last few rungs of the ladder and dusts the loose earth from his knees.

"Did you have any trouble last night?" I ask, struggling to keep my voice level.

Tom waves a fly away from his face. His eyes are underlined in shadows of exhaustion. "Didn't see nothing."

"I reckon he was sleeping all night," Leo grins. "Snoring away while them bolters had the pick of the place." He upends the bucket of earth into the cradle and I see tiny flecks of gold glitter within the soil. Once upon a time, those golden flashes felt like magic. But I've long learned they're not enough to change a life.

Tom chuckles. "It's your turn tonight, you bastard."

I hand him the sandwich, catching a glimpse of the revolver tucked into the pocket of his trousers. "How long are you planning on doing this?" I ask. "Guarding the claim at night?"

He unwraps the bread and takes a bite. "As long as we need to," he says, mouth half full. "I'm sorry, Luce. I hate leaving you alone at night. I wouldn't do it if it weren't so important."

"It's all right. I understand." I can't look at him.

"You keep the door locked?"

"Of course."

"Good." He hands me back the cloth I wrapped the sandwich in. "I won't be home too late. I'm bloody exhausted. Thanks for breakfast."

I mumble a quick goodbye, then escape the diggings before my guilt swallows me whole.

I'm halfway to Pennyweight Flat before I realise I'm going to visit Elsie.

The cemetery is ringed by trees, a stillness over the place

that feels immune to the distant echo of shovels and cradles.

Most of the children's graves are sparsely marked; small wooden crosses, or piles of rocks, weather-worn dolls and toy soldiers standing at attention. In the valley beyond the cemetery, the diggings of Moonlight Flat scar the landscape. With row upon row of neatly dug shafts, it looks for all the world like another graveyard.

I sit on the earth beside the tiny circle of stones that marks the place my daughter lies. The late morning is hot and still, insects hissing in the long grass that hems the cemetery.

In the first few weeks after Elsie's death, Tom and I always visited her grave together. An unspoken agreement that we needed each other to keep from falling. That this was not something we could do alone.

I can't place exactly when that changed. Can't remember the first time I visited the cemetery alone. I only know it's become far more comforting this way.

Tom and I have never spoken about Elsie's death, not really. Before the camp fever upended our own lives, the outbreak was all we talked about. Each night, Tom returned home with another story about who had fallen ill, and what they'd been doing before the pains and fever took root. We traced their movements like detectives, avoiding the shops and markets and taverns where we knew the sick had been. Soon, there were too many places to be able to avoid them all.

We slept with Elsie in the bed between us, and I refused to let her crawl on the earthen floor of our tent. When I unwittingly passed a man vomiting in the creek, I took off my dress and petticoats before stepping into our tent. Burned them in a bonfire in front of the door, standing there in broad daylight in nothing but my shift.

In the face of so much death, I felt utterly powerless. Tom and I prayed ourselves into exhaustion, the weight of the situation pressing down on us from all sides. The tears of loss and physical pain that drifted across the diggings were sounds I learned, out of necessity, to ignore. Barely a day went by without us hearing of another death.

By the time the sickness reached our little family, it almost felt inevitable. But I told myself Elsie's fever was just warmth from the fire. The speckled rash spreading over her skin was insect bites, or prickly heat, or my frenzied imagination. Reality was far too brutal to accept.

After she was gone, Tom and I stopped speaking of camp fever. Stopped making plans, or thinking of the future, or burning our clothing when we'd been near the sick. It was easier to sit by the fire in silence, fingers intertwined. Every possible topic of conversation felt so trivial, so wasteful. My grief was a gaping abyss; Tom's fingers between my own the only thing stopping me from falling away entirely. I took the chalk and brandy potion I'd given Elsie and flung it into the fire. Waited for the fever to take me too.

All too quickly, Tom was back at the claim, and I was left with an empty tent and an anger taking root beside my grief. Though I tried my best not to, there was more than a small part of me that blamed Tom for our loss. Blamed him for bringing us to this place. Blamed him for wooing me back in Horley, for infecting me with his blind optimism and for fooling me into coming here. Why did we go searching for riches when we already had everything we needed? How different it would have been if we'd raised our child on the immaculate grounds of Hartwell Manor. If she'd been born within solid walls, instead of in a windblown tent, with mosquitoes in the doorway and rain puddles at the foot of the bed. If she'd been baptised in a church, instead of a clearing beside the creek.

My anger at Tom never feels more acute than when I'm here at the cemetery. Is that why I came here today, I wonder distantly? Because I need to feel that anger? Because that rage will dilute my guilt over the ghost hoaxing a little? The guilt over these thoughts of Will Browning that refuse to lie down.

I stand up, dusting the earth from my skirts. I can't stay here with my daughter if I'm to let my thoughts stray away from my family. Sending a silent goodbye to Elsie, I trudge back down the hill towards town.

Tom is home early the next evening. "No need to cook tonight," he tells me. "Meg and Richard are having us for supper.

I stiffen. "No Tom, I can't."

"I already told them we'd be there."

"Well, tell them something's come up."

Tom sighs. "I don't understand this, Luce. You and Meg were the best of friends."

He understands it. I know he does. I've told him my reasons for pulling away from Meg on more than one occasion. This is not a case of him not understanding. It's a case of him not wanting to discuss what needs to be discussed.

But he's clearly made up his mind. I know there's to be no arguing. And so I take off my apron and trail him out the door.

I met Meg the day we arrived on the goldfields, and we became friends almost instantly. A handful of years older than me, and a currency lass born and raised in the colonies, she became the guide I so desperately needed. New wife, new immigrant, mother-to-be. In their tiny tent next to ours, she lived crammed in with her husband and four children, but seemed to sail through the experience with grace. She taught me to cook damper, and to pickle the mutton so nothing went to waste. Showed me how to turn the flour bags into baby clothes, and how to make a veil out of poplin to keep the swirling dust from my eyes. I would hardly have survived that first year if it weren't for Meg and her seemingly endless supply of knowledge.

When the camp fever barrelled through, it took two of Meg's sons a few weeks after it took Elsie. Our first instincts were to lean on each other, and on the other lost women who had buried their children on Pennyweight Flat. We found some fragile sense of comfort huddled in the corners of each other's tents, stumbling through our losses with cups of smoke-scented tea. All our stories were so similar; fear and denial, and the fever taking its young victims so quickly it was as though our legs had been kicked out from beneath us. A small blessing, we told each other over and over, that our children had suffered just days, instead of weeks or months. A tiny, hollow blessing.

But then those mothers, with their lukewarm tea and their suffocating sadness, they began to blame themselves. *Should have burned the clothes, should have given him more water, could have moved away…*

I stepped away from those tentative friendships, forged

in tragedy. I couldn't handle the heaviness, the reminders that came with them. I tried to keep hold of my friendship with Meg. I knew that without her in my life, the loneliness would strangle me. But enter her tent and I was back in those bleak days of our shared grief. Any small glimmers of light I'd begun to see were immediately extinguished. And I made the choice to step away.

I miss her, sometimes deeply. We carried each other through both the births and deaths of our children, and I assumed, once, that that would bind us together for life. But being around Meg draws me back into a time I can't bear to face. When we finally moved away from the tent beside theirs, I allowed myself to cry with relief.

And now here we are, following the creek to the camp in which we lived for more than two years; among them, the worst months of my life. My stomach is knotted and I feel uncomfortably hot, despite the cool wind whipping up the dust.

The sun is beginning to sink, silhouetting trees with blinding orange light. The creek is still alive with men and the clatter and sigh of the cradles.

Tom gives me a smile that feels too broad. "I'm glad you're here," he tells me.

I wonder then if this evening is his doing; did he coax Meg and Richard into inviting us tonight? Is this about his disapproval of my friendship with Clara? Or another attempt at showing me the way to be happy?

I press my lips into a thin white line and sidestep a mound of horse dung.

Meg and Richard's son and daughter are tossing a ball to each other in front of the tent, bounding after dropped catches like hares. A campfire smoulders in front of the door, meat-scented steam rising from the pot that sits on the embers. In spite of myself, my eyes drift to the place our neighbouring tent once stood. A wattle and daub shack is in its place now, smoke puffing steadily out a crooked stone chimney.

At the sound of our footsteps, Richard emerges from their tent and tosses out greetings, a blank-faced baby tucked into his elbow. I'm reminded suddenly of how Elsie looked in Tom's arms; so fragile and doll-like against his wide brown hands. I turn away quickly.

Out comes Meg, offering us a warm smile. Her eyes are bright and she's less painfully thin than last time I saw her. Straw-coloured tendrils of hair escape from beneath her cloth bonnet and blow across her cheeks. She pulls me into her arms, then steps back and gives my hands a squeeze. "How are you, Lucy?" There is no animosity in her voice; no anger at the way I cut her out of my life so completely. I am grateful.

"I'm… I'm well," I say, and I realise it's the truth. At least, it's beginning to be.

"I'm glad." She bends to stir the stew pot, then turns back to me. "Supper's not far off. But maybe a drink first?"

"I'd like that."

"Good. Jack!" she hollers at her son. "Come away from the creek! Get those clothes wet and you ain't got no more." She shakes her head in resignation and puts a hand to my shoulder, leading me inside. The men stay by the campfire, chatting between themselves. Meg uncorks a bottle and fills two cups, kicking at a mouse that darts beneath the table. "Here. Let's enjoy the peace while it lasts."

I sit, taking a small sip from the cup. I recognise the scent of Meg's homemade dandelion wine. The taste is at once both sweet and sour, and almost sickeningly familiar. I set the cup back down in front of me.

"How's the cottage?" Meg asks.

"The cottage is fine." I draw in a breath. "I'm sorry I haven't—"

She puts a hand to my wrist, cutting me off. "Don't apologise, Lucy. Please. There's no need." Her eyes meet mine and I see the deep understanding beneath them. "I'm just glad you're here."

I give a short smile, unsure if I can say the same. "I've missed you," I say instead.

"I've missed you too." She sips her wine. "Tom still working with that tin miner?"

"Leo. Yes."

"Any luck?"

"Enough to keep food on the table. Not much else."

"Well. You know how quickly fortunes can change out here."

It feels like a conversation we've had a thousand times. Everything feels like yesterday. Feels as though it has been minutes since I last sat in this chair, drank this wine, rather than a year. And there it is, that underlying pull of dread, inches beneath the surface. This is what has kept me away from my closest friend for so long. I feel it threatening to rise and consume me.

Because there, in that corner, is where Meg's two little boys once slept. Over there is where Elsie got into the potatoes while my back was turned and flung them across the tent like bowling balls. And there's the half-drunk bottle of chalk and brandy on the shelf, a tincture we learned the hard way does little to fight camp fever.

How can Meg and Richard continue to live in a place so haunted by memories?

We cram around the table for a supper of mutton stew, the children's creek-soaked boots tipped over by the door, and the baby asleep in a crib beside the washstand.

I try to find the comfort in this; in being around old friends. Old friends who know what we've been through. But this tent, so cluttered with chatter and life, it doesn't feel like what Tom and I have. Once we leave the chaos of Meg and Richard's home, all we will go back to is emptiness.

"Did you hear about that ghost sighting a couple of days ago?" asks Meg, making me straighten in my chair.

"A ghost sighting?" I repeat.

"Apparently it was a woman in an old-fashioned dress," says Meg. "Just standing there behind the tavern or something. Jenny from the grocer's was talking about it the other morning."

I try not to let the smile show on my face.

"Lucy is starring in a ghosty play," Tom announces.

I look at him in surprise. "How do you know it's a ghosty play?"

"Seen your little book lying on the table," he reminds me. "*The Lady of Fyvie*, by Will Browning."

"Oh yes," grins Meg, "Will Browning. That's that fancy fellow who started up the theatre troupe. I didn't know you were a part of that, Lucy." She leans towards me conspiratorially. "I've seen that Mr Browning about the place. Don't you think he's just ever so handsome?"

I garble something that's not really anything, relieved when the baby interrupts with a shriek.

"Sorry," says Meg, going to the cradle. "I hoped he might sleep through supper."

"He never sleeps through anything," announces Meg's daughter, Alice.

I feel Tom trying to catch my eye. Keep my eyes on my plate. Tension gathers in my shoulders. I take another mouthful of wine, but it makes me feel worse.

"Did you read any of it?" I ask him under the baby's squalling. "The play?" I don't want him knowing I'm playing the part of the Green Lady. Not yet, at least. It feels safer to keep it a secret.

Will people make the connection when I step onto stage dressed as a ghost? I know it likely. Once I reveal myself, the mystery will be gone, and the hoaxing will have to end. But this knowledge only makes me more eager to play the ghost again.

"Didn't read any of it," Tom says. "Just the cover. Why?"

I shake my head dismissively.

I try to let that piece of knowledge settle me. Try to focus on the thrill of the Green Lady being spoken of, rather than the dread this tent is dredging up within me.

"Good for you, Lucy," says Richard. "Very brave of you getting on stage like that. We'll all have to come and watch."

Tom makes a show of squeezing my hand.

"I heard there's a woman up in town holding séances in her cottage," says Meg, plugging the baby's mouth with a knotted cloth pacifier. "Jenny said her sister went up there and they tried that spirit rapping."

"The mediums sometimes hollow out the walls," I say. "Hide people in there to make the rapping sounds."

Tom raises his eyebrows. "How on earth do you know

that?"

I shrug. "Just heard it somewhere." I take another mouthful of dandelion wine, swallowing down the memories that arrive with it. But I can't get them down quick enough. There we all are, sitting around the shared campfire in front of our tents, wrapped in blankets and swatting away flies among the shrieks and laughter of three lost children.

And there is the time when Tom was everything and more to me; a time when we'd fall asleep each night with hands and legs intertwined, the feel of his heart beating beneath my fingers somehow assuring me we'd survive.

"Stop it, Jack!" Alice wails at her brother, the sound making me jump. "Ma, he's kicking me!"

I get to my feet almost instinctively. Mumble something about relieving myself and lurch out into the open air.

Meg's tent is stifling. Pulling me back down to a hell I've only just managed to poke my head out of. And before I can make sense of what I'm doing, I begin to walk. Away from the tent. Away from the diggings.

I'm beginning to see my methods of coping could use a little improvement.

I stride back into town, glancing constantly over my shoulder to see if I've been followed. No sign of Tom. How long will it take them to discover I've run off like a petulant child? I can't manage more than a small tug of shame.

I've walked with no purpose beyond escaping, and I have little thought of where I should go. I can't bear the idea of going home. The memories Tom and I have created there are hardly more pleasant than the memories trapped in Meg and Richard's tent.

I stop momentarily outside the boarding house. Consider

going upstairs to hunt down Clara. No. She is busy preparing for the opening of her shop, spending long nights with a needle and thread in hand. I've already interrupted her once this week to have her magic me into the Green Lady. Not that she needed much convincing.

I keep walking. There is the Commercial. And yes, I'm fairly sure that somewhere in my mind, I knew all along that this was where I was going to end up.

I look down at my flat, mud-streaked skirts. Try to bash the creases out of them. I can still smell woodsmoke on my skin. But I don't care. Not tonight. I walk into the tavern without a second thought.

The bar is quiet, and I feel something sink inside me when I see no sign of Will. My eyes drift to the staircase that leads to the lodgings before I hurriedly look away. I might have eradicated my nerves over stepping into the Commercial but waltzing up to a man's room is still far beyond me.

I take myself to the unaccompanied ladies' room. Sit in the corner, sipping from a glass of whisky. The room is quiet and softly lit, and a gentle piano melody floats in from the main bar. As the liquor slides down my throat, I feel a little of the tension inside me drift away. There is a newness to this place Meg's tent doesn't have. The Commercial, somewhere I've only just discovered the courage to enter, makes me think of the future, instead of the past. And there's a newness, too, to the woman I am when I'm here. She is not the most decent of women, I see that all too clearly. I see my mistreatment of Tom and Meg, and the childish rebellion of ghost hoaxing all laid out in front of me. But my time in Castlemaine has taught me that so much of life is mere survival. And right now, this person is who I need to be to survive.

So there's been talk of the Green Lady sighting. I've rattled the place, just as I hoped. Meek, invisible Lucy has made people talk. At least, the woman I pretended to be has.

Laughter floats out from the billiards room across the hall. Familiar laughter. I pick up my glass and go to investigate.

Charles and Matthew are dancing around the billiards table with cues in their hands. Charles looks up as I hover in the doorway.

"Evening, Mrs Earnshaw."

I smile. "It's Lucy."

"Come in, come in, Lucy." Matthew ushers me through the door. From his brassy voice and the half-filled glasses on the edge of the billiards table, I can tell they've been in their cups for hours. "Don't be shy. Here." He shoves the cue into my hand. "You may as well take my shot. Charlie's already wiping the floor with me."

I smile, holding the cue back out to him. "I don't know how to play."

Charles grins. "Neither does he."

"Come stand here." With a hand to my shoulder, Matthew positions me at the corner of the table. "This ball in this pocket. Take your time. Line it up."

I set my glass on the edge of the table beside Matthew's and copy the position I've seen the billiards players assume. My cue barely makes contact with the ball, which dribbles across the table for a few sorry inches. I grin. "I told you I didn't know how to play."

Matthew takes the cue back and executes a shot that is marginally better than mine. "Were you looking for Will? He's upstairs writing."

"Oh no," I say hurriedly. "I was just… passing." My cheeks blaze in embarrassment, but the two men barely react. And then, because I can't help myself, I drop my voice and say, "I went out playing the ghost this week. Got people talking."

Charles grins at me. "Didn't think you had it in you."

"A woman saw me in street," I tell them excitedly. "She ran away, all terrified. And the other morning, Jenny from the grocer's was talking about it…"

The men chuckle at my enthusiasm, and instead of being embarrassed, I'm glad to have entertained them.

"So," says Matthew, "when will we be seeing the Green Lady again?"

"I don't know," I admit. "Will wasn't all that happy about it. I don't think he wants me to do it again. And we need to use his room to get ready."

Charles snorts. "Miserable sod's probably just wishing it were him out there causing trouble."

I smile.

"You know Will's not the only one with a private room," Matthew tells me with a wink. "Why don't you and Clara come by tomorrow night? I'll clear out and let you use my room. You can give this town their ghost again."

The darkness is thick when I let myself back into the cottage. In the muted glow of the lamp, I make out the inky bulk of my husband sitting at the table. One side of his face is lit with candlelight, the other bathed in shadow.

For a rigid moment, we eye each other without speaking.

"Where in hell did you go?" he says finally. "I've been looking everywhere for you."

I almost laugh at that. I was hardly hidden away, whacking billiard balls around the table in one of the town's biggest public houses. Tom clearly did not even think to look for me at the Commercial. I'm infinitely relieved, of course, that he chose not to.

"I'm sorry," I murmur.

"You've been drinking. I can smell it on you."

I don't answer.

Tom's voice sparks suddenly. "How could you do that to Meg, when she—"

"I told you I couldn't go out there," I hiss. "I told you it was too much. But you always seem to know what's best for me, don't you. You always seem to know better."

Tom sighs heavily. He slumps back in his chair and picks at something underneath his fingernail. I grip the edge of the table, listening to the lamp hiss in the stillness. My head is beginning to ache.

"It's been more than a year, Lucy," Tom says finally.

My heart jumps because this is as close as he's come in months to speaking of our loss. *More than a year since what?*, I want to push. I want to hear him speak of our daughter. I can't remember the last time I heard him say Elsie's name. But he falls silent.

"And so?" I say bitterly. "I ought to just forget?"

Tom looks out the window into the dark garden. He rubs his stubble, not looking at me. "You ought to..." Another sigh. "Richard and Meg, they've carried on. Their new son..."

I stare him down. "And is that what you want, Tom? A new son?"

He exhales sharply. "Of course it is."

"Fine." I take off my bonnet and fling it onto the chair. "Fine. I'm here, aren't I? Do as you wish."

I stride into the bedroom and crawl onto the bed in my skirts and boots. Stare into the darkness. Tom enters the room and I feel the bed shift as he sits on the edge. His breathing is loud and rhythmic. Indecision? Isn't this what he wanted? His wife compliant and willing? Ready to give him that precious new son?

He turns suddenly, lurches, lowering himself over me. He grips a fistful of my skirts and yanks them to my waist. His hand finds the laces of my drawers, and he fumbles for a moment with the knot. His hot fingers reach beneath the waistband and I swallow my sharp inhalation. Resist the urge to pull away.

Tom releases me suddenly. He rolls over, back to me. "Go to sleep," he mumbles, letting the silence settle heavily around us.

CHAPTER NINE

Night at the diggings is the characteristic time; murder here –
murder there – revolvers cracking – blunderbusses bombing … one
man groaning with a broken leg – another shouting because he couldn't
find his way to his hole, and a third equally vociferous because he has
tumbled into one – this man swearing – another praying – a party of
bacchanals chanting various ditties to different time and tune, or rather
minus both."

Ellen Clacy
A Lady's Visit to the Gold Diggings of Australia
1852

Forest Creek, I say when I get to Matthew's room the
next night. This is where I want the Green Lady to be seen.
It's the diggings I want to terrorise. For this is the place the
holds the heart of my grief, the place that has Tom in its grip,
the place where my daughter was stolen from me. I want to

burn it to the ground.

I waited until Tom was snoring lightly to slip out of bed and dress, before making my way to the Commercial. He has always been a heavy sleeper, and I know I'll be able to creep back into the cottage in the early hours, leaving him oblivious to my adventures.

It's almost eleven, and Matthew's room is hung with cigar smoke. He and Charles are halfway through a bottle of whisky; opposite each other in matching armchairs, glasses in one hand and cigars in the other.

I sit beside the unlit fireplace while Clara and her makeup brushes turn me into a Scottish wraith. The delicate folds of the Green Lady's dress sigh against my body.

"Forest Creek?" Clara repeats. "That's miles away."

"*A* mile," I say. Maybe a little more, but she won't debate the issue. I can't imagine she's spent much time in the diggings. "People are already speaking of the first sighting," I remind her. "It'd really get them talking if the Green Lady was seen out among the mining claims. Imagine how mysterious she'd look out there."

Matthew eyes me with a grin. "You've created a monster, Clara. A *monster*." He howls with laughter. Charles, after a second of deliberation, decides to join in.

"Keep your bloody voices down," Clara hisses. "You noisy bastards want to give the game away?"

"Where's Will?" Charles asks, still chuckling mindlessly. He grinds his cigar into an ashtray on the tea table. "Didn't think he'd be one to miss a little hoaxing."

Clara dusts powder over my cheeks. "Lucy says he's being funny about the whole thing."

"He's working tonight anyway," Matthew tells us.

"Writing his new play."

Clara raises her dark eyebrows as she presses the lid back onto the jar of powder. "Can't imagine him getting any work done with you two carrying on in the next room."

Charles lurches to his feet and pounds a fist against the wall. "Will! Come on out, you prickly bastard! Don't pretend you don't love a good scare."

"Don't," I murmur, too softly to be heard. But while I know Will won't be pleased I'm playing the ghost again, I can't deny there's a part of me that's desperate to see him. When the door clicks open and he pokes his head inside the room, my stomach turns over in response.

He shakes his head at Charles. "What in hell—" His eyes fall to me. "Ah." He takes in the wide sweep of the Green Lady's gown. "I thought you were done with all this."

I hold his gaze. "I didn't say that."

"The Green Lady will be seen on the diggings tonight," Clara announces, swanning past him as she unpins my hair. It tumbles over my shoulders.

"The diggings?" he repeats. "Lucy, that's madness."

But the Green Lady makes me bold. "I wasn't asking for your permission."

Will opens his mouth, but says nothing, silenced by my sudden audacity. I don't miss the smile Clara tries to hide behind her hand.

"It's dangerous," Will says finally. "Walking among all those holes in the ground."

"Stay to the outside of the tents and you won't fall. I lived out there for more than two years."

But the danger, it's there all right. Because even though Tom is fast asleep in bed tonight, Leo is out at their claim with his eyes open for thieves. Bushrangers, bolters. And perhaps a ghost or two. Talented as Clara is with a makeup brush, I doubt the disguise will fool my husband's close friend.

But I want that danger. I want that thrill. It's part of what drew me to hoaxing in the first place. Even the thought of there being bushrangers out in the forest is not enough to deter me. Because this rush of fear and exhilaration makes me feel alive.

Will looks at me for a moment without speaking. If he's going to be angry, so be it. Acceding to him, giving in, and being what he wants me to be – where can that lead? Nowhere, while I wear Tom's ring on my finger. But playing the ghost; that leads me to a place that's dizzying in its excitement. A place where my pain and frustration is blissfully distant.

"Let's go, Lucy," Clara cuts in. "It's already past eleven."

Will's eyes dart to Charles and Matthew, then he looks back at Clara and me. "The two of you are going out there alone?"

"Can hardly take these animals with us," Clara says, waving a hand in the direction of the men. "We'll be fishing them out of the mining claims."

"You're not going out to the diggings alone," Will says firmly. "Let me get my coat."

Clara bubbles with laughter. "Honestly, Will, you're so predictable." She takes a fresh glass from the shelf and fills it, perching on the arm of Matthew's chair. "Enjoy yourselves."

I get hesitantly to my feet. "You're not coming with us?"

"All the way to the diggings?" She brings her glass to her lips. "Wouldn't dream of it."

Will strides from the room without another word, leaving me to follow dazedly. For a fleeting moment, I felt in control, but in the wake of Browning's anger and Clara's total orchestration of the situation, I feel like I'm being pulled along in riptide. But I have neither the will nor the inclination to protest a walk out to the diggings alone with Browning. My heart is thundering at the prospect.

He disappears into his own room for a moment, returning with a sack jacket and a large black greatcoat, along with a lamp he has taken from the table. "Put this on," he says stiffly, handing me the coat. I slip it over my shoulders and follow him out of the hotel.

I keep my head down and my collar pulled up as we make our way out of town. Even in the darkness, heat is pressing down on the land, but I wrap myself in Browning's greatcoat, letting the sleeves fall over my hands. His rosewater scent clings to the wool and I draw in a long breath to drink it in.

The lamp in his hand does little to cut through the night as we leave the streetlamps behind. Sparse clouds drift in front of the moon. The horizon is glowing with the campfires of the diggings, but they're too far away to offer much light. The bush on either side of us rustles and sighs, alive with unseen animals.

We walk close together, our shoulders brushing against each other's. I glance his way, but his eyes are fixed to the path ahead, jaw set firmly.

"Are we going to walk in silence all the way there?" I ask finally.

He eyes me. "I don't think you should be doing this."

"I know you don't. But you volunteered to come out here, remember?"

"Well. I could hardly let you and Clara go alone. What kind of man would that make me?"

"Is that why you don't want me to play the ghost?" I ask. "Because you think it dangerous?"

"It is dangerous."

I say nothing. Our footsteps crunch loudly on the dry dirt road. Will lets out a sigh. But then he says, "Charles tells me you're a better billiards player than Matthew."

I eye him. "Apparently that's not difficult."

He gives a short chuckle. Looks at his feet. "I'm sorry I missed you," he says after a moment. "I would have come down if I'd known you were there."

I feel a smile on the edge of my lips. Feel a little of the tension drain from my shoulders. "Can I take that to mean you forgive me for going hoaxing?"

He returns my smile tentatively. "Let's not get carried away."

I pull his coat tighter around me. "They said you've been writing?"

"Yes. A new play."

"About the supernatural?"

"Not this time. My time here has inspired me to write something a little more realist. Something a little more challenging. An exploration of how we're shaped by the natural world around us."

I look ahead to the firelit plain of the diggings where the trees have been torn from the earth. "I would have thought rather the natural world is shaped by us."

Will hums in thought, shifting the lantern from one hand to the other. "Yes, in a way. But don't you think the harshness of this land strengthens us? Makes us capable of more than we would otherwise have been?"

I almost laugh at the searing truth of his words. Look at me, in the Green Lady's dress, walking shoulder to shoulder with a man who is not my husband. Here in this new life of mine, I'm certainly capable of more than I once was.

I've been shaped, I suppose, by the world I'm in. After all, it's this town, this land, these infested, sun-bleached goldfields that were supposed to give us everything that I blame for all I've lost.

"You're right," I say, and I'm glad for the cordiality we seem to have rediscovered.

From out of the dark comes music; an undulating vocal melody, sung in Irish beside the diggers' campfire. Though I don't understand its meaning, the sadness is inescapable. I can feel it in my chest.

I first heard the Irish keening days after we arrived on the goldfields. A funeral of sorts, Meg explained. A way for the Irish to honour their dead.

"Do you hear it?" I ask softly. "The keening?"

"Yes. It's very beautiful. Very haunting."

And it's this I will focus on tonight; the otherworldly atmosphere the singing creates. Not the memories that come with it. How many nights did I lie in our tent, listening to the Irish mourn their dead through song? Those plaintive voices became the sound of my own grief.

But not tonight. The Green Lady's costume shields me from those memories. Tonight, the keening just creates a world in which people are willing to believe in ghosts.

It's not just the Green Lady's costume that shields me from the memories, I realise as I walk. It's Will Browning's presence, and the way he drags my mind out of the past.

When I'm with him, I'm so intrigued by the present that I don't feel so trapped by what has come before.

"It must have been a challenging life out here," he says.

"In some ways." I keep my voice light in an attempt to scramble past the subject.

"Do you miss England?" he asks.

"Sometimes. In parts." I miss not knowing the hollow ache of losing a child. But I don't miss scrubbing dishes at Hartwell Manor, or winters so grey you can feel it in your bones. And nothing in England ever thrilled me as much as sneaking out here to the diggings with Will Browning, about to play the ghost. "And you?" I ask.

As he opens his mouth to speak, an owl lets out a hoarse shriek that sounds like someone's just been done in.

He smiles wryly. "I miss not fearing for my life whenever I go for a stroll."

I laugh. "It's just an owl. We used to hear them all the time from our tent. I'd rather be strolling out here than walking through London at night. All those dark little streets and alleys. Bet there's far worse things than owls hiding in there."

He grins. "Why do you think people believed in Springheeled Jack for so long?"

"*Mysteries of London* was my favourite Penny Blood," I tell him. "I was reading it right up until we came out here."

He raises his eyebrows. "Didn't pick you as a Penny Blood reader."

"I used to steal them from my older brother when I was a girl. I'd read them before bed and scare myself silly."

He laughs. "I loved them too. Although I have to say, *Mysteries* went downhill somewhat after they changed authors.

You haven't missed much."

I smile to myself, imagining Will as a boy, hiding under the covers to read Penny Bloods, just as I used to do. Perhaps we're not from such different worlds after all.

"Are you angry with me?" I dare to ask.

He gives a half-shrug. "It's like you said, you don't need my blessing."

"That doesn't really answer my question."

"I just don't want to see you get into trouble," he says. "But if this is something you need to do…"

Something you need to do.

What does Will Browning imagine it is that made me need to play the ghost? I've told him nothing about Elsie. Nothing about the grief that was pulling me below the surface until I found the Green Lady. I don't want him to look at me with pity. But perhaps I've already said too much.

His eyes on me feel suddenly piercing, and I have to look away. "It's nice to be someone else for a while," I say, not wanting to go further.

"Even if she's dead?"

I laugh a little. "Yes, even if she'd dead."

His hand brushes against mine as we walk, and for a fleeting second, our fingers intertwine. So brief I can't tell if I imagined it. I feel my body pull instinctively towards him. Feel a tug deep inside me of something I distantly recognise as desire.

How dare you?, says that faraway part of me that is still Lucy. But the part of me that is someone else is winning. Whatever this woman does, it doesn't seem to matter. When the sun comes up, it will all be relegated back to the world of myth and fairy tale.

A loud argument crashes through the melody of the keening. The shouting is coming from somewhere near the creek. I strain my ears, but I can't make out the words.

"Is it always like this?" Will asks. "Are the miners always so angry?"

"People are on edge," I say. "There's been a lot of thefts lately."

"Thefts? Among the miners?"

"No one's sure. Word is it could be bushrangers."

He frowns. "I think we ought to leave."

"No." The word is out before I can even think about it. My tone leaves no room for argument.

Will nods faintly. I can tell he has witnessed something behind my eyes. Something darker than he was expecting.

He puts down the lamp and takes a step closer to me. Folds my hand in both of his. I see a new seriousness in his eyes. "Be careful, Lucy, won't you. If anything were to happen to you…" He swallows. "I would feel horribly responsible."

I nod. "I'll be careful."

I go to step away, but he keeps my hand in his for another moment. Gives my fingers a gentle squeeze. A bolt of energy tightens my shoulders.

I didn't believe it. Not really. Didn't believe that a man like Will Browning might be drawn to a woman like me. Didn't believe he could find a single thing among my stumbling sadness that might make him look at me twice. But in the way his thumb glides over my knuckles; in the way he looks at me as though he's staring into my soul, I know that Will sees more in me than I see in myself. At once, I'm terrified; I'm flattered; I'm grateful. And I want to take this nervous excitement that is charging through my body, and use it to play the ghost.

I slip the coat from my shoulders and hand it to him without a word. I breathe deep and force myself to move slowly. A ghost among the wilderness. I keep myself close to the thick white trunks on the edge of the diggings, giving stray eyes nothing but a hint of a flowing green skirt.

No one is close, but I see clusters of men around the campfires in the barren plains among the claims. I think of all those nights I spent in our little tent out here, falling asleep to the distant laughter of men at their fires. Listening to them curse and chatter in the strange, wide accent of the currency lads. Soothing Elsie's tears each night she was torn from sleep by the emptying of the guns.

I tried, in those first two years. I tried so hard. Tried to share Tom's enthusiasm, his drive, his belief that this was the right thing to do. I told myself it was only a matter of time before he came home with those nuggets in his pocket, and we'd have the riches we craved.

I was ignoring reality long before I pulled on the Green Lady's gown.

I continue my walk around the rim of the diggings, past campfires surrounded by miners; past men on sleeping mats, their hands folded over their pistols. Careful to keep my distance from Tom and Leo's claim. Careful to stay away from Meg and Richard's tent.

No one looks up as I pass. No one pauses in conversation or turns at the crackle of twigs. My footsteps are too careful, too silent, and the moonlight is not falling the right way to light the mint-coloured folds of my dress.

I make out the figure of a man up ahead, back to me as he pisses against a tree. He'll see me, I realise, when he turns around. What will he make of me?

I take a step closer, partially hiding myself behind the silky trunk of a gum tree. I position myself for full effect, the ethereal fabric of my skirts whipping against the bark.

Patience.

As the man turns back towards the camp, he stops walking. And he sees a ghost.

"Christ Almighty," I hear him hiss. He stumbles backwards, shoulder bumping against a tree in his shock. And then he is off into the dark, without looking at me again.

Before my image can be scrutinised, I grab my skirts in my fist and run into the blackness that enfolds me.

I dodge tents and trees with little more than instinct. When I am surrounded by silence, I stop running, gasping down my breath. I feel oddly exhilarated. Strangely buoyed by the knowledge of how easily I could have plummeted into an open claim. A laugh escapes me – what a dramatic end that would have been to the story of the Green Lady.

I turn in a circle, trying to get my bearings. The campfires behind me tell me I've run farther away from town, out towards where the forest thickens. I walk back in the direction of the camp. I feel as though I'm hovering somewhere between this world and the next.

The diggings are quieter now, many of the campfires reduced to embers and much of the chatter silenced. The tents dotted around the claims are dark.

On the edge of my vision, I see a flicker of light. A pinprick of white moving along the ground. So fleeting and fragile it flits in and out of my sight.

I think of the night fossickers; the men who creep out to the goldfields in the dark and dig up other people's claims by lamplight. Night fossickers were seen on Moonlight Flat the night of Fred Buckley's burial, and on several occasions since. Is this what I'm seeing?

I creep towards the lamplight and peek out from behind a tent. I need to watch. I know how rattled Tom is over these thefts. If there's a chance I can catch a glimpse of who is responsible, I have to try.

My heart thunders. Am I watching a bushranger at work? Perhaps even Fred Buckley's killer? My palms prickle with sweat.

A broad figure emerges from the earth, a lamp in hand. And as he hauls himself from the claim, the light flickers over his features.

I swallow my gasp.

Though he is dressed in black rather than his trooper's uniform, I have no trouble recognising Constable Stone.

I grip my skirts in my fist as I turn this discovery around in my head. Maybe Stone is out here in an official capacity. As part of an investigation.

Maybe not.

I take an involuntary step backwards, earth crunching beneath my boots. Stone looks up suddenly. And his eyes meet mine. Is that recognition in his gaze? Surely not. I barely know the man, and my disguise is a good one. But his eyes seem to pierce me. And as though I'm the one who has seen a ghost, I turn and race out across the diggings, back to where Browning is waiting.

When we get back to the hotel, I hurry upstairs to change, wiping off my makeup with the cloth beside the washbin. I shake off Will's insistence to walk me home and rush back to the cottage.

A part of me is desperate to tell Tom what I saw. But how could I explain what I was doing out on the diggings? Tom can never know I was ghost hoaxing in the company of another man.

I slide the key into the lock and creep inside, pulling off my dusty boots.

As I push open the bedroom door, my heart jolts. The bed is empty. Tom was asleep when I left, so he must know I've been out of the house. Has he gone out to find me?

I throw off my dress and yank the pins out of my hair. I ruffle it up, in what I hope makes it look as though I've been asleep for hours.

How long has Tom been gone? Does he know I've been out for most of the night? Or did he wake just minutes ago and notice me missing? I have no way of knowing.

With my shawl wrapped around my shoulders, I open the front door and peer out into the street.

"Tom?" My voice disappears into the night and a shiver goes through me. I know there are plenty of indecent things going on in that darkness. After all, I'm a part of them.

I go to the gate and peer into the street. Everything is still, and I can hear insects flitting around the streetlights, frogs clicking in the creek. I start at the sound of footsteps, letting out my breath at the sight of Tom emerging from the shadows. He hurries towards me.

"Lucy. Where the hell were you?"

"I… I couldn't sleep. I just went for some air. When I came back to bed, you were gone." I hold my breath, waiting for him to dispute the matter.

"Some air?" he repeats.

"Yes."

His eyes flicker over me. Does he believe me? Strangely, I can't tell. I have always been able to read him.

"You shouldn't be out this time of night," he says. "Especially not now. With all that's going on."

"I'm sorry. I didn't mean to worry you."

Tom opens his mouth, but he decides against speaking. "It's very late," he says finally. "Let's get back to bed."

"'Perhaps the Green Lady will forever walk,'" Ollie croons, staring into the distance with what I assume is supposed to be a look of deep contemplation.

We've made it to the end of rehearsal and, somehow, miraculously, the play. All without Will Browning speaking directly to me. With just three other performers in the show, I'm certain this level of snubbing takes a special kind of talent.

Maybe I'm mistaken. Maybe my new theatrical self has become too precious for her own damn good. Nonetheless, my heart is thudding when I make my way towards him as the others file off the stage.

At the sight of me, he folds his arms across his chest. "Well done, Mrs Earnshaw," he says stiffly. "You acted well today."

I blink, words dying in my throat at his brusqueness. What happened to that comfortable chatter we found on the way to Forest Creek?

"Thank you," I spit out, but there's not an ounce of gratitude in my words. I march off stage and grab my bonnet, clenching my jaw in anger. I can't help another glance back in his direction, but he's poring over his script like he's never seen anything so exciting in his whole damn life. Rage shoots through me. Am I truly so dispensable? So easy to push aside? Or is this coldness my punishment for defying him by playing the ghost?

"What happened out at Forest Creek last night?" Clara asks as we walk to the door. "Why's Will so wound up?"

I snort. "Damned if I know."

She gives me a wry smile. "These fickle theatre types are trouble. You ought to stay away from them."

Though I know she's half-joking, she's also right. I should stay away. After all, why in hell should I care if Browning is being cold to me? What I really ought to be thinking about is what I'll make for supper tonight. With not much growing in the garden beyond potatoes, it'll likely be Irish stew again.

Yes, good. This is much safer. Onions, potatoes, a little smoked meat…

"I heard some chatter about the Green Lady at the market this morning," says Clara, voice low. My thoughts about the stew disintegrate. "A ghost peering out among the mining claims. You've certainly got people talking."

"Good," I snap. Because much of my need to play the ghost is built on anger and frustration. And Will Browning is digging a hell of a lot of both up inside me right now.

I can't resist another glance over my shoulder as we leave. Will has disappeared backstage, but I can hear his footsteps clomping around on the floorboards.

Clara pushes open the door, orange dusk flooding inside. "You'll come to the shop sometime this week? Help me set things up?"

I nod. "Yes, on Thursday."

"Perfect. Shall I see you home?"

I shake my head. "I can make my own way."

I watch as she disappears back towards the boarding house. And I stand outside the theatre, caught in indecision. Because what I really want is not to return to the cottage and make another damn pot of Irish stew. It's to march back inside the theatre and demand to know why in hell Will Browning is being such a bastard. The intensity of the thought shocks me. I don't *march* anywhere, and I certainly don't *demand* anything. But maybe I should.

I shove open the door before I can change my mind. Stride back down the aisle.

Will is carrying a small tin of paint onto the stage, large swathes of painted cloth spread out at his feet. His eyes meet mine for the first time today, and somehow, infuriatingly, it drains away my resolve. Suddenly I'm tearing through my thoughts, trying to determine what I might have done wrong to make him act so distantly. What might have turned our night at Forest Creek into two hours of stilted silence.

"You're back," he says. His eyes give nothing away.

I make my way towards him, the click of my boots echoing in the empty space. The ghost light paints a frayed gold circle in the centre of the stage.

"What's this about then?" I ask, my voice far less assertive than I hoped it would be. "I thought we were all right."

He holds my gaze for a moment. "We," he repeats finally. "There is no 'we', Lucy."

I grit my teeth. "You know what I meant."

He sets down the pot of paint and looks at me with

faintly apologetic eyes. "Would you like to help me?"

I open my mouth, caught off guard. "Help you with what?"

"Painting the set."

"You're doing that yourself?"

He kneels beside the paint tin and pries it open with the end of a pencil. "Just one of the challenges of starting at the bottom again. No one to do these things for me."

I hover at the foot of the stairs that lead up to the stage. Fold my arms across my chest. "I don't know anything about painting."

"Nor do I. I'm banking on the fact that no one in this town does either." He holds out a paintbrush, a wordless peace offering with the faintest of smiles.

I take my bonnet back off and put it on the floor in the corner of the stage. I take the brush, my fingers grazing his.

"Here," he says, pointing to the large sheet of calico at our feet. A neat stone wall has been outlined across it. "You can paint the bricks. I've outlined them already. They just need filling in."

I kneel beside the cloth, dipping the brush into the pot of sand-coloured paint he sets beside me.

"I had no idea you were making all this," I say, in spite of myself.

"I made Clara buy me this fabric when she put in her last order. I'm afraid it won't look quite as solid and professional as I'd like, but it ought to create something of an atmosphere at the very least." He kneels beside me, painting carefully around the hanging hooks at the top of the fabric.

"Am I painting the walls of Fyvie Castle?" I ask, tracing the outline of a turret.

"You are." He dips his brush into a pot of water. "I visited the castle as a child. And I always remembered the turrets. They felt like something straight out of a fairy tale. I made up a story about a prince who could turn into a dragon." He smiles to himself. "My imagination always was a little peculiar."

And how is it that we're back here, in this compatible comfort, talking about dragons and fairy tales and castles with turrets? I don't know, but I'm glad of it. I need this, I realise. I need this easy, warm conversation. Need conversation that makes me think, makes me someone I never used to be. I need to feel that light inside me that comes from looking forward instead of back.

And I need someone to look at me the way Will Browning does.

"If you want me to stop hoaxing, I will." The words are hard to get out. Because there's an exhilaration to playing the Green Lady, whether out on the diggings, or on the stage of the Theatre Royal. A blissful thing to be taken from my real life for a time. It doesn't matter that it's into this story of betrayal and despair. Because funnelling my own gloom into the Green Lady eases it from my body. Makes me feel a lightness I can barely remember feeling. When I'm lost in the world of Fyvie Castle, I don't think of Constable Stone crawling from the claim. I don't think of Tom either, or that questioning look in his eyes.

But I don't want all that if it means losing this unnameable thing that's simmering between Will and me.

For several long moments, he doesn't speak, just runs his paintbrush over a wild twist of ivy. "You shouldn't stop on account of me," he says finally. "I know playing the ghost has its way of… making you forget your troubles."

A splodge of water plops off my brush and makes the painted bricks look rain-washed. "Why are you so against it?" I ask. "It's not just because you think it dangerous, is it. There's more to it than that."

Will lets out a soft sigh. His gaze is fixed to the darkened auditorium, to the rows of empty seats. "I suppose it reminds me of a time in my life I'd rather forget."

Something tugs inside me. "The failure of your plays."

He nods. "When my first piece was a success, I thought I'd made it. But I couldn't seem to replicate the quality of it again. And the more bad work I produced, the more the reviewers crucified me. It took away the love I had for the theatre. Took away my passion for what I do. I felt a great anger at that. At the critics. And at society as a whole for rejecting my work." When his eyes meet mine, he looks suddenly young and vulnerable. "I suppose playing the ghost was a reaction to that. A way of rebelling against society. And escaping the harshness of reality for a time." He rinses his brush and sits back on his heels, his arm grazing mine. "It's foolish," he says. "I know."

"Well," I say, "it may be foolish. But I understand."

"You do." It is not a question.

Perhaps it's not my grief he can see. Perhaps it's my attraction to him that is simmering beneath my skin. I've not done much to hide it. Perhaps he does not imagine it's grief I'm escaping, but rather, my marriage.

Perhaps he is right.

I sit back too, and my shoulder presses against his. Will Browning is utterly magnetic, and I can't manage to put space between us.

"When I saw you go out there to play the Green Lady, it just reminded me of that time in my life when I felt the need to go hoaxing. Reminded me of everything I hoped to forget by coming to Australia."

"Then I won't do it again," I say firmly. "I can't bear the thought of making you feel that way. And I don't want this coldness between us each time I play the ghost."

"No, Lucy." He puts a hand out suddenly, gripping my forearm. "If you need to do it, you should. I apologise for my coldness. Truth be told, it had less to do with the ghost hoaxing, and more to do with the fact that…" He swallows visibly. "That I enjoy your company far more than I ought to." He gives a humourless laugh. "I know I may have a strange way of showing it. But last night, when I was out there with you, I felt…" He clears his throat, his words dying away. "Well, what I felt is neither here nor there. You belong to another man. I just thought it best to keep my distance."

I can't look at him. Who knows where that might lead? My heart is thundering so loudly I'm sure he can hear it. Finally, I murmur, "I enjoy your company far more than I ought to as well."

My words hang in the silence, above the pearly glow of the ghost light and the painted walls of Fyvie Castle. I'm frozen in place, knuckles white around the paintbrush, too afraid to move, to speak.

Will jumps suddenly to his feet, dragging the cloth to the edge of the stage to dry. The biting smell of wet paint wafts into the air. "The pieces I did yesterday are dry," he says, a little too brightly. "Shall we hang them up and see how they look?"

He disappears backstage before I can respond and

returns with several folded-up pieces of cloth. When he opens them out, I see they're painted with the same bricks and narrow windows as the section we have just finished.

He passes me the cloth and goes backstage again, returning with a ladder. He climbs to the top and I pass up a corner of the fabric, allowing him to hang it from the rail at the back of the stage. When one wall of Fyvie Castle has been erected, he moves the ladder to the other side and we repeat the process.

I stand at the front of the stage, turning in a slow half circle, a smile on the edge of my lips. Shadows shift on the makeshift walls, transporting me to Scotland, and the cloud-drenched world of Fyvie Castle. Motes of dust sparkle in the lamplight. I know this is as close to home as I'm ever likely to get again. But right now, it's enough.

I want to ask Will whether *The Lady of Fyvie* has helped him rediscover his lost passion for the theatre. Whether it's possible to come back from a despair so deep it threatened to swallow you whole. But I don't want to break the silence. It feels almost otherworldly.

I sense his presence behind me. And I take a step in his direction.

I understand what kind of person this makes me. I understand the crushing shame I ought to feel. But I want it; deeply, desperately. I want closeness, intimacy, to feel another's skin against my own. Want someone to take me out of my own head and look at me with lust in their eyes. I want all those things Tom and I have lost.

He is close. I can feel his breath flutter the hair at the back of my neck, as though he is daring himself to touch – or trying to prevent himself from doing so. My heart is loud in my ears.

And then his hand moves against my shoulder, wrapping around the curve of me. Seeing his paint-splattered, imperfect fingers against my body gives me the courage to turn and face him. To look up and meet his eyes.

He presses a palm to my cheek. "Tell me to stop and I shall."

No.

There will be consequences, of course. There always are. But perhaps these are consequences I'm willing to accept. A fair trade.

I lean forward to meet him, my lips to his. A kiss that thaws me from an eternal freeze. My mind is blissfully blank. All I'm aware of is the sensation of being alive.

When Will pulls away, I hear a murmur of disappointment escape me.

He leans his forehead against mine and tucks a strand of hair behind my ear. "Lucy, I…"

I take a step back, and that action is enough to silence him.

I can't ask him to be this man. Can't ask him to dive into this; a thing which can never be. Not out in the daylight. Dizzying and blissful as my lips on his felt, we can only ever exist in that place beyond reality.

I run down the steps and off the stage. Leave without another word.

CHAPTER TEN

I rush from the theatre and the rippling walls of Fyvie
Castle. Weave between streetlamps so I might avoid their
scrutiny. I dart off the road as a carriage rattles past.

And I stop abruptly at the sight of my husband walking
towards me.

"What are you doing here?" I ask.

Tom's hands are dug in the pockets of his coat, collar
turned up against the wind. "I came to walk you home from
your rehearsal. I wasn't sure what time it finished. I suppose
I'm a little late."

I wrap my arms around myself, unable to look at him. It
feels like he knows, he knows, he knows.

How could he know?

"Is this because you don't like me being friends with
Clara?" I ask stiffly. "Because she already left. I—"

"I just thought it might be a nice thing for me to walk my
wife home. I know I've been out at the claim a lot." After a
moment of silence, he sighs. "I'm trying, Lucy. I'm really

bloody trying."

Guilt cuts me and I take a step closer to him, looping my hand around his arm. "I know you are. I'm sorry."

It's sure as hell more than I can say for myself.

"How was your rehearsal?" Tom asks as we walk.

"Fine."

"Good."

And at this moment, I'm infinitely grateful for the pattern of small talk we've fallen into. Small talk, I realise, is an easy thing to hide behind.

Somewhere far away, thunder rattles the sky.

"Weather's turning," says Tom.

"Mm." I notice a dribble of paint on my skirts and shift my arm to cover it.

At the top of our street, Tom stops walking. "Is that…"

I freeze. Constable Stone is on our doorstep, a large cloth bag at his feet. Tom strides down the street and I hurry after him, dread knotting my stomach.

"What the hell do you want?" Tom hisses at the trooper. I'm taken aback by the venom in his words.

Stone looks past him and gives me a thin smile. "Mrs Earnshaw."

"Constable." My voice is tiny.

He nods toward the sack. "I've laundry that needs doing."

Not once in three years has Constable Stone ever come to me for his laundry. I know it no coincidence he has appeared tonight.

"Don't be ridiculous," says Tom. "It's late. Come back in the morning."

Stone's eyes meet mine.

"It's all right, Tom." I grab the bag. "One shilling."

"Lucy," Tom snaps, but Stone is already pressing the coins into my hand. I pull out my key, fumbling as I shove it into the lock. "I'll deliver it to you when it's done."

"Good. You can bring it to the police station." He takes the bag of laundry from my hand. "I'll carry it inside for you."

He saw me playing the ghost. More than that, he knows I saw him climbing out of that claim. Of these things, I have no doubt. What I do not know, is what he will do with this information.

This is not a visit for the sake of his laundry, of that much I'm certain. Is this little house call to warn me against telling anyone what I saw? Or to let me know that I've been caught?

I know there are ghost hoaxers in England who faced the courts, but surely I won't suffer the same fate. Those English hoaxers were arrested for assault, for breaking and entering, but I've not broken any laws. All I've done is stir up a little gossip and create a bit of a scare. Still, I know the people of Castlemaine will have something to say about it if they discover what I've been doing. If I'm to keep hoaxing until the play, I need to keep the Green Lady's identity a secret.

Stone's message is clear enough: if I open my mouth, he will open his. And neither of us want that.

He looks me in the eye, the faintest hint of a smile on his lips. Yes, message received. But there is something else in his gaze; a searching look, as though he's trying to determine what led me to do what I did. As though catching Tom Earnshaw's mousy little wife playing the ghost among the claims at midnight is a thing that requires an explanation. I suppose it is. But it is not an explanation I'm about to give.

Tom presses his palm flat to Stone's chest to prevent him

from entering our cottage. "Leave it," he says tersely. "I'll carry it in."

"Very well." A smile on the edge of Stone's lips. "If that's what you want." He drops the sack, and it thuds softly on the doorstep. Thunder rolls again, closer this time. I can smell the rain on the air.

He turns and marches down the front path and I realise I'm barely breathing.

"Listen to that rain," Tom says the next morning. "I guess you'll not be doing Stone's laundry today."

I watch from beneath the blankets as he climbs out of bed and pulls on his trousers.

"I'm going to take it back to him," he says. "Tell him to wash his own damn clothes and stay the hell away from us."

I sit up, taken aback by his fervour. "You don't have to do that."

Tom tucks in his shirt. "He's a corrupt bastard, Luce. I don't want you anywhere near him."

I wonder if my husband has any idea of the extent of Stone's corruption. "Tom." I reach for his forearm. "Please. It's just a little laundry. I'll do it tomorrow and be done with it. Besides, we could use the money." I look at him pleadingly.

He sighs. "Fine. But if he comes here again, you tell him you're not available."

I nod wordlessly, not sure it's a promise I can keep.

Tom pulls back one curtain and shoves open the window. The cool change has blown in overnight and the bedroom fills with rain-scented air. Water streams down the glass. He curses under his breath. "No going out in this. Claim'll be half underwater."

"Maybe it'll clear," I say, clinging to the possibility. "You know what the rain's like in this place. Pouring one minute, dry the next."

I can't bear thought of being trapped in the cottage with Tom all day. Especially now my head is so full of Will, and all that passed between us last night. I was awake hours before dawn, trying to find the guilt I know I ought to feel. Told myself I ought to step away from the play, and never go near Will Browning again. My new rebellious side refused to listen.

Tom hovers at the window for another moment, then climbs back into bed. I lie frozen beside him, arms held across my chest. When he shifts on the mattress, I flinch.

"Don't worry, Luce," he says dryly. "I wouldn't dare."

The coldness in his voice makes my chest ache.

After just minutes, he is out of bed again. I follow him into the kitchen and light the fire. Set a pot of porridge simmering on the stove. Rain thunders against the windows, punctuating our silence.

The day stretches out bleakly before us. There is painfully little space between the two of us as I boil the tea and make the porridge. As Tom goes from window to window, watching the rain. By the time I serve up the food, it feels as though the walls of the cottage are closing in on me. Making it hard to breathe.

"I'm going to the market," I say, after a few spoonfuls of porridge.

Tom doesn't look up from his bowl. "It's pouring rain."

"Yes, well. We still need to eat." I take my cloak from the hook beside the door. "I'll be back soon."

Tom looks up at me for a long second, and I see an unspoken apology in his eyes. As though he knows I'm leaving to avoid being around him. But he doesn't open his mouth. Doesn't attempt to find the words to make me stay.

The barrage of rain has turned the unpaved streets to swamp, and I pick my way between shop awnings, water rolling steadily off the brim of my bonnet. The boggy roads are barely accessible, and the town feels oddly empty without the constant rhythm of horse hooves and wheels.

When I return to the cottage, my skirts are soaked, and half the main street is caked to my boots. I shoulder open the door, lugging in the basket I'd filled with food we didn't really need. I'd just craved the space the market would provide.

Tom leaps from his chair and takes the basket, carrying it into the kitchen and setting it on the floor. The contents of the money box are spread out over the table; coins stacked in neat columns, a few scraps of gold beside them, ready to be weighed and banked.

"You're soaked," he says. "Come and get dry."

I shrug off my cloak and hang it back on the hook. Kick off my muddy boots.

"I made tea," Tom tells me. "Should still be hot." He lifts the kettle from the hook and refills the pot while I unpack the basket, my wet stockings leaving footprints on the floorboards.

Tom sets my tea on the table for me, then sits and brings his own half-drunk cup to his lips. "Looks as though the rain's set in. Real waste of a day."

My gaze drifts to the small knots of gold on the table, vividly lustrous against the rough-hewn wood. My chest squeezes. "Tom," I say carefully, "you know it's not your fault, don't you? That you've not found a big haul yet?"

I hold my breath, half expecting him to fly into a rage, or veer wildly away from the subject. Instead, he just puts down his teacup and sighs.

"I know," he says. "I do. I just… I just wish things were different."

I put my hand to his forearm, feeling its broadness. *I wish that too.* It doesn't need to be said.

A violent shiver goes through me, and I pull my hand away.

"Take that dress off," says Tom. "You'll catch a chill. It's cold today."

I go to the bedroom, unbuttoning my wet dress and petticoats and hanging them over a chair to dry. I slip my flannel robe on over my shift and drawers.

My script is poking out from under the bed. The sight of it brings that powerful desire to lose myself in the world of the play and all it has come to represent. I force the urge away. Pad back out to the kitchen and sit at the table beside Tom.

Maybe this is what we need; to be held prisoner in our little cottage for a time. Maybe then we'll find a way to have those conversations we ought to have had months ago. Conversations where we speak our daughter's name and let the other peek inside our head for a moment. Those conversations that might somehow lead us back to each other. But is that really what I want? I can't tell anymore. And that doubt is more than a little terrifying.

Tom scoops the coins and gold pieces back into the box and sits it on the shelf behind him. He reaches into the drawer beneath the cupboards and pulls out a pack of cards. He begins to deal. "You remember how to play All Fours, don't you?"

I smile. "Of course." Tom taught me to play on the voyage, and we passed endless hours of ocean with cards in our hands. Our games were slow and chatter-filled, and half the time we'd end up rolling around beneath the blankets before we declared a winner.

I look across the table, trying to see him as I did back then. Trying to remember what it felt like to be so besotted with Tom Earnshaw that I had to toss down my cards and fling myself into his arms mid-game.

That little crease of Tom's brow as he looks down at his cards, the way he scratches the place his beard meets his neck; I remember that. Remember watching him so closely I might memorise every detail of him. And though I remember that attraction, that need to feel his skin against my own, I can't quite recall how to feel it.

Rain drums against the glass as we pore over the cards. The earthy smell of the burned-out fire is thick in the air.

"You let me win," I say, counting up the points.

"I wouldn't do that."

"You always let me win when we played on the ship."

He chuckles lightly. "Well. I had other things on my mind back then. Today you just outplayed me." He scoops up the cards and begins to shuffle them. "Another round?"

I nod.

A knock at the door interrupts us. Tom gets to his feet, and I tug my robe tighter around my body.

My shoulders tighten at the sound of Constable Stone's voice. What is he doing here? Is he after his laundry? Surely not. Nothing will dry in this weather. There must be another reason for his visit. I get to my feet. If Stone is here to see me, I need to interject in the men's conversation somehow. There's far too much he could tell my husband.

But then I hear a second voice. Stone is not alone, and the realisation goes some way to easing my panic. Surely he'll not speak of that night in the presence of another trooper. Stone is a former convict. If he were found guilty of night fossicking, he'd be hauled out to Port Arthur, or somewhere equally as hideous.

"We can speak outside," Tom says, and the door closes neatly behind them. I strain my ears to catch a thread of their conversation. But their words are muffled by distance, and the faint patter of the easing downpour.

"What did they want?" I demand, the moment Tom comes back inside. Rain has darkened the shoulders of his faded blue vest.

"It's all right." He puts a hand to my shoulder. "They just had some questions about Leo and these driving accusations the Tipperary boys are making against him. Thought there might be some connection between that and the night fossicking."

My heart quickens. If Stone is pointing the finger at Leo for his own crimes, there's no way I can stay silent about what I saw. "Surely they don't think Leo's involved?"

"I doubt it. They're just clutching at straws if you ask me. I told them Leo never had nothing to do with any driving. Couldn't imagine anyone less likely to be a thief." He takes his coat from the hook beside the door and slips it on. "I'd best let him know the coppers were asking after him. Warn him to keep out of trouble."

"Please, Tom," I say suddenly. "Stay."

My own words surprise me. I can't remember the last time I craved my husband's company. But I want him here now. Want to sit at the table with him and play All Fours. Our strange, unexpected compatibility feels precious. Fleeting.

His lips part, as though he's surprised by my request. "I can't," he says after a moment. "I'm sorry. If it were me the coppers were asking after, I'd want Leo to tell me right away."

"Of course." My voice is thin.

Tom hovers in front of me for a moment, as though caught in indecision. "I'll be back as soon as I can."

I feel a hollowness inside me as the door thumps shut. Clinging to these moments of happiness with Tom feels like trying to catch hold of the wind.

CHAPTER ELEVEN

"What do you think?" Clara leads me into her dressmaker's parlour. The building has just been completed, sunlight spilling through large windows and lighting the chaos of chests, fabric rolls and wooden mannequins. A large oak table is pushed up against one wall, supporting a tower of boxes.

I look around incredulously. "Where on earth were you keeping all this while you were living at the boarding house?"

"Some under the bed. Some in Will's room at the Commercial. Even hid some things in here once it had a roof. Don't think the builders even noticed. Mind you, most of this fabric didn't arrive til yesterday."

I peer through the door at the back of the parlour. It leads into small living quarters; a fireplace in one corner, a sleeping mat in the other. A small table sits in the centre of the room, a crimson and white bodice and skirt laid over a chair beside it.

"The place looks wonderful," I tell Clara. "I'm so happy

for you."

"The outfit on the chair," she calls, teetering towards the back room with a box in her arms. "Try it on. I need to see how it looks on a real person."

I run a finger over the vividly coloured fabric. I've never worn anything so vibrant. Everything I own these days either started life as, or has ended up, the colour of mud.

She dumps the box in a corner of the living quarters and picks up a wide hooped underskirt that's leaning against the wall. She holds it out to me. "Wear it with the crinoline cage."

I eye the cage warily. I'm not the kind of woman who wears hoop skirts. I'm not even sure how I might get into the thing. "Really?" I ask. "I'm not sure I…"

Clara rolls her eyes impatiently. "Honestly, Lucy, don't be so mopesy. Everyone's wearing them these days. This one's just come in, all the way from London."

I take the cage, suddenly embarrassed by the dowdy flatness of my own skirts. Tom has always been adamant that I dress for safety rather than fashion – we both know women who near burnt themselves to a crisp strolling through the campfires of the diggings in wide, fashionable skirts.

But there are no campfires here in Clara's parlour. My husband is not here either. And perhaps with a little concentration, I can manage to wrangle myself into a hoop skirt.

I take the clothes into the corner of the living quarters and dress myself carefully, stepping into the cage and fastening it at my waist. Then I attempt the crimson skirts and bodice.

Buoyed by the crinoline, the skirts swell around me in a bell-like shape I've never dared to wear. I catch a glimpse of myself in the mirror that leans against one wall. Against the deep red, my skin looks fashionably pale, and my blue eyes seem brighter than I remember. I smile at my reflection.

Clara comes in, hand on her hip as she inspects the dress, a frown of concentration crinkling her nose. She tugs the bodice down towards my hips. "It's not sitting right." She rifles through a box, emerging with a pincushion. Then she comes to stand behind me, pinching and pinning the pleats at my waist.

The front door clicks open. "Anyone here?"

At the sound of Will's voice, something flips in my chest.

"In here," Clara calls. She moves around to face me. "Will's bringing Charles and Matthew to help me shift that dreadful table." She frowns at my expression, making me suspect I've done quite a terrible job of looking unflapped. "There's no problem is there?"

"No," I garble. "Of course not."

I've told Clara nothing of what passed between Will and me at the theatre. I think perhaps I'm wary of her questions. Questions with answers that are too confronting to say out loud.

He appears in the doorway of the living quarters, Charles and Matthew in tow. The three of them are dressed casually in rolled-up shirtsleeves and simple linen waistcoats, yet still manage to look like they've just danced out of the pleasure gardens.

"Lucy," Will says in surprise. "You look beautiful. I mean… the dress, Clara," he stumbles. "You've quite a talent."

Clara almost manages to hold back a laugh. "The table's in the front room. It needs to go in the other corner. I tried to move it myself, but I could barely shift it an inch."

"What happened to the window frame?" Matthew asks, joining Will in the doorway. "Why is it covered in white paint?"

Clara shakes her head. "Just a little trouble from the locals."

I frown. "What happened?" I didn't notice the paint on the way in.

"Someone painted a few choice words on the window frame," she tells me. "The white paint was all I could find to cover it. I'll have to fix it later."

"Those bastards," says Will. "Do you know who—"

"It's fine, Will," Clara cuts in. "Just help me with the table. You can put the boxes in the corner."

"As you wish." His eyes meet mine for a second, then he quickly looks away.

I hear a dull thud as one of the boxes hits the floor.

"Careful!" barks Clara.

"How goes the ghost hoaxing, Lucy?" Charles calls over his shoulder as he heads into the front room. "You giving the good people of Castlemaine a decent scare?"

I think of Constable Stone crawling from the claim. Think of the vandals at work on Clara's window frame. "They deserve a good scare."

Charles laughs.

I lean forward, trying to catch Will's reaction. I hadn't intended on bringing up hoaxing again – at least not within two minutes of his arrival.

Clara jabs me in the side. "Stand still."

I'm statuesque as she steps back again to inspect the adjustments she's made. I hear the men mutter and curse as they heave the table across the outer room.

"That's sitting better now," says Clara. "You can change back if you like. Just be careful with the pins when you take it off."

I open my mouth to tell her there's no way in hell I'm changing my clothes out in the open now Will is here, but she's already charging out into the parlour, berating the men over where they've put the table. I scramble out of the crimson skirts and back into my own clothes so fast I'm surprised I don't get vertigo.

"I'm glad we got to see this shop of yours finished before we went back to Melbourne," I hear Matthew tell Clara. "You certain you don't want to come with us, Will? Haven't you had enough of this outpost yet?"

My stomach plunges, but Will says, "I'm happy where I am for the moment. Besides, I told you, I'll be down in Melbourne for a few days next week. Get my dose of the place then."

"You're going to Melbourne, Will?" asks Clara. "No, that's too close to the window! I already told you, it needs to go in the corner."

I hear one of the men groan.

"I'm going to see George Howard's new play at Astley's Amphitheatre," Will says. "They're using both the ring and the stage. It's supposed to be quite the spectacle."

Clara snorts. "George Howard? The man's a bastard. Wouldn't even give me an audition."

"You'd much rather be working for me anyway," Will teases her.

"Indeed. It's always been my dream to act alongside greats like Ollie Cooper."

He laughs. "Well, you've already scared Arthur off. I'm sure with a little focus you can get rid of Ollie too."

I fasten the last of my buttons and catch a glimpse of myself in the mirror. Out of the crimson gown, I look decidedly plain and colourless. But when I step out into the parlour, Will is deliberate in looking my way. And suddenly I'm back on the stage at the Theatre Royal with the castle blowing around us and his lips against mine. I shake the thought away hurriedly.

A thing that can never be.

"Lucy," Clara calls, snapping me out of my haze. "The blue gown I showed you last week. It's in the chest over by the window. It needs to go on the mannequin."

I scurry obediently to the chest, glad for something to do. I find the gown and unfold it carefully, sliding it over the wooden bust of the mannequin at the front of the shop. Realising I've forgotten the underskirts, I go back to the chest to fetch them, and when I try to tie them beneath the gown, I somehow manage to entrap myself in reams of blue and white fabric.

"It's not right," I hear Clara say. "Maybe the table was better where it was. Move it back. Come on, Charlie. Quickly."

"Save me," Will murmurs, appearing at my side.

I emerge from the skirts and offer him a grin. "She just wants everything to be perfect."

"She's terrifying." He lifts the blue skirts, allowing me to straighten the petticoats.

"When will you go to Melbourne?" I ask as I work.

"I thought to leave on Monday. Perhaps see the performance on Tuesday afternoon."

"I've heard Astley's Amphitheatre is quite something."

"It is. And the performance of *Joan of Arc* I plan to see has been getting fabulous reviews. They say the staging is breathtaking."

"It sounds wonderful."

For a moment, Will doesn't speak. He glances over at the others before looking back at me. "You could…" He falters. "You could always come with me." His voice is barely a whisper. "You'd have your own private room, of course. I wouldn't…"

My mouth opens and closes, caught off guard by his invitation. I can barely believe I've heard him correctly.

For a moment, I allow myself to imagine what it would feel like to accept. But no, I can't follow this thought too far. It will lead me to places I can absolutely, positively never go.

Places like Astley's Amphitheatre with Will Browning.

Impossible, of course. For so many reasons, not least the scraps in our coin box. I shake my head. "I don't have the money."

"Don't worry about that. I…" He looks down for a moment, then back up at me shyly. "I'd like you to come, Lucy. Very much." He swallows. "Perhaps you might think about it?"

And though I try my hardest not to, I think about it. I think about it when I'm whacking filthy shirts against my washboard. Think about it when I'm lying frozen in bed beside Tom. And I'm thinking about as I stand in Clara's parlour a few days later, waiting for her to put the finishing touches on the crimson skirts.

"It looks good on you," she says. "I want you to wear it in Melbourne."

"How did you—"

"Oh please. I have ears. And eyes. I can see the way you and Will look at each other."

I flush. I'd convinced myself I had been discreet. Kept my feelings to myself. Kept what happened at the theatre well hidden. "There's nothing between Will and me," I say.

"Is that so?" Clara kneels at my feet to stitch up the hem.

I trace a finger over the delicate embroidery along the neckline. "He did invite me to Melbourne," I say finally. "But it's not as if I can go."

"Why not?"

I don't know why I'm still shocked at her bluntness. But even though there's a part of me that wants to, I just can't see the world as Clara Snow does. Can't just leap inside a carriage with a man who's not my husband and clatter off into the sunset.

Clara pulls out a pin and digs it into her apron. "You deserve to be happy, Lucy," she says. "We all do. Every one of us that ended up out here."

I've said nothing to Clara about the sadness that follows me like a shadow. How much of my pain do my eyes give away?

"I think maybe you were as reluctant to come here as I was," she says.

I swallow heavily. "That's not true."

"Well," she says finally, "you deserve to be happy in any case."

I was happy once; I remember it like a fading dream. I

was happy with Tom, dizzy in his company. We lost that happiness when we lost Elsie and have never been able to find it again.

But when I'm around Will, when my mind is full of new ideas and new possibilities, I catch fleeting glimpses of a future in which I'm not tied to my grief. A future in which I might find a way to be happy again.

"I can't go with Will," I say. "I'm a married woman."

Clara stops stitching for a moment and looks up to meet my eyes. "Do you love your husband, Lucy?"

The question is like a blow to the chest.

And so is my hesitation.

I think of the warmth I felt when Tom and I sat together playing cards by the fire. But was that happiness based on nothing but a memory? Was I trying to catch hold of joy that has long passed? Once, I loved him with such intensity it almost scared me. A love I thought would see us through anything. And while it's turned out to be a love that has buckled under the strain of loss, I'm far too scared to cut myself loose from it completely. While I'm anchored to my grief, I'm also anchored to Tom, and the security that comes with being a wife in this strange land. "Yes," I say finally. "I do love my husband. Of course I do."

Clara doesn't answer at once. She steps back, then walks in a slow circle around me, inspecting the hem of the dress. Then she goes to the cupboard and returns with a small jar filled with dried leaves.

"I want you to take this."

I frown. "What is it?"

"Thunder god vine. From the apothecary at the Chinese camp. Stops an unwanted child."

My eyes widen. "What are you talking about? Why are you giving me this?"

"I just thought that if you do decide to go with Will, it's best if you—"

"I'm not going with Will!" I cry. "And I'm certainly not… I certainly don't need this!" I feel my cheeks blazing. With anger or shame, or something else entirely, I can't tell. "I love my husband," I gush. "I do. And I would never…"

"All right," says Clara. "I'm sorry. I didn't mean to offend you."

"Well, you did." Without bothering to remove the crimson gown, I grab my own clothes from the floor and charge out of Clara's shop.

It's not til I get back the cottage that I realise I've brought the jar of thunder god vine home with me. I shove it into the back of the cupboard, catching a glimpse of my reflection in the window. In spite of my anger at Clara, I have to admit the gown is stunning. Like nothing I've ever worn in my life. For a fleeting moment, I imagine walking the streets of Melbourne on Will's arm, these fine skirts swelling around me. I shove the thought away. I can't allow it to take shape any further than it already has.

The door flies open and Tom charges into the house, leaving a trail of muddy footprints behind him. He disappears into the bedroom.

"Tom?" I call. "Are you all right?"

He grunts in response.

I hurry into the bedroom, steering my hooped skirts past the side table. Tom has pulled the washcloth from the basin and holds it to his eye as he paces back and forth across the room. I can see flecks of dried blood on his knuckles.

"What happened?" I ask.

"Nothing. It's fine."

"Were you in a fight?" In all the years I've known Tom, I've never once seen him be aggressive. "With who?"

He sighs heavily. Puts the cloth back in the basin to dampen it. I can see a bruise beginning to swell beneath his eye. The skin below his temple has split, leaving a rusty streak down his cheek.

"Jesus, Tom. Sit down. Let me clean you up."

Reluctantly, he sits on the edge of the bed. I dip the cloth back in the basin and sponge the blood from his cheek.

"Who did this?" I ask.

Tom hesitates. Is he truly going to be closed up about this? But then he says, "Clyde."

"You got into a fight with Clyde? Who started it?"

"Really, Lucy? Do you need to ask that?"

Yes, I do. Because I've never known my husband to come home with bloodied fists before. Have rarely known him to even raise his voice. What are the goldfields turning him into?

I lower the cloth so we can look eye to eye. His swollen by Clyde's fists, and mine full of guilt. After all, the secrets I'm keeping are far greater than why Clyde smacked my husband in the eye. But truth-telling is becoming more complicated by the day.

"He's been going around interrogating us all," Tom says finally. "Asking us what we seen, what we heard, like we're all guilty men."

"And so you started a fight with him?"

"He swung the first punch," says Tom. "I just gave him

a bit of a shove. Told him I didn't appreciate him making accusations."

I think of Constable Stone climbing from the claim by lamplight. "No, I'm sure you didn't." I wrestle my skirts aside as I bend to wash out the cloth.

"What on earth are you wearing?" Tom asks with a dull chuckle.

"Clara made it. She thought I might like it."

He begins to unlace his boots. "This isn't the place for a dress like that. You'll go up in smoke if you're not careful. Besides, it's not really you, is it. Take it off."

I clench my teeth. "I'd like to go to Melbourne for a few days," I blurt. "With the theatre."

Tom looks up. "Melbourne?"

"Yes. To see a play at Astley's Amphitheatre. There's a play on about Joan of Arc that uses both the stage and the ring. We're going to use the theatre's funds to pay for the trip."

"The theatre's funds?" Tom repeats.

"Mr Browning says if we see real actors and actresses perform, it will help our own performances." I realise I'm talking too quickly.

"Does he now?" Tom uses one boot to kick off the other. I can practically see his thoughts churning. Can tell he hates the idea. And yet he was the one to nudge me in the direction of Will and the theatre troupe in the first place.

"I'm not sure that's appropriate," he says finally.

"In England, perhaps," I say. "But things are different here."

"Not so different."

I wring out the bloodstained cloth.

"You're a married woman," says Tom. "You shouldn't be gallivanting about the colony without your husband."

I hold his gaze. "Come with me then," I dare him.

Tom gives a snort of laughter, as though taking me to the theatre is the most insane idea he's ever heard in his life. "Who will be going?"

"Everyone," I say, wincing inwardly at the lie. "Clara and Mrs Markham and Arthur Wallace…"

I am the worst of people; I see this with such clarity that I'm on the verge of taking it all back and admitting to my lies. This is not who I want to be; this I know with certainty. And yet I can't deny the excitement that floods me when Tom finally nods in agreement.

CHAPTER TWELVE

Will and I are in the stagecoach at dawn. The sun is a faint glow behind the cloud bank, but there's a fragrant thickness to the air that promises heat. The coach is full, and there are one or two familiar faces among the passengers. Men and women I've passed at the market, seen in church services.

I pretend Will and I are nothing more than acquaintances. Nods of greeting, *good morning, Mr Browning,* and we take up seats on opposites sides of the coach.

Though the day has barely begun, I can hear the rattle of mining cradles as we pass Forest Creek. How many mornings have I been woken by that sound? That rhythmic scrape and thud that's as familiar to me as breath.

I look out over the scarred landscape, dotted with tree stumps and holes in the earth. At the hint of mountains behind the morning haze. We wind past the blue shadow of the hills and past plains golden in the sunrise. Kangaroos make tiny silhouettes, flying away across the paddocks as the carriage rattles past.

The further we get from Castlemaine, the more the tension in my shoulders begins to melt away, replaced with nervous excitement. As I peer out the opposite window at the wide, rusty landscape, my eye catches Will's and he flashes a quick smile.

The Black Forest creeps up on the carriage like fog; a few trees breaking the monotony of the plains, then more, until we are surrounded by bush and the soft daylight has drained away.

I've passed through the Black Forest before, on our first journey to the goldfields. The place unnerved me then, and that was before I heard all the stories of the bushrangers who hide in the caves, attacking gold-laden carriages on the way back from the diggings. Though Captain Melville has supposedly cleared out of the forest to wreak havoc on the coast, there's no shortage of stories from people who've experienced a holdup here.

A restless energy hangs in the coach as we rattle down the narrow dirt road, people murmuring under their breath, ladies clutching their reticules a little tighter. The horses' hooves beat a steady rhythm that rattles alongside my heart. I press my forehead to the window, eyes darting, trying to catch hold of the shadows flitting between the trees.

I'm glad when the branches of the Black Forest part and sunlight spills over the coach. I catch a glimpse of searing blue sky and release the breath I'm holding.

By the time we reach Melbourne, I'm exhausted, my eyes heavy from the early start, and my bones rattled by hours in the coach. When I make my way to the door of the carriage, Will is waiting for me at the steps. Offers me his hand to help me climb down.

Melbourne is all sound and colour. Carriages pass below domes and spires that look transplanted from England, bright painted signs above doors announcing the barbers, the tailors, the dispensaries. The lamplighter moves through the purple dusk, climbing his ladder and coaxing the streetlights to life.

Will nods at the three-storey building beside the Cobb and Co terminus. A grand archway welcomes us to the Albion Hotel, decorative balustrades hemming semi-circular balconies. Men in top hats and frock coats spill from the adjoining bar.

"I stayed here the night I arrived in the colony," Will tells me. "I think you'll like it. It's rather beautiful inside. And there's fine views from upstairs."

I follow him into the hotel foyer, terrified of catching sight of anyone I know. The thought is laughable of course; I don't know anyone in Melbourne, nor do I know anyone who spends their time in places like the Albion. Besides, what do I have to hide? I'm just a woman travelling to town to see a show at Astley's Amphitheatre.

Maybe if I tell myself that enough, it will somehow become true.

My eyes shift around the foyer, taking in the rich polished oak of the woodwork, the delicate lace curtains fringing the arched windows. A different world from the leaky lodging house Tom and I stayed in on our first night in Australia. We told ourselves that when we next returned to town, we'd be staying in places like the Albion. The irony brings a wry smile to my lips.

Will moves away from the front desk and comes towards me with a smile on his face. He holds out a key. "Here. I've got us both rooms on the top floor. Overlooking the river."

I shoot a hurried glance to the man behind the counter. Is he watching me? Judging? But his eyes are turned downwards as he writes in his ledger. I'm sure this town of new wealth has seen far madder things than me.

And up the stairs I go behind Will, gripping the bannister like it's a life raft.

When we reach the top floor, he stops at a room on the corner. "This is yours," he says. "I'm two doors down. Room three-one-four."

I grip the key in my clammy palms. "Thank you," I manage. "For all of this."

"Of course." He hovers awkwardly for a moment, and I can tell neither of us have any thought of how this is to proceed. Are we to pretend this is just a thing of private rooms, and separate seats on the coach? Am I to pretend my heart's not speeding beneath his gaze; and that surely, surely, he can sense it?

"I thought to go down to the supper room," he says. "Have a little food. Will you join me?"

But with his closeness, with this sudden upturning of everything I've so far been, my stomach is cartwheeling. I can't tell if it's excitement or dread. All I know is I can't bear the thought of food. Nor can I face, right now, the possibility of where this thing might lead. And exactly what it might mean.

"I think I'd rather just go to bed," I say. "If you wouldn't mind? I'm exhausted."

"Of course." Is that relief in his eyes? Does he feel the weight of this too? He pecks my cheek. "Good night, Lucy. Sleep well."

And before I can reply, he is gone.

In my palatial bed, I barely sleep. I tell myself it's my nagging conscience keeping me awake, and not the thought of Will in bed a few doors down the hall. Because I most certainly am not the kind of woman kept awake by thoughts of men who are not her husband.

Nor am I the kind of woman who wears crimson and crinoline cages. But here is my reflection, fastening the row of tiny buttons up my chest with Clara's cherry-red gown exploding around me. I'm wearing the simple white day bodice she made to match the skirts, and with my skin safely covered to my wrists and neck, it feels like a far less daunting outfit to wear to breakfast than the eye-catching eveningwear she pinned me into at the shop.

When I arrive downstairs, I find Will sitting at a table by the window, a notebook open in front of him. He is scrawling in it furiously. A stray piece of hair falls over his eye and he tucks it thoughtlessly behind his ear, without the pen leaving the page. For a moment, I just stand watching him, not wanting to interrupt. Wanting a silent moment to take him in. I can't believe I'm in his company.

Alone, in his company. I feel oddly outside myself.

Will looks up. At the sight of me, his face brightens.

"Good morning." I feel his eyes taking me in. "You look lovely."

I lower my gaze shyly. "Clara's dress."

"Ah. Yes. It's stunning."

I hover, uncertain if we ought to be seen sitting together,

but Will pulls out the chair beside him, answering my silent question. I perch tentatively on the edge with as much grace as I can muster. Before we left, Clara put me through a vigorous training regime in which I practiced hoicking up the back of the crinoline cage to wrangle myself onto a chair. I'm terrified of giving the breakfast room an eyeful of my underwear.

"You're writing?" I ask Will.

"Yes. I always find a change of scenery is good for motivation." He closes the notebook. "But I'll have plenty of time to do that later. How did you sleep?"

A waiter appears at the table, filling my cup with coffee.

"I slept well," I lie. Telling the truth will get us into questions like 'What kept you awake?' and no way in hell am I going there.

"I'm glad to hear it." He plugs the cork into his ink pot. "And your room? Is it to your liking?"

Are we really having a conversation so mundane and simple? And why does it not feel completely wrong? Because the strangest part of all this is that somehow, as we sit here drinking coffee and speaking of the views from our bedroom windows, Will and I have managed to find a sense of comfort. The unease I felt in the hallway last night has vanished with the sun. Somehow, so subtly I can barely place it, being around him has become easy.

Will Browning is the man I could once barely speak to. But as I sit here with him, in a scene that belongs in someone else's life, I feel an unexpected sense of peace. A peace that even my raging conscience can't disrupt. Escaping my life for a time – and yes, escaping my marriage – feels like the air I have been craving for far longer than I've dared to acknowledge.

"I understand you not wanting to be seen with me in the coach," Will says as we walk into the theatre that afternoon. There is a smile on his face. "But do you think we might sit together for the show?"

I am awed by Astley's Amphitheatre; by the huge circus-like ring that unfolds before us; by the curtained archway hiding a stage I suspect is enormous; the chandelier glittering from a mile-high roof. I point everything out to Will like an overexcited child. Tiers and tiers of velvet-lined seats. Benches so close to the ring they must make you feel a part of the show. And would you just look at all these people?

I suspect Will might be regretting his request to sit to beside me.

He chuckles gently at my enthusiasm. "Did you never go to Astley's in London? It served as a model for this place."

I give a short laugh. "I'm from Horley, remember? I've been to London twice in my life. And the only time I ever went to the theatre back home was when our church put on its Christmas play."

"Oh yes," he chuckles. "The angel in the nightgown. Where you got your start in this fine industry."

I burst out laughing. Mercifully, I'd forgotten I told him all about the Christmas play after a little too much wine at the Commercial that first night. I can't believe he remembers.

We take our seats on the second level. They have a fine view of both the stage and the ring. A hush falls over the audience as the great chandelier above our heads dims and the curtain rises.

The show is like nothing I've ever seen. Armies and horses

engulf the ring and make me feel a part of the battle, while the actress playing Joan of Arc is breathtaking. It's all smoke and light and music coming from an orchestra hidden in the wings.

And yet I find my gaze drifting to the man beside me. His eyes are fixed on the stage, lips parted slightly. His gloved hand rests on his knee, inches from mine, as though tempting me to take it.

My thoughts pull towards Tom like a compass towards the north. The man I promised to love until I died. But these memories I have of him, of us, they are founded on something that no longer exists. And now all that's in their place is guilt and regret and that horrible suffocating silence. Conditions in which a person cannot survive.

I reach over and cover Will's hand with my own. Though his eyes remain fixed to the stage, I don't miss the small smile that appears on the edge of his lips. And when his fingers slide between mine and give an almost imperceptible squeeze, I can think of nothing but the coiled desire inside me, threatening to tear itself free.

"Quite something, don't you think?" Will murmurs in my ear as we stand with the rest of the audience to applaud the performers.

"Amazing, truly."

"And to think this is all happening so far from England. Whoever thought we'd make a civilised land of this outpost?"

"Strange what a little gold in the earth will do."

The curtain falls and the applause peters out. Will puts a light hand to my back as we funnel towards the doors with the rest of the crowd. "One day soon," he says, "it'll be my work performed here at Astley's. Just you wait and see."

I look over my shoulder to catch his eye. "I have no doubt."

I feel his fingers move against my back, an almost imperceptible movement.

"How is the new play coming along?" I ask, as the corridor widens and we're able to walk side by side.

"I believe in it," he says. "More than I've believed in anything I've written for a long time." His voice thickens. "This is the work that's going to reinvent my career, Lucy. I feel sure of it."

I take his arm instinctively and press myself closer to his body. I feel stirred by his enthusiasm, his ambition. This is who Will Browning is, I see then; he pours passion into everything he does, even a play written for arguably the world's most dreadful amateur theatre troupe. Little wonder he took it so hard when his career stalled. How brutal that criticism, those accusations of fraud must have been for him. Enough to drive him to rebel against society. Enough to drive him to play the ghost.

But it isn't just in ghost hoaxing that Will Browning seeks to rebel, I see then. It's in every aspect of the way he lives his life.

With your husband or without.

Rules are made to be broken.

I don't mind being a part of his rebellion. After all, he is part of mine.

But Will's rebellion, I soon learn, goes only so far. Because after a meal in the Albion's supper room, he walks me upstairs and stops outside my door. For a long moment, he holds his lips against the edge of mine, his fingers curling around my ribs. Then he murmurs a goodnight. Disappears into his room without another word.

From this, I understand two things. The first is that Will Browning will not come to my room tonight. The second is that if I can somehow find the courage to go to his, my advances will not be rejected.

I stand with my back to the door. Close my eyes and tighten my fist around the key. The urge to go to him is overwhelming. I try to find the self-loathing I know should accompany my desire. But I can't quite make myself feel it.

I am supposed to feel like a terrible person. But I just feel human. So desperate for happiness I can hardly breathe.

In two days' time, I will go back to that grease- and ash-scented cottage in Castlemaine. I will sit around the table with Tom and serve the same mutton stew I serve every Thursday. I will listen to him talk about how tomorrow will be the day that he will find a nugget and everything will change. In his eyes I will see the same strain and tension I know he sees in mine, and I will drown under the weight of it.

This moment here, now; it feels like my only chance to take in the air I need to survive.

I think of Elsie. This woman I am becoming is not who I wanted her mother to be. But Elsie is gone. She won't see. She will never see. Perhaps this was about her once – perhaps in so many ways it still is. But right now, it is about me. And it is about Will. And about taking the chance to live before I die.

There's an inevitability to this, I tell myself as I step out of my room. Of course there is. Did I not toss the jar of thunder god vine in my luggage? Pretend it a last-minute impulse, when I knew it anything but?

Will doesn't look surprised to see me. He stands in the doorway, still dressed in his shirt and waistcoat. I step forward and begin to open the buttons at his chest.

His hand catches mine. "Are you certain?"

And I nod because I can't bear to look again, or to analyse, or even think. I rise on my toes and press my lips to his.

Just for now, I'll simply let myself exist.

CHAPTER THIRTEEN

The night blurs. Hands and undone laces; lips finding places that have not been found in so many cold and lifeless months. Will lavishes me, pushes me, makes me bold; and I sense, in his wordless gasps, and the racing heart I feel when I drag my hands over his chest, that impossibly, I'm doing the same for him.

The pleasure is shocking, and almost-new. The air I need. And I'm unable to get enough.

After a few short hours of sleep, I feel the morning sun against my cheek, and for a moment, I'm afraid to open my eyes.

How will this look in the harsh light of day? With my eyes closed and Will's warm shape beside me, I can find no regret. But I can't stay here forever.

When I finally open my eyes, the room is hot with late-morning sun. In the hazy pink light, it's easy to convince myself I'm still dreaming. Easy to tell myself this is all a fairy tale, and that nothing I do here matters. Easy to roll back against Will's body and feel my skin against his, feel the weight of his arm as he pulls me into his chest.

I let myself exist in that fairy tale for the rest of the day; as we sit at the breakfast table with our knees touching. As we walk hand in hand along the river, and through gardens alight with colour. As we explore the neat grid of a city that gold has drawn on the map. In this fairy tale, there is no past and no future, and I'm so close to joy it's almost frightening.

"I've had a wonderful few days," Will says that night. "Being here with you." We are in a palatial dining hall at the top end of town, not far from Astley's Amphitheatre. It's a place of marble stairs and white tablecloths, and velvet chairs so lavish I'm almost embarrassed to sit on them. The kind of place Tom and I dreamt of frequenting once he pulled our riches from the earth. The kind of place I never truly imagined myself going. But this grand dining hall, like the wine in front of me and the roast pigeon on my plate, are all things I've come to accept as pieces of the fairy tale. Pieces I know will inevitably give way to the mutton stew and mining cradles of reality.

"Champagne! More champagne!" bellows a man a few tables over, waving broadly to get the attention of both the waiter and the entire restaurant. He's new wealth, that rare success story – I can tell by both the pristine, barely worn clothes he and his wife are wearing, and by the excited curses he drops when the new bottle of champagne is brought to his table. Curses that flow like water from the mouths of the men on the diggings.

"Good for him," says Will, laughing lightly. He turns his wine glass around by the stem. "After the play," he says carefully, "I may move down here. Try my hand at bigger things."

Something sinks inside me. I look out the window and watch a coach roll past. I can't pretend to be surprised by this, of course. A man like Will is far more at home walking the streets of Melbourne than traipsing through the mud of the gold diggings. And he was clear about his ambitions at Astley's yesterday. But I can't help the sudden pain that lodges in my throat. With Will gone, Castlemaine will be a bleaker place. I keep my eyes averted for a moment too long.

His hand covers mine. He has removed his gloves, and his skin is warm against my own.

"Lucy," he says. "Look at me."

I do.

"You could always come with me."

I smile, though I pull my eyes away instinctively. How can he dare to speak of such things? It brings this far too close to reality.

"Would that please you?" he asks.

"You know it would." My voice is almost a whisper.

"Then perhaps—"

"No," I say. "You can't talk of these things. I'm married."

"But not happily."

The knot in my throat tightens. At his boldness. At his truth. "What does that matter?"

"What do you mean, what does that matter?" He squeezes my fingers. "Happiness is everything. It's all that should matter."

"To you, perhaps. Your life has been all… well, it's been all theatres and hotels and places like this. But that's not what my life has been."

"I don't think my life has been quite as easy as you think," Will says gently. "I've had my share of challenges. Believe me. But that's exactly why I believe we should strive for happiness above all else."

I feel oddly irritated. Because this enormous proposition has not only thrown me completely off balance, it has also reminded me of the world that lies outside this blissful bubble we've created over the past two days. A world in which I have sworn myself to Tom Earnshaw for as long as we both should live.

"Do you feel no guilt?" I ask softly, gently. "At asking me these things? All the while knowing I have a husband back in Castlemaine?"

He lets out a humourless laugh. "Guilt?" he repeats. "Lucy, sometimes all I feel is guilt. I know this is wrong."

"And yet?" I ask, because I can sense that coming. That *and yet*, that reason why we both ought to push through our guilt and seek the happiness we crave. That happiness we cannot find within the confines of an orderly, moral life.

I'm not the kind of woman who…

How many times have I told myself this lie? Told myself I'm not the kind of woman who does these immoral things? But this is exactly who I am. Telling myself otherwise doesn't make it any less true.

But I can't shake the exhilaration, the happiness I feel when I'm with Will; that same rush that comes from playing the ghost. Upturning the way things are supposed to be.

Being a troublemaker.

Will looks across the room for a moment, eyes drifting over the digger who's refilling his glass of champagne. "Would you start again, Lucy? If you could?"

But what's the point of thinking *if you could?* Because I can't, can I. None of us can.

I shake my head, unable to look at him. "I can't."

"But what if you could?"

I let his words hang between us for a long time. A part of me desperately wants to agree to his request. Take me away, to this place where I'm happy. But I know I can't outrun the past, or the sadness that comes with it. We are shaped by what has come before. Wherever I go, I will take my memories. I know that if I were to make a life with Will, I could not hide my loss from him forever. As much as I wish it to be otherwise, I know my grief goes a long way towards defining me. But it's a part of myself I never want him to see. I don't want his pity.

"A marriage is for life," I say, staring into my half-empty wine glass.

"It doesn't have to be. And I think perhaps a part of you knows that. Why else would you be here with me?"

I dare to face him then. Because I know he's right. Deep down, a life without Tom is exactly what I have been seeking.

But walking away from a marriage is not something decent women do. At least, not in the life I know. The only women I have ever known to leave their marriages were those terrified wives who raced through the diggings and hid in each other's tents to escape their violent husbands. Or those sorry women put up by their men for sale. But Tom has never laid a hand on me. And he's not the kind of man who would take his wife to market. I'm far more responsible than him for the disintegration of our marriage.

But I am coming to realise that the life I know is one that encompasses the smallest fragment of all there is to experience. And perhaps if I were to peek into this vast array of possibilities, I would see a world in which I could truly move on. These past few days have made me feel far more alive than any other day I've crawled through since I lost my daughter. Maybe I can't live by the rules anymore.

Will lifts my hand and brings it to his lips. "I know it's a lot," he says. "But just think about it. There's no need to make a decision now."

Knocked off kilter by Will's proposition, I drown myself in wine, and when we emerge into the street an hour later, the edges of reality feel blurred and malleable. A policeman rides past on horseback, and the clops of hooves echo inside my body.

As we meander back in the direction of the Albion, a broadsheet plastered to a brick wall catches my eye.

Madame Moulin, Revelations of a Spirit Medium. A list of dates is printed beneath, tonight among them.

I snatch Will's arm. "Oh look! Madame Moulin's séance! Isn't that who Charles and Matthew saw?" I point at the broadsheet, bouncing quite drunkenly on my toes. "Her next sitting is at ten. Let's go and visit her."

He chuckles. "I don't think that's a good idea."

"Why not?"

"Because her séance parlour's on Lonsdale Street. That's far too close to the… less savoury parts of town."

"Less savoury parts of town?" I raise my eyebrows. "Do you truly think I've not been in worse places on the diggings? Come on, Will," I push. "You adore all this spiritualist business." I squeeze his arm. "Please?"

He shakes his head and sighs, though there's a smile on

his lips. He glances at his pocket watch. "We'd best hurry then," he says finally. "It's almost ten." He offers his arm and we begin to walk briskly through the lamplit streets. "Why are you so interested in spiritualism all of a sudden?" he asks. "You and your rational brain."

Me and my rational brain. Why am I so interested? I'm not quite sure. I only know that the night feels like an adventure, and I don't want it to end. Besides, my rational brain has become somewhat scrambled by all the wine I've scarfed since Will so politely invited me to leave my husband.

Madame Moulin's séance parlour is in an unassuming townhouse in a residential part of the city. Will and I arrive breathless a few minutes after ten. A young man dressed entirely in black stands guard at the door.

"Have you reserved a place?" he asks us in a deep, theatrical voice.

"I'm afraid not," says Will. "Is there any way you might find room for us?"

The man makes a show of counting the tickets in his hand, then says, "Two shillings each."

Will hands him the money and he steps aside, allowing us to enter.

We follow the dull smoulder of light down a passage and into the parlour. A long oval table sits in the middle of the room, a single candle sighing in the centre. Dark drapes block the window, and an odd smoky fragrance thickens the hot air. There are seven or eight others inside, already seated around the table. Two couples among them; one close to my age, and the other several years older. The rest of the crowd is made up of elderly women wearing dark shapeless dresses and veils.

Have these people come in hope of receiving a message from a lost loved one? Or are they, like me, just here for the spectacle? A thing of curiosity? Either way, these ladies in widows' weeds make an easy target for Madame Moulin.

One of the women shuffles onto the chair beside her, allowing Will and me to sit together. Will gives her a nod of thanks.

I take my seat, glancing around the parlour. I think of what Charles told me about people hiding in hollowed-out walls. I squint into the darkness, searching for any hint of movement behind the wallpaper, but the single candle flickering in the centre of the table leaves most of the room in shadow.

Slow footsteps click down an unseen hall and here is Madame Moulin, a predictable cliché of dark skirts and silver hair. She sweeps into the room and takes a seat at the head of the table.

"Welcome. Tonight, we seek to uncover the mysteries of the other side." Her accent is unplaceably odd – I guess it European of some kind. I also guess it to be fake. I exchange humoured glances with Will.

Eyes darkened with lampblack peer across the table, inspecting each of us in turn.

"Please place your hands on the table." We all do so obediently. "Close your eyes." Madame Moulin takes a long, dramatic breath. "I now call forth the spirits."

Silence settles over the room, so intense I can hear the candle sighing. I open my eyes, peering curiously around the table. Will winks at me and nudges my knee with his.

"There is a spirit with us now," says the madame suddenly. Cue a chorus of gasps and murmurs. "The name is

John. Who here has come to speak with John?"

"John? My husband, John?" an older woman speaks up.

I roll my eyes. Madame Moulin's séance is just as Charles described it.

"Are you willing to speak with us, John? One rap for no, two raps for yes."

Two raps, of course, coming from the wall behind the madame.

Poor John's wife barely swallows a wail. My gaze drifts past Madame Moulin, straining into the darkness in an attempt to see the wall. Is the wallpaper moving, breathing, as if there is someone behind it? I can't be sure. The dark is too thick.

"Tell us, John," says Madame Moulin, "are you suffering?"

One rap. No.

"And do you miss your dear wife?"

I can barely hold back a snort at the madame's inane questions.

Two raps and his wife is in tears, no doubt with a sizeable gratuity for the medium as soon as this charade is done.

A bell rings from the darkness above our heads, bringing gasps from the sitters. And with my eyes open, I catch it; that faint shift of the madame's skirts. The slight movement of her thigh to pull on that unseen thread.

Madame Moulin is no more real than the Green Lady.

This feels like a joke. A mockery to all those of us who have lost our loved ones. Is this what I'm doing when I go out playing the ghost? Making a mockery of those who believe? Playing on their fears to satisfy my own need to rebel?

Shouldn't I know better?

Perhaps. But I also know it's because of Elsie's death that I need to play the Green Lady.

Madame Moulin's eyes turn upwards to the bell. "There are more spirits with us here tonight." She draws in a deep breath and closes her eyes again, keeping her chin tilted upwards. Begins to sway back and forth. The silence is almost tangible, broken only by the squeak of Madame Moulin's chair. Candlelight flickers on faces, casting shadows beneath eyes. I see fingers curl against the tabletop, but otherwise, the attendees are frozen. Subjects in a death photograph.

The madame reaches for the slate and chalk sitting in front of her on the table. Eyes still closed, she holds the tip of the chalk to the slate. It begins to move between her fingers.

At first, nothing appears on the slate but a chain of loops and curled, meaningless figures. And then, with excruciating slowness, there are letters.

I am here.

And in the corner of the slate, in a strange childlike hand: *Mama.*

On the other side of the table, a young woman cries out. The word knifes me, and I close my eyes, forcing away tears.

"Ask the spirit their name," the woman sobs.

The anger that tears through me is hot and fierce. Anger at Madame Moulin for preying on these people in mourning. Angry at these wailing women for falling for her tricks. Most of all, I'm angry at myself. Because I'm watching that young woman stare at the slate, and I can see her hoping with every inch of her being that her lost child's name will appear there in front of her. And yet I can't make myself believe.

I want to, desperately. Want that possibility that perhaps, against all reason, my daughter is in this room with us. That she might be just inches away, through a veil so thin I can almost reach her. But all I can see is trickery, and a world in which Elsie is gone forever.

I make suddenly to stand. Will's hand covers mine.

"What are you doing?" he murmurs.

"I want to leave." The room feels hot and airless and full of lies, and I suddenly want to be anywhere else.

Madame Moulin's eyes spring open. "There must be no breaking the circle," she says sharply. "Doing so will invite the spirits to take hold of you."

I clatter to my feet, stumbling out of the smoky parlour. The doorman looks at me in surprise as I blow past him.

"All right, ma'am?" he asks, in a broad London drawl that's completely different from the persona he affected when we first arrived.

I don't answer. I just hurry down the street, in a desperate attempt to escape the séance parlour.

I hear Will's footsteps behind me. Feel a pull of dread. Because how am I to get by now without telling him of all I have lost? And how can I share Elsie with him when I can't even share her with her father?

But there are no questions. He just wraps his arms around me, pulling me close. I catch his rosewater scent, laced with the fragrant smoke of the séance parlour. I am so grateful for his silence, his lack of questions. There is an unspoken understanding between us that, deep down, we are strangers, each with our own secrets and pain.

And right now, that is enough.

CHAPTER FOURTEEN

*"The police are making efforts to clear Little Lonsdale Street of
the dens which at present disgrace it."*

The Australian Star
30th December 1889

"Are you all right?" Will asks finally.

I step back from his embrace. "Yes. I'm sorry. I didn't mean to embarrass you. Or… break the circle."

He chuckles. "I'll take my chance against the spirits taking hold of me."

"It's a scam," I say bitterly. "A joke."

"Yes. A very elaborate one."

"I thought you were open-minded about these things," I say.

"I am. But I'm not a fool. Madame Moulin's séance was clearly full of theatrics." He reaches an arm around my shoulder, pulling me close. "Let's get back to the hotel."

"No. Not yet." I don't want to go to bed with the dead at the front of my thoughts. These past few days have been such a blissful escape, and I need that to continue. I don't want to be pulled beneath the surface by Madame Moulin and her hollowed-out walls. I need something to take my mind off the letters that appeared on that slate.

I start walking, with little thought of where I'm going. There are no carriages on this street, and the men gathered outside a building on the corner are without the top hats and silk of the people we have been surrounded by for most of the evening. The trails of light from the lamp on the main street are all that illuminate the shadows.

Will jogs to keep up with me. He takes my arm, forcing me to a halt. "Lucy, stop. You're upset, I can tell. Let's just go back."

"I'm not upset."

His look clearly says he doesn't believe me. "I'm sorry for the things I said. For suggesting you leave your husband. I can tell it's rattled you."

"I don't want you to be sorry," I say. "I'm rattled because… because I'm thinking of it."

"You are?" I hear the spark of hope in his voice.

"Yes. And I'm not ready for our night to be over."

"All right," he agrees. "But this is a terrible part of town. Let's head back towards the Albion."

I peer across the road at a narrow doorway. I watch two Chinamen enter, followed by a group of white men. It's a strange sight; I've never seen the Chinese miners mingling with our kind in Castlemaine.

"What is that place?" I ask Will.

He examines the building, then shakes his head. "Never mind. Come on. Let's go back."

I raise my eyebrows. Keep my feet planted on the ground.

"It's an opium den, I imagine," he says finally. "They've become quite the rage since the Chinese brought the stuff over. All underground, of course. Seems as though the police are turning a blind eye to what's going on in this part of town."

Full of curiosity, I dart across the road and step inside before Will can stop me. He calls my name. Hurries after me.

The den is candlelit and full of shadows. A thick fug of smoke stings my eyes. Men lounge on divans and benches covered in straw matting, bringing long pipes to their lips. I notice a few women among them. There's a dull hum of chatter in the hot floral air. I glance at Will. I half expect him to demand we return to the hotel, but there's a look of interest in his eyes.

"Have you tried it?" I ask him. "Opium?"

He laughs. "Where do you think all that rubbish about Lady Fyvie's visions came from?"

"What's it like?"

"You've not taken laudanum before?"

"Well, yes, but not for… pleasure."

He hesitates for a moment. "Then I really don't think you need to—"

"Mr Browning," I say with mock sharpness, "it's far too late for decorum. You've already swept me away from my husband under false pretences. You've watched me play the ghost. Do you really think me so innocent?"

The words sound like more like Clara's than my own. If

that colourless kitchen hand from Horley saw me now, she wouldn't recognise herself.

Will's hand finds the bare curve of my neck. "No, Lucy," he murmurs, close to my ear. "I've no illusions of your innocence."

My body sears with both shame and desire, but before I can speak, Will has a hand to my shoulder and is ushering me further into the den. He pays the Chinaman behind the bar, who gestures for us to sit on a narrow divan in the corner of the room.

Will and I sit close together, our legs pressed against each other's and our hats and gloves strewn in a careless pile beside us. The man appears with a long bamboo pipe in one hand and an oil lamp in the other, a candle flickering inside it. He sets them on the small table in front of us.

Will nods his thanks. With practiced ease, he heats a dark knot of opium paste over the lamp, then places it in the bowl of the pipe. Leans back to take a long, slow draw. He blows a line of sweet-smelling smoke into an arc above his head. "I find it quite relaxing," he tells me. "Good for the creativity."

"I want to try it."

He hands me the pipe. "Not too much," he warns.

My throat burns as I inhale, but a warmth comes over me almost immediately. I feel the edges of the world unravel a little, and my anger at Madame Moulin fade. I lean against Will, feeling his arm wrap around my shoulder. Enjoying his solidity, his aliveness.

I open my eyes, picking out shapes in the shifting shadows of the den. The patrons are slow-moving, and the hum of voices is almost musical. Tonight, with the edges of reality softened, I am not so afraid of the Chinese men floating past me. Tonight, we feel like one and the same.

"Do you really believe there are people who can speak to the dead?" I ask Will. In the back of my mind, I see Madame Moulin's chalk meandering along the slate.

I am here.

Mama...

His fingers trace slow circles over my bare forearm. "Perhaps. I know most mediums are just performers. It's all trickery and theatre for the sake of those in mourning. But can we truly claim to know so much about the universe that we can definitively declare it's impossible to speak to the dead? What about men like Andrew Jackson Davis? Some of his revelations are so eye opening I believe there's every chance they come from the spirit world, as he claims. And several men of the cloth have claimed it to be a true phenomenon. After all, does the Bible not speak of ghosts?"

But I've stopped listening. Because through the sea of smoke-hazed figures is a face I never imagined I would see again.

Impossible.

Fred Buckley died six weeks ago when black powder exploded in his claim. We saw his remains buried in the cemetery on Campbell's Hill. And I listened to Clyde try to coax his ghost into rapping on the broken windlass. Two knocks for yes.

And yet there he is, walking past the bar and looking as real as Will and me. His long chin and fire-coloured hair leave me in no doubt. Fred Buckley has a face that's hard to forget.

He turns a corner and disappears. Instinct takes over and I scramble to my feet. Charge after him. I hear Will call my name, but I don't look back. I chase Fred Buckley down a dark, narrow passage. What I will do if I catch him, I have no thought, but I need to know if I saw what I think I did. Need to find that hazy line between reality and fantasy.

I break into a second smoke-filled parlour at the back of the den. Buckley is about to sit on a divan in the corner when I reach out and grab his arm, making him whirl around in shock.

"You're Fred Buckley," I say.

He chuckles at my look of horror. "Afraid you've seen a ghost?"

"You died in Castlemaine," I say. "I attended your burial." And then my thoughts catch up with me from the smoke-frayed world they've been languishing in. "You're not a ghost."

He barks a short laugh. "No missy, I ain't." He sinks back on the divan and waves to an approaching server to put his pipe and lamp on the table in front of him.

"You faked your own death?" All too easy, I realise then, to throw black powder down into a claim. No one would question the lack of a body. "Why?"

Buckley lifts the pipe and leans forward to hold the opium over the lamp. Candlelight flickers beneath his eyes. "Leave me alone, woman. It's none of your business."

"Please. Tell me why you did it." Beyond the opium haze, my mind is beginning to race. All is not well on those diggings. I need to know what caused Buckley to stage his own demise. Did it have something to do with the thefts? With Constable Stone and the night fossicking? Or am I just jumping to conclusions?

"What's it to you?"

I suck in my breath. "I'm Tom Earnshaw's wife," I say,

eyes pulling downwards with shame. "I'm worried for him."

Buckley's eyes flicker with recognition. And more than a little surprise. "Is Tom here?"

My face heats. "No," I say. "He's… He's not here."

Buckley just nods. What does he care about my infidelity?

"Did it have something to do with the police?" I press. "With Constable Stone?"

"Constable Stone," he snorts. "He's nothing."

"He's corrupt," I say.

"Of course he is. They say he beat a man half to death to get sent out here."

"Is he the reason you did what you did?"

Buckley shakes his head dismissively. "Just stay away from the police, Mrs Earnshaw. That's all you need to know."

"Stay away from the police? What do you mean? All of them? I—" Dizziness presses down on me suddenly and I stumble forward, bumping into the edge of the divan.

"Steady on there," says Buckley with a dull chuckle. He takes my elbow to steady me. "Why don't you head on back to whoever it is you're here with and leave me in peace?"

I feel the evening's bedlam of wine and opium lurching up inside me. I fly to the door at the back of the parlour. Stumble into a narrow lane and retch, surprised when nothing comes out. I lean against the brick wall, resting my head against my arms. I try to pull Clara's crimson skirts closer to my body. She won't be impressed if I bring them home smelling like whatever the hell is in that bucket beside the door.

I swallow hard as the stench turns my stomach again. Fred Buckley's words are thumping around in my brain.

Stay away from the police.

He's mistaken, surely. Misguided. Or trying to cover for his own crimes. The Castlemaine troopers are decent men.

But I realise I have nothing with which to back up that belief. Really, I know nothing of the Castlemaine police; not their names, barely their faces. Not beyond Constable Stone at least. But the men in uniform; aren't they the ones we're supposed to trust?

I feel a hand on my arm and dare to look, half expecting Will. Instead, it's Fred Buckley standing over me with a cup in his hand.

"All right?" he asks. He hands me the cup and I bring it gratefully to my lips before realising it's full of liquor. I groan and shove it back against his chest.

I straighten and look sheepishly at Buckley. "Thank you for coming after me."

He shrugs. "Well. Could get yourself in all sorts of trouble if you're not careful. I'm sure Tom wouldn't like you being alone out here." He eyes my plunging red neckline. "Especially dressed like that."

My cheeks flush and I fold my arms instinctively across my body. "The police are the ones behind the thefts?"

"I don't know why it surprises you. Greed is what keeps the goldfields alive."

I look at him squarely. "I need to know why you did what you did."

"Why?"

I close my eyes for a moment. Breathe deep to steady myself. "I caught Constable Stone night fossicking a few weeks ago," I say. "He knows I saw him. He's made threats… of sorts. And I need to know what I've gotten myself involved in."

Buckley's eyes take me in and he gives a single, short chuckle. "Didn't know Tom was married to such a menace."

I grit my teeth. When I don't answer, Buckley sighs.

"I made a stupid mistake. Got into a fight with one of the other diggers. Beat him up real bad. The troopers threw me in the cells. I thought for sure I were going to end up breaking rocks at Port Arthur. But the officers made me an offer. Said they'd let me go free if I went to work for them."

"Work for them?" I repeat. "Night fossicking?"

"At first. Then other things."

"What things?"

Buckley hesitates. "They're running a racket in the Black Forest," he says after a moment. "They send men out to hold up the coaches to and from the goldfields. A cut of the takings goes to the coachmen in exchange for their silence. And to keep them from firing a shot."

No. This is too much. "We passed through the Black Forest on the way here," I say. "Didn't have a single problem."

"Lucky you." He snorts. "It's happening, Mrs Earnshaw. Believe me. I were one of the poor bastards the troopers sent out there. Hold-ups once a month, all prearranged to make sure the right men are driving the coaches."

"The right men?" I repeat. "You mean the ones willing to stay quiet?"

He nods. "First Monday of the month, Castlemaine to Melbourne. Third Friday for the return journey." He smiles wryly. "No one notices the regularity because the hold-ups ain't hardly ever reported. Coachmen are paid to keep their mouth shut, and the passengers, well they just want the whole thing over and done. They know once their treasures are in the hands of bushrangers, they ain't getting them back again."

But my thoughts are caught on *third Friday for the return journey.*

The third Friday of the month is in two days' time.

We're due to take the coach back to Castlemaine tomorrow – Thursday. Can I convince Will to stay another night? I need to know if Buckley is telling the truth. Need to know the kind of place I'm living in, and just what I've entangled myself with.

"They gave you a cut of the takings too?" I ask.

"A few scraps. Most just goes into the officers' pockets. I only did it to stay out of the penal colonies. They're doing the same thing to that poor bastard Stone. Forcing him to get his hands dirty and giving him pennies in return."

For several moments, I say nothing, my mind struggling to make sense of all he has told me.

"And you couldn't get out?" I ask finally. "That's why you did what you did?"

Buckley nods. "I'd just finished my sentence before I went out to the diggings. I didn't want to live a life of crime no more. I knew if the Gold Commissioner ever learned of the racket going on under his nose, we'd be in no end of trouble. The officers'd likely get a slap on the wrist, but lags like me and Stone, we'd be off to the hangman. I tried to leave one night, but the coppers must have got word I was leaving. They caught me on the road out. Said they'd kill me if I left. I suppose they was worried about who I might tell. So I set off some black powder in my claim. Made it look like I done myself in. I—"

"Lucy!"

I whirl around at the sound of Will's voice. His hand

slides around my arm. "What the hell are you doing out here?" His eyes fall to Buckley. "Who is this?"

"It's no one," I say hurriedly, turning from Buckley and ushering Will away. "I just wasn't feeling well." I feel a hand on my other arm, yanking me back.

"Mrs Earnshaw," Buckley says, his voice low, "you can't tell a soul what I just told you. Any of them coppers find out what you know, you won't see another day."

"What is he talking about?" Will demands.

I shake free of Buckley's grip. "I have to tell Tom," I say, my voice rattling. "He needs to know he can't trust—"

"No, you don't," Buckley snaps. "You just tell your husband to keep his head down and stay the hell away from the police."

CHAPTER FIFTEEN

My encounter with the all-too-unghostly Fred Buckley is enough to make me flee the opium den. The smell of the sea hangs on the wind and I lift my face to the sky. Try to order my thoughts.

Will appears behind me with our hats in his arms. He hands me my bonnet and gloves. "What was that about?"

"It's nothing," I say. "Just take me back to the hotel. Please."

He asks again when we're back in his room, my opium-scented gown flung over a chair in the corner. He stands close to me, lamplight painting shadows on his bare chest.

"That man knew about the thefts on the gold diggings," I tell him. I don't want to go into any more detail. The thefts are on one side of my life. Will Browning is on the other.

"You're worried for your husband," he says.

"Yes," I admit. "But that doesn't mean I…"

"I know," he says gently. "It's all right. I understand."

The silence seems to thicken, to tense. I don't want thoughts of Tom intruding into this room.

I shuffle closer to Will. Tug at my laces, releasing my corset.

In the darkness I feel his lips against my own, but my thoughts are wandering, wandering, to Buckley, to Tom, to crooked troopers and the Black Forest racket.

"What do you think about staying one more night?" I blurt.

"Don't you need to get back?"

"Not urgently. I'll just tell my husband the coach was delayed. I've had such a wonderful time. I don't want it to end."

It's not a lie, I tell myself. Two days in Melbourne with Will have left me feeling lighter than I remember feeling in forever. But I need to know if Buckley is telling the truth.

"Well," he says, "we've to be back in Castlemaine by Saturday for rehearsal. But I don't see why we couldn't manage one more night."

By Friday morning, my nerves have caught up with me. Am I really doing this? Knowingly climbing onto a coach that in all likelihood is to be set upon by bushrangers?

It's too late for regret. Before we left the hotel this morning, I slipped off my wedding ring and tucked it into the bottom of my case. Made sure I have a few coins in my pocket to hand over to the highwaymen.

"Are you all right?" Will asks as we wait at the terminus for the coach. "You're quiet this morning."

I pace in impatient circles. Manage a smile. "A lot on my mind is all."

He nods, pressing my hand between both of his. I let myself enjoy that fleeting feel of him. By the end of the day, we'll be back in Castlemaine, and I will go back to being Tom's wife.

At least for now.

The coach rattles up to the terminus, pulled by two large brown horses. Will helps me into the coach and I take the seat beside him. Things have gone too far for false propriety. There are no familiar faces in the carriage, and besides, if we really are about to be set upon by bushrangers, I want him beside me.

As the coach pulls away from the terminus, my pulse begins to thunder. Is this the most foolish thing I have ever done? There have been so many contenders over the past few weeks it's difficult to say.

I glance at the chain of Will's gold watch hanging from his pocket. "Perhaps you ought to hide that," I say. "Just in case."

He gives me a quizzical smile but unhooks the watch all the same.

I sit stiltedly beside the window, toes tapping nervously. The neat chaos of Melbourne vanishes over the horizon. Ahead, blue-grey mountains are half hidden by cloud.

I close my eyes and try to breathe.

Like it or not, I'm involved in this tangled mess of thieving that is going on in Castlemaine. Perhaps I ought to go to Constable Stone and speak openly. Promise him my silence. If Buckley is telling the truth, and those who claim to uphold the law in Castlemaine are doing anything but, surely the town is not a safe place to be. I fear for Tom, sleeping out in the open with his revolver in hand. If he and Leo continue guarding their claim at night, how long will it be until they catch a glimpse of a thief? Catch a glimpse of the truth?

And this truth – if that is really what it is – is a dangerous truth to know. The miners have had more clout since the uprising in Ballarat a few years ago, but it's still the men in uniform who hold the power. A miner who knows too much could be taken care of with minimal fuss.

And so could his wife.

Here is the forest. Muted sunlight struggles through the branches, painting long shadows over the road. Light rain has begun to fall, speckling the windows and blurring my view of the trees that lie beyond. The horses continue their steady rhythm, drawing us deeper into the forest. I realise I'm holding my breath.

The coach careens to a sudden stop, bringing a cry of shock from several of the passengers. I grip the edge of the seat to avoid being thrown forward.

"What's happening?" another woman asks shakily.

But I do not need to be told.

Horses appear on either side of the carriage, ridden by men in tatty, colourless coats and trousers. They both wear wide-brimmed hats pulled down low over their foreheads, neckcloths tied over their mouths and noses to hide their faces. Each has a pistol in their hand. One fires a shot into the sky, making the passengers gasp. Birds shriek and vanish. Will slides his hand into mine.

One of the highwaymen leaps from his horse, his boots crunching loudly on the road. The door of the coach clicks open and he's inside in a single, swift movement. With the pistol still between his fingers, he reaches into his coat and produces a small cloth sack. He strides through the carriage, directing the nose of the gun at a gold ring on one lady's finger. She slides it off tearfully and tosses it in the sack. The highwayman steps slowly through the carriage. A hat pin. A watch. A gold necklace.

Before he reaches me, I fumble in my pocket for the coin pouch. I've played this moment over and over in my head; walked into it headfirst, but I'm still hot with fear. I shove the pouch into the bushranger's sack, rigid in my seat.

Almost as quickly as they appeared, the highwaymen are gone. Around us, the forest is still, the clatter of hooves fading and becoming silence. For several moments, the only sound is the heavy breathing of the passengers, and the muffled sobbing coming from the woman who gave up the ring. Faint rain patters against the glass.

"Are you all right?" Will murmurs.

"I'm fine."

But it's a grand lie. The highwaymen appeared at the exact time Fred Buckley said they would. Coincidence? Hardly.

And that means there is every chance his other tales are also true.

The coach begins to move again, pulling us back towards Castlemaine. And the knot in my stomach grows a little tighter.

CHAPTER SIXTEEN

"The nuisances caused by the Celestials are becoming so serious that unless some measures are adopted to check their increase, a very pretty quarrel will happen ... and result in something unpleasant. The Chinese are congregating around Forest Creek in great numbers, disgusting by their filthy habits the decent diggers among whom they happen to squat..."

Mount Alexander Mail
Castlemaine
13th October 1854

"A hold-up?" says Tom. "Oh Lucy, that's awful."

I arrived home to an orange dusk, just minutes before Tom returned from the diggings. At the sight of me in the kitchen, a day late, he pulled me into his arms, catching me by surprise.

I'm glad the news of the hold-up has taken his focus off my late return. Glad he hasn't stopped to poke holes in my garbled story of the coach's delay.

He unlaces his boots and kicks them under the table. "Did they hurt you?"

"No." I dump a handful of limp carrots into the soup pot. "And they only took a few coins. I hid my wedding ring in the bottom of my case before I got in the coach."

"Smart girl. You must have been terrified."

I stir the soup, not answering. I feel as though I'm seeing the town with fresh eyes. Seeing the dark current beneath the surface. Maybe I can't be surprised. As Fred Buckley said, this is a place grown on greed. Everyone came here hoping for a better life. And for those of us who have been unable to find it, it's only a short step to immorality and crime.

Tom smiles at me as I set his soup bowl in front of him. He's washed his hands and face for supper, changed into a clean shirt. The bruise beneath his eye has lightened to a faint shadow.

"How was the theatre?" he asks.

"Wonderful," I say, unwilling to go into more detail.

Tom tears the end off the loaf of bread. "I saw that woman from your theatre group at the dispensary. Clara."

The kitchen feels suddenly cloying. "Yes?"

"She didn't go to Melbourne with you?"

"No. She decided to stay. Make sure everything was ready for the opening of her shop." The lie comes to me too easily.

"I see."

Does he believe me? I can't tell.

There is nothing but warmth in his voice. But perhaps he's testing me. Perhaps I'm not the only one who's learnt a few acting skills over these past bitter months.

"Have there been more thefts?" I ask.

"A couple of tents were robbed out by Pennyweight. Nothing major. Clyde reckons he saw that Chinaman Ah Tam out at Forest Creek, sniffing around in other men's claims."

I shift uncomfortably. "Is he certain?"

"You'd have to ask him that," says Tom.

"Have you been guarding the claim?"

"Every second night. Alternating with Leo."

I stir my soup, my appetite gone. "You ought to give them what they want," I blurt. "The thieves. If they want to raid your claim, just let them." My voice wavers.

Tom frowns. "Why in hell would I do that?"

I grit my teeth. How desperately I want to tell him of Fred Buckley and all I have learnt. But Buckley's warning rings in my ears. *Any of them coppers find out what you know, you won't see another day.* There's so much I need Tom to hear. But so much I can't speak of. It would just put him in danger.

"These thieves," I say instead, "who knows how violent they are? Who knows what they're capable of? If they want to dig in your claim, you should just let them do it."

Tom gives a thin smile and turns back to his soup. "Don't worry, Luce. There's nothing in my claim but mud anyway."

I go to Clara's shop the next morning. The place is far more orderly than it was last time I saw it, with mannequins arranged in the windows and the reams of fabric lined up neatly in one corner. A broadsheet advertising her wares is plastered to one window, and the white patch on the front door has been painted over in a handsome grey-green.

I find her sitting at the table in the corner of the shop, sketching the beginnings of a new design. I hold out the gown and hoop skirt.

"Here. Thank you for lending them to me."

Clara nods, barely looking up from the page. "Just put them on the chair over there."

I set the skirts down and hover beside the table. "How have your first few days of business been?"

"A decent start," she says. "I've commissions from two of the ladies I used to sew for."

"That's wonderful." I shift my weight, making the floor creak noisily.

Finally, she looks up. "Is there something else you need, Lucy?"

"When you've the time," I begin awkwardly, "will you take me to the Chinese camp? Show me where to get the thunder god vine?" My voice is impossibly small.

Clara smiles to herself, tapping her pencil against her chin. "You had a good time in Melbourne then?"

I nod faintly. I can't go into more detail. Can't speak of what Will asked me to do. Speaking of it makes it far too real.

"Good." Clara eyes me, but when it becomes clear I'm not going to offer any more information, she lets the matter slide. She puts down her pencil. "Let's go now. I've a client coming for measurements in an hour."

Off we go in the direction of Clinkers Hill, where the Chinese miners have made their camp, away from the settlements of the white men.

I've heard stories about the mysterious tonics and

potions to come out of the Chinese apothecary, cures much more outlandish than the fish oil and earthworms on the shelves of the dispensary in town. Before Clara had tucked the bottle of thunder god vine into my hand, I'd always brushed their concoctions aside, put it down to a quirk of their culture. Even when Elsie fell ill, venturing to the Chinese camp for a cure had not even crossed my mind. What kind of person would feed their child something that came from this unknown race?

But I do not have the same fear for myself. Moments before I crept into Will's hotel room, I tossed back the thunder god vine without a second thought.

Through the warren of tight huts, I see the dark heads of the Chinese moving through the streets. Though they have swapped their pointed hats for woollen caps more like our own, their unfamiliarity is unnerving. I feel wildly out of place.

"Let's just go back," I say suddenly. "I'll… I'll just take the risk."

Clara frowns. "What are you so afraid of?"

I hesitate. I can't place it. But it has something to do with that terror wrought by strangeness, by the unfamiliar. That same terror that has us transplanting myths of haunted castles across the seas to unknown lands.

There's been talk of the Chinamen luring unsuspecting ladies to their tents. Talk of them having the power to wipe a woman's senses clean. But the rational part of me knows this is little more than gossip. It also knows that this is not what's causing me to be afraid. This is just fear of the foreign.

Clara loops her arm through mine and keeps walking. "You're being stupid," she says, and that's the end of the matter.

I try to conjure up the apathy towards the Chinese I felt swanning through their opium den on Little Lonsdale Street. It's much harder to do without lungs full of smoke and a head full of wine.

The Chinese apothecary is a primitive, windblown place, like the tented shopfronts that lined Forest Creek when Tom and I first arrived. A rickety shelf teeters at the back of the tent, a makeshift wooden counter in front. An older man stands behind it, threads of grey streaking his long queue.

I stare at my feet, far too overcome with fear and shame to make eye contact with anything other than the floor.

"Good morning," says Clara.

I glance up curiously to see the man nod in response.

"Thunder god vine," Clara tells him.

He nods again. Disappears behind a flap at the back of the tent. I hear him murmuring to someone on the other side.

The man returns with a small jar. He puts it on the counter and holds up one finger.

Clara nudges me. "One shilling."

I fumble in my purse and dump the money on the counter. I slip the jar into my reticule, nod my thanks and rush from the shop.

In my hurry to escape, I narrowly miss colliding with a Chinese woman and her child. I stumble, caught off guard by the sight of them. I'd not realised any women and children had made the journey out here with their countrymen. Certainly, I've never seen them in town.

"I'm sorry," I murmur, holding up my hand in a gesture of apology.

The woman nods, bowing her head. Then she looks up,

her eyes meeting mine. I feel a sudden, unexpected moment of connection; as an Englishwoman, I feel like a novelty among all the men here on the diggings – I can hardly imagine how it must feel for her.

She steps inside the apothecary, passing Clara in the doorway.

I whirl around at the sound of footsteps, wild voices. One of the Chinese diggers thunders past, pursued by a group of white men. The Chinaman skids on the loose earth as he rounds the corner, falling to his knees. One of the men leaps on top of him, pinning him to the ground.

"Bloody thief," the Englishman hisses. "Stay the hell away from our claims." He brings back his fist, pounding the Chinaman's nose. Blood spurts onto the footprinted earth.

This man is innocent. I know it. He's being punished for the crimes of Stone and the other troopers.

Open my mouth and my secrets will spill. But how can I allow this?

Before I can change my mind, I race towards the men. "Stop!"

The attacker turns to give me a fleeting glance. The rest don't even acknowledge me.

The Chinaman groans as a boot flies into his side.

And then, more footsteps; more men approaching. Tom is among them. At the sight of me, he stops in surprise.

"What in hell are you doing here?"

I'm breathless. "They're attacking the wrong man."

"How do you know that?"

The Chinaman is coiled, pleading, shielding his face from the men's wild kicks.

"Do something!" I cry, pushing past Tom's question.

"They're going to kill him!"

Before he can reply, the police arrive on horseback, firing a shot into the sky. Like frightened dogs, the men scatter, leaving the Chinese digger curled up on the ground. Two of his countrymen hurry to his side, helping him to his feet. They rush him into a nearby tent, a stream of blood running down his face and blackening the collar of his shirt.

The police horses canter up the hill towards us.

"Why are you here?" I ask Tom, my voice low. "Did you come to attack that man?"

Hurt flashes across his eyes. "Is that what you think of me now?"

I falter. I don't want to believe Tom has it in him to attack another man. But I think of the night he came home swollen-eyed, with Clyde's blood staining his knuckles.

"Leo told me a group had come here to confront Ah Tam," he tells me. "I came along to—"

"To watch?"

"To hear what he had to say for himself. I didn't expect them to just jump him like this."

I let out my breath. I can't tell if my husband is naïve or a liar.

"Lucy?" says Clara. "Are you all right?"

"She's fine," Tom cuts in tersely.

I give her a strained smile. "I'm all right. Thank you. You ought to get back. You don't want to be late for your meeting."

Clara hesitates for a moment, then nods, turning and disappearing between the huts. Hot wind blows up the hill, whirlpooling the dust.

Suddenly I want nothing more than to escape the

Chinese camp, with Ah Tam's blood black on the ground. I start to walk, Tom jogging to catch up to me.

For several long seconds, we walk in silence, our footsteps crunching rhythmically.

"How do you know they were attacking the wrong man?" asks Tom.

I watch at my feet as I walk.

Telling him everything Fred Buckley told me is too dangerous. But I have to give him something.

I stop walking, tugging him into a narrow alley behind the marketplace. The stench of boiling meat floats out from a cookshop and makes my stomach roll.

"I saw Constable Stone night fossicking at Forest Creek. Three weeks ago."

For a moment, Tom says nothing. "Stone," he repeats.

I nod.

"How do you know he wasn't just on duty?"

"He wasn't wearing his uniform."

"That doesn't necessarily mean—"

"He's involved in this, Tom," I push. "I know it. I saw him climbing out of another man's claim in the middle of the night. Alone. You have to believe me. The Chinese miners are innocent. Tell the other men not to go after them again."

For several moments, Tom just stares at me, his face unreadable. We are standing toe to toe, and I can feel the heat rising from his body. Can see the dark flecks in his blue eyes. And the coldness.

"What in hell were you doing out at Forest Creek in the middle of the night?" he asks finally. There's a strain to his voice, as though his control is about to tear loose.

"I came out there to find you. You were guarding the

claim that night." A lie, yes, but how could he know this? "You left your coat and I was afraid you might get cold in the night…" My words are thin with guilt.

"You never brought my coat to the claim."

"I know. After I saw Stone fossicking, I got scared and ran."

He rubs his square jaw. Tries to take a step back from me, but his spine meets the wall of the hut he stands in front of. "Why didn't you tell me this earlier?"

And the answer to that, well, that comes easily when I think of Constable Stone on my doorstep with threats in his eyes. When I think of Fred Buckley hurling black powder into his claim to escape the troopers' clutches.

"I was afraid. Afraid of what he might do if he found out I'd told anyone."

Of all the lies I've just spouted, it's this truth that brings the look of doubt to Tom's eyes. I can see it all – the anger, the hurt, the questions. But he doesn't voice any of it. Instead, he just nods stiffly.

"Stone," he says again.

"I'm telling the truth, Tom. You have to believe me."

"Why would I not believe you?" The words are spoken so simply, but I can hear everything that lies beneath them. My late-night rehearsals and midnight walks for air, and *I saw that woman from your theatre group at the dispensary.*

He starts to walk. Impulsively, I follow.

I glance sideways at him. His eyes are storm clouds, face furrowed in a deep frown.

"Tom," I say. "You can't tell anyone what I just told you. Promise me. It's very important."

He doesn't answer. Doesn't promise. Instead, he says,

"Why were you at the Chinese camp?"

"I went to their apothecary. Clara said they could give me something for… headaches." My fingers tighten around my reticule, tracing the shape of the jar inside.

"You were visiting someone, weren't you," Tom says suddenly. "Out at Forest Creek. The night you saw Stone fossicking. You were visiting another man."

I feel his words like a physical blow. Hear my involuntary inhalation.

"I came to bring you your coat," I manage.

Tom breathes heavily through his nose. "Were you visiting the same man you went to Melbourne with?"

Heat courses through me. "I went to Melbourne with the theatre group."

But I can hear the waver in my voice. And I know my husband can hear it too.

CHAPTER SEVENTEEN

Tom does not come home for supper. The stew I've cooked sits congealing on the range. I stare mindlessly at the pot, letting flies gather around the rim. My throat is thick with tears.

I try to tell myself this is what I wanted. For Tom to discover my secrets. In fleeting moments since I returned to Castlemaine, I've even imagined him being the one to cast me out of the house. Then I could disappear off to the salons of Melbourne with Will, the decision made for me.

But Tom's absence leaves a deep coldness inside me. How much does he know? How many conclusions has he drawn?

I turn the pages of my script and recite my lines. But it brings me none of the usual joy. The Green Lady fails to pull me from reality like she has always done.

Craving company, I leave the house and head for Clara's shop.

Though it's getting late, I can see through the window that she's still working, stitching buttons onto a waistcoat on one of her mannequins. Her dark hair hangs in a long plait down her back, a frown of concentration creasing the bridge of her nose. At the sight of her entrenched in her work, I turn to leave. I can't bother her with troubles I've brought on myself.

As I reach the corner, I hear the front door click open. She steps out into the street, calling me back.

"You're busy," I say. "I didn't mean to disturb you."

"It's all right, I could use a break. Come in. I'll make us some tea."

I follow her back into the shop. She carries the lamp into the living quarters and sets it on the tiny table. Stokes the fire and hangs the kettle above the flames.

The back room is chaos. Petticoats are strewn over the unmade bed, swathes of fabric draped over chairs. A half-drunk cup of cold tea sits in front of me at the table, among a pile of hairpins, scissors, and a copy of yesterday's *Mount Alexander Mail.*

"How was the meeting with your client?" I ask.

"Fine." She takes the dirty teacup and rinses it in the trough. "Has your husband found out you were with Will?"

"Is it so obvious?" I play with a splintered edge on the table. "He doesn't know it was Will. He just suspects I've been with another man."

"How did he find out?"

I rub my eyes. "I told him you were coming to Melbourne with me. And then he saw you at the dispensary."

"Oh hell," says Clara. "I'm sorry, Lucy. I—"

"Don't be foolish. It's not your fault. And I told him I was out on the claims one night and he thinks I was out visiting."

"Why in hell did you tell him that?"

"It's a long story. That man they attacked at Clinker's Hill today…" I fade out, not wanting to revisit the whole sorry mess.

"Maybe it's for the best," says Clara. "You and Tom are unhappy, that much is obvious. Maybe you'd both be better off finding your own way."

The thought brings sudden tears to my eyes. "A marriage is for life," I say, for not the first time.

Clara shakes her head. "Open your eyes, girl. Whatever precious little bubble you existed in in England, it's gone now. Things are different here. People are not so stuck in their ways. Not so worried about what society thinks of them. Look." She flips through the newspaper lying on the table and scans the page. "Here. *To my wife Margaret Owens, having gone away with Peter Worthington, I declare myself no longer responsible for your debts and financial upkeep.*"

I frown. "That's dreadful."

"Is it? Sounds to me like Margaret Owens and her husband might be far happier without each other."

Perhaps she's right. But the thought of Tom posting such a message fills me with unfathomable shame and sadness.

My tears spill suddenly, and I swipe at them with the back of my hand. Clara lifts the kettle and fills the teapot, placing a cup in front of me on the table. She presses a hand to my shoulder for a second.

"Let's go back to the front room," she says. "It's too hot back here." With the lamp in one hand and her teacup in the other, she leads me back out to the parlour. "What do you think of this?" she asks, handing me a sketch of a pin-striped gown. "Too garish?"

"Not at all," I say. "In Melbourne, the women were wearing—"

My words are lost beneath a sudden crash, and I feel glass graze my cheek. A large rock thumps against a mannequin, knocking it to the floor amongst shattered pieces of the window. I stumble backwards, tea spilling down the front of my dress.

Clara tears through the front door. "You bastards!" she yells into the street. "Come back here and show your damn faces!"

She comes back inside and slams the door, cheeks flushed.

"Did you see who it was?"

She shakes her head. Closes her eyes for a moment and leans against the door. Her jaw trembles, then she clamps it closed.

"Are you all right?" I ask gently.

She opens her eyes. Nods. Then she kneels carefully among the glass, shifting the mannequin and its waistcoat away from a pool of spilled tea.

I kneel beside her and touch her wrist. "I'm sorry," I say. "We'll fix this."

"Of course we will," she says, picking at the glass shards with hard eyes. Earth-scented wind gusts through the broken window and blows our hair back from our faces. My hand tightens around her wrist. "Don't let these men stop you."

I expect some sharp retort from Clara – *no, of course I won't* – but her lips are pressed into a thin white line. She reaches for another piece of glass, cursing as a shard slices into her finger. A bead of blood appears on her pale skin. I stand carefully, holding out my hand to help her to her feet. "Come on," I say. "I'll help you clean this up."

"Are you coming to the hunt?" asks Tom.

Every few months, the diggers shoulder their weapons and charge out to the bushland to blast possums from the trees. First man with a hit gets his drinks paid for all night.

Tom stands by the door with his revolver in hand, looking at me expectantly. I'm not sure what game we're playing. Am I to pretend there are no secrets between us? Or am I to demand that we throw things out in the open? Tell my husband everything and let whatever is to come of it come?

No. I can't do that to Will. Can't throw him in the path of Tom's wrath. Nor can I face the confrontation of it. After a year of small talk, the thought of having a real conversation with my husband terrifies me.

Pretending feels like the only way forward. Pretending everything is fine. And pretending I don't think running through the dark with rifles and chasing some poor creature up a tree isn't the stupidest thing I've ever heard.

"Of course I'll come," I say, taking my bonnet from the hook.

I follow Tom out of the cottage and through town towards the scrub on the edge of Moonlight Flat. The streets are busy, loud. Men stride past, laughing and chattering, bottles in one hand and rifles in the other. A thin crescent moon hangs among an explosion of stars, silently watching the chaos below.

I can feel tension pouring from Tom's body. "Slow down

a little," I say, jogging to catch up with him.

He stops charging. Still doesn't speak.

"I wonder if Leo will win again this time," I say, trying for lightness.

Tom grunts noncommittally. He shifts his revolver to his other hand, widening the space between us.

A crowd has gathered among the trees, shining lamps up into the branches. An unseen creature rustles the silver leaves.

"Careful, man," someone calls, "ain't you heard there's ghosts out here?"

A roar of laughter.

A shot echoes into the sky. Tom hurries after the crowd as they chase the animal further into the bush. I let myself fall behind.

A group of men have their rifles raised towards the dark silhouette of a tree. I hope the poor creature manages to outrun them. I also hope Tom won't raise his weapon, but just watch proceedings as he did the last time we came to one of these debacles. I don't like the sight of my husband with a weapon in his hand.

Last time we were here, we stood on the edge of the cluster, arm in arm, buffering each other against our fresh loss. We had gone to watch the hunt in hope it might distract us. And yes, for a few hours, it did. Because standing there arm in arm with Tom, with the rest of the settlement cheering and howling around us, it felt like us against the world. How have we taken such a wrong turn?

Tonight, Tom is not just watching proceedings. Not that I expected him to. He lifts his revolver and fires, barely even aiming.

"Take your time, Tom," I say. "That was a terrible shot.

You'll hurt someone."

He holds the weapon out to me. "You want to try?" Bitterness in his words.

I wrap my arms around myself. "Of course not."

He turns back to the trees. Fires again. This time his shot is so wild it brings laughter from the men standing beside him.

"All right, Earnshaw, that's enough," Clyde barks. "You ought to listen to your wife. She's right, you'll have someone's head off." He waves at Ollie, who's standing to Tom's left. "You're up, Cooper."

Tom steps back, shifting the revolver from one hand to the other. I watch as Ollie carefully lines up his shot and pulls the trigger. He curses as the possum darts away again. Laughter ripples through the crowd.

"That creature's too smart for you all," I say to Tom, forcing a smile.

He doesn't look at me.

"Are you ignoring me?"

"I'm not ignoring you. I'm hunting."

I wrap my arms around myself. "Speak to me then."

"About what, Lucy? What would you like to speak about?" He looks at me fleetingly, before turning back to the hunt.

My throat tightens, and I blink back tears. "Speak about anything," I cough. "Anything at all."

He turns to me then, and the coldness in his eyes makes him look like a stranger. "Anything? How about we talk about whose bed you've been rolling around in?"

Dread sears through me. Eyes pull towards us, before hurriedly turning away.

"Jesus, Tom," I hiss, pulling him backwards, away from

the crowd. "Keep your damn voice down."

"Am I embarrassing you?" he says loudly. "Isn't this what you wanted, Luce? For me to talk to you?"

Rage shoots through me. "You're a bastard." In an instant, my guilt is gone. I can't bear to be around him for another second. What was I thinking, coming out here with him tonight? Trying to save something that cannot be saved. Something I don't even want to be saved. My hatred for Tom is suddenly blinding.

I whirl around and begin to charge back towards town. He snatches my arm.

"Where are you going?"

"Anywhere!" I cry. "Anywhere away from you!"

Tom lowers his voice. "I don't want you running around out there on your own."

I shove him away. "I don't care what you want! Stay the hell away from me." I've never spoken to my husband like this before. Would never have dared. But what do I care now? It's only a matter of time before he's posting a message in the newspaper to let the world know he's washed his hands of me.

I'm running down the dark ribbon of the road before I'm fully aware of what I'm doing. I'm beginning to make a habit of running away.

I wait for Tom's footsteps behind me, but they don't come.

When I reach the edge of town, I stop to catch my breath. I hear drunken shouts coming from the hunt, gunshots piercing the sky.

The hatred inside me builds, threatening to consume me. Hatred for this place, with its hollow earth and desperate men, and all those lost children buried on the hill. I snatch a stone from the side of the road and fling it wildly to let a little of the rage loose from my body. It strikes a drinking trough with a violent, satisfying clang.

I run to Clara's shop and pound on the door. Squint impatiently through the window that's not boarded up. I can see faint lamplight coming from the back room.

"I need the Green Lady's dress," I say when she answers.

"What in hell, Lucy?" She ushers me inside, locking the door behind us. "Are you all right?"

"Where's the dress?" I gulp down my breath. "I'm going to play the ghost."

Clara puts her hands to my shoulders. "You can't go out hoaxing in this state," she says. "Why don't you come and sit down? Tell me what happened."

I shake my head. I've already done far too much talking tonight. I need to disappear into a world where reality is a little more distant. "Where's the dress?"

"It's in the back," Clara says after a moment. "I'll get it for you. Just stay here."

She returns a moment later with a half-filled glass of gin. She nods to the chair beside her work table. "Here. Sit down and drink this. Might relax you a bit."

"Where's the dress?" I ask again.

"I said I'd get it for you. Just sit down."

I sit, finally accepting the glass. Pulling off my bonnet, I take a sip, listening to Clara's footsteps disappear into the living quarters. The liquor burns as it slides down my throat.

I can't go home yet, not after the way I spoke to Tom. Nor do I want to. I can't bear the thought of crawling into bed beside him. What would happen if I disappeared for the night? Would he tear the town apart looking for me? Or would he leave me to my own devices? Wash his hands of his unfaithful wife?

I realise the shop has fallen quiet. I call Clara's name, but there's no response. I get to my feet and peer into the back room. It's dark, except for the muted glow coming from the remains of the fire. Has she gone out the back door? I barely heard a sound.

The door bursts open suddenly, and she flies back inside, Will in tow.

No, no, I don't want him here. Around Will, I have always hidden the most damaged parts of myself. And I am acutely aware they're on glaring display right now.

But when he pulls me into his arms, his touch is so filled with care and affection that it makes my throat seize with pain.

"Tell me what's wrong," he says, impossibly gently.

"Nothing's wrong. I want to play the ghost." My voice is muffled against his chest.

"I don't think that's a good idea."

I slide out of his arms. "Don't you?" I say tautly. I look back at Clara. "Is that why you fetched him? So he could tell me what to do?"

"Of course not," she says, "I—"

"Have you seen the men out on their stupid possum hunt?" I demand, uninterested in their response. "Running around like children and scaring the life out of these poor sorry creatures? Maybe they need to be given a bit of a fright themselves."

I rub my eyes, trying to calm myself. Like it or not, if I'm to go out hoaxing, I'll have to get past these two gatekeepers first. And to do that, I'll have to show them I can keep myself together.

"I need that escape," I admit. "I need to forget everything for a time."

Will nods faintly. I can tell he knows he's played a role in my internal chaos. That his offer to build a new life with me has rocked me at my foundations. And I can see the wordless apology in his eyes. I don't want him to feel regret. Because right now, his offer of a new life is the only thing keeping me afloat.

"Yes," I say suddenly.

He steps back, hands still around my forearms. "Yes, what?"

"I want to go to Melbourne with you. I want everything we spoke about."

He catches Clara's eye for a moment, and she disappears into the shop. Maybe she's finally going for the damn dress.

Will runs his thumb over my cheek, smooth as silk compared to Tom's rough skin. "Nothing would make me happier," he says, "but you're in a state, Lucy. I'm not sure you've thought this through."

I exhale sharply. It feels like I've done nothing but think. Nonetheless, I understand Will's reluctance. I suppose I was something of a walking disaster when I came charging into the shop. "It's what I want," I say, levelling my voice. "But if it makes you happy, I'll think it through some more tonight."

Will holds his lips to my forehead. "Good." And then a firm kiss against my lips. I hear myself murmur against him, my fingers making a tight fist around the hem of his jacket. He tucks a strand of hair behind my ear. And just when I expect him to talk me out of going hoaxing tonight, he gives me an empathetic smile. "Shall we find out where Clara's keeping that dress?"

I step out into the street, reams of green skirts flowing behind me. Lilias Drummond, the poor Green Lady, betrayed by her unfaithful husband and doomed to wander the halls of Fyvie Castle forever. I wonder, as I glide past the stables of the Commercial, whether Lilias Drummond really existed. Was she once as earthly and human as me? Or is she like so many of the stories told in this place; nothing but a myth? A way of making sense of the world; of our fears, our regrets, the darker sides of ourselves we hide beneath the surface?

The street is a little busier than when I raced to Clara's shop in disarray. Apparently people are growing bored with the hunt, though I can still hear plenty of pistol shots coming from Moonlight Flat. Still hear plenty of drunken, boyish laughter. For a second, I wonder what Tom is doing. I push the thought away quickly. When I'm the Green Lady, there's no room in my head for Tom, or for Will, or even for Elsie. That is part of the allure; this blissful emptiness, as playing the ghost consumes me.

I have an eerie glide down to a fine art. Tiny, slow steps that look for all the world as though I'm floating along the street. As always, I keep to the alleys, to the narrow lanes. Let those walking the main thoroughfares catch no more than a glimpse of me.

The woman who sees me tonight belongs at Madame Moulin's séance table. Hunched shoulders and darting eyes, her small body swamped in widow's weeds. At the sight of me gliding down the alley, she lets out a sharp cry, a hand pressed to her chest. She turns and stumbles back in the direction of the main street, and I instinctively hide myself in the narrow gap between two houses.

The woman is crying now, dreadful searing wails. Though I can't see her, the nearness of the sound makes me certain she is still in the alley. Footsteps thump towards her.

"Ma?" says a young man's voice. "What's happened? What on earth are you doing down here?"

The woman replies only in sobs.

"Has someone hurt you, Ma? Who's there?"

I hold my breath.

Between the woman's wails, I make out, "The lady."

"Which lady?" asks her son. "Who?"

I glance over my shoulder. I can't disappear this way. The only way out is back through the alley.

"Come on, Ma," I hear finally. "Let's get you home." The crying gets gradually softer. Finally, it disappears.

I close my eyes, trying to slow my heart.

Though there's a thrill to being seen, I can't help but feel guilty at the woman's distress. Perhaps the Green Lady has been out for long enough tonight.

I slip out from between the houses and head in the opposite direction to where the woman disappeared. Back towards Clara's parlour.

And out I float into a lane behind the shop, rounding the corner and coming face to face with one of the possum hunters. I stop abruptly. I did not expect anyone to be here, and I try not to let my surprise show on my face.

He stares at me for a long second, eyes wide and lips parted. The terror on his face makes me feel powerful.

And next, well, does it happen as though in slow motion, or does it all happen at once? I don't know. Hand in his pocket. Pistol in his hand.

And that terror in his face, that fearful instinct; it makes him fire.

The sound is deafening, distorted, my brain registering the noise at the same time it grasps the blaze above my hipbone. I look down to see a bloom of crimson creeping over the pale green bodice of my dress.

And then I am falling, the man cursing, stumbling; my earthly, flowing blood bringing far more horror to his face than the sight of the Green Lady.

CHAPTER EIGHTEEN

*"For God's sake bring me a light, for we have caught Springheeled
Jack here in the lane."'*

The Times
London
22nd February 1838

The shooter's face swims in and out of my vision.

"I didn't… I thought…" He is dithering, hand-wringing,
face white with panic.

"Get out of here." Will shoves him away. Kneels at my
side. He's asking me questions, whipping off his neckcloth
and pressing it to my hip. His words all seem jumbled. All I
can make sense of is the roar of pain in my side.

I hear Clara's voice too: "I'll go for the surgeon."

And then I'm in Will's arms, being carried away from the

glare of the streetlamps and through the back door of Clara's shop. I close my eyes, feeling every jolt in my body. Will lays me gently on the bed and smooths my hair from my forehead. Kneels at my side with words I'm sure are supposed to be calming, but the panic in his voice betrays him.

The door cracks open as Clara charges through it. "Surgeon's on his way." She reaches into her reticule for a small bottle and hands it to Will. "Give her this. It's laudanum. For the pain."

He pulls out the cork and holds the bottle to my lips. I gulp down a few drops, a trickle running out the side of my mouth. For a second, I wish desperately for Tom.

"Am I going to die?" I ask.

"Of course not." I hear the waver in Will's words. He strokes my hair with an unsteady hand. I close my eyes, desperate for the laudanum to have a scrap of an effect.

"There are police in the lane," says Clara. "We ought to tell them what happened."

Panic grips me. I don't want those corrupt troopers anywhere near me. Who knows what they're capable of? "No. No police." I try to sit, but pain rips through my body, making me cry out. "Please."

Clara and Will exchange glances. I can see their unasked questions. And I sure as hell am not about to answer them now.

Without releasing the pressure on my hip, Will wipes a damp cloth over my cheeks and forehead. To calm me, I think at first. Or is it? As he dips the cloth back in the washbin and continues to scrub at my skin, I realise he is cleaning my face of makeup. Washing away the Green Lady. Hiding any hint of what I've been doing.

And then there's another person in the room. A man leaning over me. Mr Hamilton, the settlement's surgeon.

"What happened?" he asks.

"Possum hunt," I manage.

Will presses a gentle hand to my shoulder to still me. "An accidental shooting," he tells the surgeon.

Hamilton lets out a grunt that says he knows we're lying. The hunt is taking place all the way out on Moonlight Flat. Too far from Clara's shop for my story to be believable.

Scissors slice through the fabric over my hip, freeing me from the Green Lady's gown. Blood trickles down my side.

I close my eyes against the violent tilting of the world. Fragments of the surgeon's verdict reach me through my haze.

Hit above the hip, clean entry.

And then there are hands on my shoulders, holding me to the bed. A cloth held over my mouth and nose, damp, with a sickly-sweet smell. The chloroform struggles to drag me down, the burning in my side refusing to let me slide into unconsciousness. I'm hovering, somehow, on the edge of two worlds. A place of haunted castles and ringing bells, and Elsie's name appearing in chalk on a slate. I'm in an opium dream I can't break free from, charging through the Black Forest and hearing myself scream. I see men in the earth and piles of gold I can't quite reach, and an empty wooden box going down, down into Fred Buckley's grave. And then, mercifully, the dark swallows me and I'm aware of nothing more.

When I open my eyes, Will is sitting on the edge of the bed, my hand between both of his. His jaw is tight, his eyes dark with worry.

"Is it over?" I ask. I'm scared to move.

He nods. "How do you feel?"

My hip is pulsing and I can feel tight strapping around my middle. I dare to glance down. Blooms of crimson still blot the sheets, the stained dress of the Green Lady in pieces around my body. I try to tug the blanket upwards to hide myself. Will eases the covers up to my shoulders and gently smooths my hair. "Mr Hamilton says you ought to make a full recovery. He took the ball out cleanly." He holds my hand to his lips. "I'm so sorry, Lucy. I should never have let you go out there tonight. I should never have let you play the ghost in the first place. I always knew it was a bad idea…"

His words make rage flare inside me. It was my decision to go out there tonight. I didn't go seeking his permission. But I'm too exhausted for anger. "It wasn't your fault," I croak. My mouth feels impossibly dry. Before I can ask for water, a violent rush of sickness tears up from inside me. Will gets to me with the chamber pot just in time. I empty my stomach into the pot, then roll onto my back again, wincing at the pain.

"I'm sorry," I groan, swamped in embarrassment.

"There's no need to be sorry." He presses a cup of water to my lips. "Here, drink this. Mr Hamilton said the chloroform will make you a little nauseous for a while."

"How long have I been out?"

"Less than an hour." Will tugs at his collar, as though caught in hesitation. "Shall I fetch your husband?" His voice is thin.

"No," I say hurriedly. "Just take me home."

"I can't do that. Mr Hamilton said you're not to be

moved for at least two days."

"I can't stay here for two days," I hiss. "I have to get home. Tom will…" I try to sit up, pain knifing my side and making my head spin. I feel Will's hand slide behind me, lowering me back down to the mattress.

"Lucy," Clara speaks up from the other side of the room. I didn't realise she was there. "You told me Tom already knows you've been unfaithful. What difference does it make if you stay here?"

"Your husband knows you've been unfaithful?" Will shakes his head. "I'm sorry. I… That's not important right now." But I see his jaw tighten.

Tears well up behind my eyes. "He suspects. But he can't know any of this. He can't know I've been playing the ghost. He'd be so ashamed. I couldn't do that to him." I turn my head on the pillow as my tears spill, feeling the need to hide. How can I let Will see how much my betrayal of Tom is breaking me?

"You don't think he'll notice when he sees the bullet wound in your side?" he asks, trying to bite back his sharpness.

"I'll think of something to tell him."

Clara lets out her breath. "Lucy, that's ridiculous. You—"

"It's not your problem," I snap. I wipe my eyes, regretting my outburst. "I'm sorry, I… Please. Just help me get home."

Reluctantly agreeing to help me in case I try and get home myself, Clara and Will ease me back into my shift and dress and help me to my feet. I lean on them heavily for several moments, the lamplit shop tilting around me. Finally, I dare to take a step, grateful when my legs hold beneath me.

We step out into the lane behind the shop. At the end of the alley, I see the main street filled with people. The tavern is overflowing, one man standing with an ale in one hand and the body of a possum in the other. My eyes dart across the crowd, but I don't see Tom.

By the time we reach the cottage, the pain is far too consuming for me to care who the hell sees me. Tom included. My fingers dig into Will's arm as I try to keep upright. The noise from the main street has become muted, and my breathing is thunder in my ears.

"The house is dark," says Clara. "I don't think your husband is home." She reaches into my reticule for the key and unlocks the door.

The house is black and airless. Will fumbles through the dark and lights a lamp in the kitchen, before Clara guides me into the bedroom.

Will hovers in the doorway. I understand his reluctance to enter. Tom's shirt on the chair, Tom's scarf on the hook, Tom's shaving mirror on the washstand. Even in his absence, my husband inhabits this room. Clara helps me out of my dress, then eases me onto the bed and pulls the blanket to my chest. She hands me the bottle of laudanum. "Take another drop. It will help you sleep."

I bring the bottle to my lips.

"That's enough." She pulls it away quickly. Looks over her shoulder at Will. "You ought to leave. In case her husband returns."

He looks down at me, indecision darkening his face. I see the worry and the affection he has for me, and I hate that I've brought him here, to stand in my husband's bedroom.

Finally, he nods. He comes to the bed and bends to kiss my forehead. "Take care, Lucy," he says huskily. His footsteps echo across the room and out of the cottage. I feel a dull ache in my chest.

"You should go too," I tell Clara, eyes closed against the drumming in my hip.

"Don't be mad. I'm not leaving you on your own."

"I'm all right. I promise. I just want to sleep." When she doesn't respond, I say, "Please. This will be easier to explain to Tom if I'm alone."

Clara hovers by my bedside in indecision. "Fine," she huffs. "Fine. If that's really what you want. I'll come by and check on you in the morning."

Despite the laudanum in my blood, and the remnants of the chloroform, the pain keeps me awake for most of the night. I hear Tom clatter through the front door sometime in the early morning and it takes all my willpower to stifle the groan when he flops onto the mattress beside me. He is snoring in minutes, the smell of ale and sweat rising from his skin.

By the time dawn filters through the curtains, I'm exhausted enough to drop into a broken, and painfully short-lived sleep.

Tom hauls himself out of bed, making the mattress lurch. "Lying in this morning, Luce?" His voice is full of bitterness. "You have a busy night last night then?" He yanks back the bedclothes. "Up you get. Those clothes ain't going to wash themselves."

I try to sit, gritting my teeth against the wall of pain. Tom turns and frowns down at me.

"Lucy?" The anger is gone from his face. "Are you hurt?"

"Hurt? Of course not." I try to keep my voice light. "Cramps, that's all."

Tom nods faintly, but I see the doubt in his eyes. "Is there anything I can do?"

"No. I'll be fine. Really." I sit slowly, trying to keep the grimace from my face. "I'll get you some breakfast."

Tom puts a hand on my arm to stop me. "I can feed myself. You stay in bed. You look as though you need it."

Too exhausted to argue, I nod. Ease myself back onto the mattress as Tom makes his way to the kitchen. Some distant part of me is glad for the pain. It prevents me from thinking too hard about the vicious fight I had with him last night. And what in hell he would do if he discovered the bullet wound in my side.

Somewhere in my hazy thoughts, I wonder whether people are talking about the shooting. Sightings of the Green Lady always generate gossip, so I know there's every chance this will too. My only hope is that the man who shot me is keeping himself hidden. I have no idea whether there were any other witnesses. I was not aware of any other people in the alley. But the gunshot brought Will and Clara running. It's unlikely the incident went by unnoticed.

But for now, I can't think that far ahead. For now, I just have to hide a gunshot wound from my husband.

Tom pokes his head back into the bedroom. "I can stay here today," he says, "if—"

"No," I reply, too quickly. My secrets are far too close to

the surface. We'd never get through the day without them spilling over. "I'm fine," I say. "You go the diggings."

"Are you sure?"

"Of course."

Tom hesitates a moment longer, then turns without another word and disappears out of the house.

Later in the morning, there's a knock at the door. I've been lying in bed for hours, unable to get anywhere even close to sleep.

"I'm not working today," I croak.

"Lucy? It's me." Clara. I take fresh swig of laudanum and get shakily to my feet. I pull my flannel robe on over my shift and shuffle to the door.

"You look like hell," she says when I answer.

"Thank you. I feel it."

"Is Tom here?"

I grip the doorframe to keep my balance. "No. He's gone to the diggings."

"Did he suspect anything?"

I let out a humourless laugh. "I'm sure he did. But I think he's learned better than to ask questions."

Clara puts a gentle hand to my shoulder and ushers me inside. "Come and sit down. Shall I make us some tea?"

I nod. My mouth is parched and I'm lightheaded from the laudanum I've been tossing back like it's barley water. Leaning heavily on Clara, I settle into a chair at the table, directing her to the teacups on the shelf.

"Will came to see me this morning," she says, crouching to light the fire. She hangs the kettle on the hook. He's very worried about you. He wanted to come and see you. I told him that wasn't a good idea."

I'm grateful. The last thing I need is Will Browning appearing on my doorstep and crossing paths with Tom. My eyes fill suddenly with tears, and I blink them away. What right do I have for tears? I brought all this on myself.

Clara stands over me, watching as I wipe my eyes. "Shall I send Mr Hamilton over?"

"Yes," I say dryly. "Tell him I want another hit of chloroform."

"Take the laudanum I gave you."

"Will you fetch it for me? From the nightstand."

Clara disappears into the bedroom and returns with the tiny bottle. "Have you taken any this morning?"

I shake my head. Tell myself those couple of mouthfuls I've had don't count.

She sits the bottle on the table beside me. "Just a few drops," she warns. "Or a ball in the side will be the least of your troubles."

I nod obediently.

She fills the pot from the cannister of tea Tom has left on the table and pours the boiling water in. Hands me a steaming cup.

I pull the stopper from the laudanum bottle and ease a few drops into my tea, aware of Clara's watchful eyes on me.

She sits beside me, turning her cup around in her hands. "Will asked you to move to Melbourne with him? He asked you to leave your husband?"

I nod.

"And you're going to go?"

I remember it now; the promise I made to Will last night when I was fired up with rage at Tom. Full of a desperate need to play the ghost and upturn the world. Is it still what I want in the harshness of morning? My thoughts are too clouded to tell.

"Will cares about you very much," says Clara. And this I know, even with my drug-addled brain.

"I care about him too. I care about him so much it's frightening."

"Why did you do it?" asks Clara. "Lie with Will? And play the ghost? Is it because you married the wrong man?"

I squeeze my eyes closed. Admitting I married the wrong man feels far too brutal. I tighten my grip on my teacup. "I lost my daughter," I say finally. "A year and a half ago, in the camp fever outbreak. And since then, I can't seem to find my bearings. I needed a way to escape the grief."

The words feel strange on my tongue. I can't remember the last time I spoke of Elsie. For so many months, she has existed only within my memories.

Clara lets out her breath. "I'm so sorry, Lucy."

I stare out the window. Behind the cottage, the fronds of my little vegetable garden bend in the wind. "I know it's no excuse. Hundreds of other people lost their children in that outbreak. And none of them are running around playing the ghost. Or crawling into bed with men who aren't their husbands."

"How do you know what all those people are doing?" Clara asks gently. "You don't see into their lives every day."

"I see my husband every day," I say. "And he's not falling apart. He's getting up and going out to his claim and trying to find our fortune." I hear the bitterness in my voice. The anger. And for a second, I do not feel bad for lying to Tom. Do not feel bad for going to Will's bed. Because it feels as though Tom needs to be punished for the way he glided past our daughter's death. His life has gone on just as it did before Elsie died. And for that, I feel a tangled mix of jealousy and rage.

"Playing the ghost," I say, "it felt like a way of getting back at this place. Punishing it for all it's taken from me."

And is Will a way of getting back at Tom? For bringing us out here? And for not caring enough about losing our child? Perhaps somewhere in the back of my mind, he was once. But it goes far deeper than that now. Will Browning has awoken something in me that had been long dormant. Something I'm not sure I have the strength to give up.

I stay at the table for what feels like hours, turning my empty teacup around and around between my hands. It's far too hot in the fire-warmed kitchen and I wish I'd asked Clara to open the windows before she left. A headache thumps steadily behind my eyes.

"Mrs Earnshaw?" Constable Stone's commanding voice is accompanied by a loud knock. I stumble to my feet, clutching the wall for balance as I hobble to the door.

Stone is alone. At the sight of me, he gives a brisk nod. He doesn't look at all surprised to see me in my robe in the middle of the day, my hair hanging limp and tangled down my back. I can barely muster a greeting.

"Last night two women claimed they witnessed a man shoot the Green Lady in the alley behind Hargraves Street. The shooter has been taken into police custody."

"And you're here to ask after my wellbeing?" There's a coldness to my voice, but I see a flicker in Stone's eyes that looks oddly like compassion.

"Does that surprise you?" he asks evenly.

"It does," I say. "I know you're not the most honest of men."

"But not entirely without morality."

"I find that hard to believe." If he is to speak openly about the night we caught each other out at Forest Creek, I will do the same. "You're letting other men take the blame for your night fossicking. A poor Chinaman was nearly beaten to death."

"Well. I can't control the way the colony feels about outsiders."

But of course, I have spoken out of place. Stone has little control over anything. My anger is misplaced. No doubt he was sent out to Forest Creek that night by his superiors. What did they threaten him with? I'm sure those corrupt officers above him could make life hell for a trooper with the convict stain.

"I could easily have killed you," he says coolly, "the night you saw me at Forest Creek. But I chose not to."

I let out a mildly hysterical laugh. "Why are you telling me this?"

"To show you I do have a little morality. To convince you that I do in fact have your best interests at heart."

"Is this an official police visit?" I ask doubtfully.

"No," he admits. "No one else in the police force knows who the Green Lady really is."

I swallow. "I'm not going to tell anyone I saw you fossicking. I swear it."

Does he know I'm lying? I've already told my husband.

Stone gives a faint nod. "I'm not here to threaten you, Mrs Earnshaw. I really am here to ask after your wellbeing.

And to find out whether you plan to lay charges against the shooter."

"Of course I don't."

"I see."

"What will happen to him?" I ask finally. "You said he's in the cells."

"Well," says Stone, "he won't be charged if no victim comes forward. There's no evidence that a crime took place."

"No victim is going to come forward." I make to close the door, but Stone holds out a broad hand, preventing it from closing. "Are you certain you're all right? You really don't look well."

The concern in his eyes catches me off guard. Convict, corrupt trooper, yes, but I see a glimmer of decency behind Stone's eyes. Has that always been there? I've never looked this closely before. Perhaps he's like so many of us here; our morality hidden behind desperation.

Yes, he could easily have killed me that night. Put a bullet in my chest and carried me out to the bush to be lost among the wilderness.

I squeeze my eyes closed, swamped by sudden dizziness.

Stone dives forward, gripping my arm to stop me from falling. "Maybe you ought to sit down."

I follow his gaze. Blood has soaked through my shift, flecking the front of my robe. And before I can speak, before I can sit, I feel myself swallowed by dark.

CHAPTER NINETEEN

I wake up in bed. Tom is on a chair at my bedside, a deep frown crumpling his forehead. I shift at the sight of him, and pain grips my body.

He presses a hand to my shoulder. "Lie still."

My heart races. How much does he know?

I close my eyes against the afternoon light streaming through the gap in the curtains. "What are you doing here?" I ask. It feels like a foolish question.

"Constable Stone found me on the diggings. Said he came here to bring you his laundry and you collapsed at the door."

I close my eyes for a moment, grateful for Stone's discretion. And, I suppose, for hauling me off my doorstep.

Tom holds up the empty laudanum bottle. "I found this on the table. Did you take it all? No wonder you've been out for hours." He lifts a cup from the side table and slides a hand behind my head to lift it. "Drink some water." He drizzles the liquid down my throat, and I gulp at it thirstily.

I dare to glance down. The blankets are curled around

my legs, and I see the ink-dark blood staining my shift.

"I sent for Mr Hamilton," Tom says, voice low. "He changed the dressing of the wound."

I turn my head on the pillow.

For long moments, there is silence. I can't bear to look at Tom. I know he's waiting for me to speak. Waiting for me to cobble together some kind of explanation. He lets out a small sigh.

"What happened?" he asks finally.

I say nothing.

"Lucy. Please. Did someone hurt you?"

The worry in his voice fills my throat with tears.

"Was it the man you…?"

I close my eyes. "No."

The silence is thick and heavy. Haunting.

I dare to glance up at Tom. He is leaning close, his blue eyes dark with worry. He clears his throat. "I know we don't… That we've not spoken much lately. And that… there are things in your life I don't know about." He lets out a breath. "I don't care about any of that now. I just need you to tell me what happened to you. Please."

I want more than anything to tell him the truth. To tell him I took a bullet in the street. But how can I do that without revealing everything else I've been a part of? Besides, if he learns of the shooting, he'll go straight for the police. And there's no way I can let that happen. I don't want my husband anywhere near those crooked troopers.

My tears escape, and I turn my head on the pillow, unable to look him in the eye. I know I owe him at least an attempt at an explanation, but where do I even start?

Tom's chair squeaks noisily and I dare to face him. I

realise he has a fresh nightshift laid across his knees. His fist tightens around it. "I thought you might want a change of clothes."

I glance down at the blood staining my hip. Nod slightly.

He eases his hand beneath my shoulders, helping me sit. He grasps tentatively at the hem of my stained nightshift and then stops, as though suddenly uncertain. I suppose I can't blame him. I've barely let him close to me in months. Instinctively, I put a hand over his.

Tom," I say, "it's all right."

He swallows visibly, easing the shift up over my head. His rough fingers graze the side of my ribs, and I hear my sharp inhalation.

"Am I hurting you?"

"No." It was the feel of him that caused my breath to leave me. The strange newness of his skin so gentle against mine. Suddenly, I miss him deeply. And I'm achingly glad he's here.

He pulls my clean shift over my head and eases me back onto the mattress. "All right?"

I nod, throat stabbing with unspoken words. He brushes his hand across my forehead, through my hair.

"I'm sorry," I cough. "I'm so sorry."

Tom gives the faintest of nods. His lips part, and I hold my breath, each of us waiting for the other to speak. "Get some rest," he murmurs at last.

I close my eyes, wait for him to leave. Wait for the creak of the floorboards, the dull thud of the door. But there is nothing. Just his steady breathing, the creak of his chair and his constant, wordless presence.

For almost a fortnight, as I lie in bed, Tom asks no more questions. He refuses to go to the diggings, instead staying home and haunting my bedside. Neither of us speak of the night of the shooting, and though there is now another huge addition to the pile of *things we don't talk about*, we manage to fill the days with chatter that is almost civil. Almost warm. He tells me about Leo's latest run-in with the Tipperary boys, and the new lemonade stand that's popped up near his claim. I tell him of Clara's shop, and the trouble she's had with her former clients. Our conversations would almost be easy if it weren't for the poisonous topics we have to constantly veer away from.

I wonder if, outside, people are talking. Did others witness the shooting of the Green Lady? There's a chance of it, I know, and I'm glad Tom is here, away from the gossip of the town.

When I'm able to manoeuvre around the cottage without leaning on my husband or the wall, I send him back to the claim.

"Are you certain?" he asks, hands on my shoulders.

"I'm fine. Go."

When Tom leaves, my first instinct is to open my script. Somewhere, at the back of my mind, is the knowledge that the performance of *The Lady of Fyvie* is planned for tomorrow. I have no thought of whether it's still to take place. Though Clara has been at my door several times during the past week, asking after my recovery, we never touched on the play in front of Tom.

I skim through the words of the script. I know my lines

as though they're a part of me, and I feel physically strong enough to appear on stage. But the prospect of the play is tinged with bitterness now. And maybe a little fear. My hand moves across my body, finding that place above my hip where reality came crashing into the Green Lady's world.

In the afternoon, I build up the courage to step out of my cottage.

After Tom has sat at my bedside for two weeks in the face of my silence, visiting Will feels like the worst of betrayals. But how can I stay away? When Will last saw me, he watched the surgeon pull a bullet from my side. I can imagine his worry. Perhaps his guilt.

I can't bear to hurt either of them.

I pass Clara's shop on my way to the Commercial. And I stop in horror. The mannequins from the window display are strewn over the floor, their fine gowns and waistcoats in shreds. Reams of fabric have been unrolled across the floor, long jagged tears down the middle. Design sketches and broadsheets have been ripped from the walls and windows.

I rush through the door, calling Clara's name. She's sitting on the floor in the back room, huddled against the wall with her knees pulled to her chest. She looks up at the sight of me, hurriedly wiping away tears. Hair is coming loose from the tangled knot at her neck, curls clinging to her wet cheeks. Her eyes are red and swollen. I've never seen her like this; so broken and defeated.

"What happened?" I ask. "Are you hurt?"

She shakes her head. I lower myself carefully onto the ground beside her. Cover her hand with mine.

"They broke in while I was at the bank this morning,"

she says after moments of silence. She coughs back tears. "They've destroyed months of work. In broad daylight, if you can believe it."

"I'm so sorry," I murmur.

Clara turns her face away, pressing a palm to her eyes.

"Do you have any thought of who it was?" I ask gently. "Mr Wallace…" I fade out. Though I know Arthur Wallace and Clara have never seen eye to eye, he doesn't seem the kind of man to break into her shop and destroy her work.

Clara gets to her feet and goes to the drawer of her nightstand. She pulls out a handful of folded pages. "It's not just Arthur Wallace," she says, tossing the pages towards me. "These are from men whose wives have commissioned me. Men who were once punters of mine. They make their feelings quite clear."

I open the letters, one after the other. They're full of thinly veiled threats, and words like *disgrace* and *whore*. *Dressmaking is a domain for the upper classes; I'll not have my wife seen in such company; women like you bring a bad name to this town.*

Two of the letters are unsigned, others marked with names I vaguely recognise. Men who, like Arthur Wallace, hold positions of power within the town.

"I'm unwelcome here, they say," Clara snorts. "Don't remember them saying such things when they were panting all over me with their arses in the air. A whore is most welcome til she starts making something of herself. Starts showing her face in the daylight." She sits beside me again and taps a long finger against one of the pages. "This fine chap," she says bitterly, "refused to pay his wife's credit. Left me five pounds out of pocket." She leans her head against the wall. "Don't know which one of them did this. Or who they sent to do it for them. But it hardly matters."

"Have you been to the police?" I ask.

She nods. "They said they'd be by shortly. Not that I'm expecting them to do much. Can't hardly see the coppers going round questioning men like Arthur Wallace over an attack on some lag, can you?"

I don't answer. Just reach an arm around her and hold her tightly. "What will you do?" I ask.

She rubs her eyes. "Close my doors for a while. I've no choice. I've barely anything left to sell. And even if new commissions came in, I'd have no fabric to make them with until I can get another order from Melbourne." She takes the letters from me and puts them on the table. I wonder if she kept them because she foresaw something like this.

"I thought I could start again," she says, her eyes fixed to the letter at the top of the pile. "I really did. I thought once my sentence was over, I could put the past behind me." There's something new to her voice; at least, something she's always kept hidden from me. Vulnerability, grief. I see the cracks in that shield she puts up with her sharp tongue. "These men," she coughs, "do they really think I chose to make my living the way I did? Do they not think I was dying of shame every time I so much as looked at their faces?" She sighs heavily. "I thought it was all for a purpose. Thought it would get me what I wanted. But look at this place." She waves a hand at the devastated parlour. "Look at all I've got to show for myself. And here I thought I could start again."

I don't speak, sure I'll never find the right words.

Maybe there's no such thing as putting the past behind us. No such thing as starting again. Without our pasts, we'd be different people.

Maybe that's what Clara is seeking.

Maybe that's what I've been seeking too.

The front door clicks open and she gets quickly to her feet, glancing in the mirror and trying to scrub the tearstains from her face. She looks into the front room. "Troopers are here. For whatever good they'll do."

Troopers.

My stomach lurches at the mere thought of their presence.

Clara holds out a hand, helping me stand. "There's no need for you to stay," she says.

I hesitate. Half of me wants nothing more than to put as much distance between me and the troopers as possible. The other half can't bear to leave Clara alone with them.

I tell myself she's in no danger. It's only the men involved in their thieving racket who end up in pits full of black powder. Or who pretend to, at least.

Clara heads out to meet the troopers, while I stand dithering in the doorway, a hand pressed to my aching hip.

I eye the two policemen. Their bearded faces are vaguely familiar, but I've no idea of their names. No idea whether they're part of this racket. They follow Clara around the shop, listening as she describes her return from the bank to find the back door broken and the place in disarray.

While the police are picking their way through the chaos of the window display, Clara joins me in the doorway. "There's really no need for you to be here. I can manage." She lowers her voice. "Have you been to see Will?"

"Not yet. I was on my way…"

"Go. He's been very worried for you."

I nod, eyes down. "And the performance?" I dare to ask.

"Is it to go ahead?"

"I'd say that depends on you."

I draw in a breath. "Shall I come by in the morning? Help you clean the place?"

Clara gives a short smile. "I'd like that."

I pull her into a quick embrace, then hurry towards the front door.

The officer looks up as I pass. "Leaving, Mrs Earnshaw?"

My heart speeds. "How do you know my name?"

He looks amused at my question. "It's our job to know everyone in this settlement."

Is there something behind his eyes? Something I can't quite catch hold of? Perhaps just my imagination. Nonetheless, it makes me dart from the shop like my skirts are burning.

CHAPTER TWENTY

I'm still jittery when I arrive at the Commercial. Jittery when I climb the stairs to Will's room. I knock lightly. He opens the door, letting out his breath at the sight of me.

"Lucy. I'm so glad to see you. How are you feeling?"

I try for a smile. "I'll live."

He steps aside, gesturing for me to enter. He closes the door behind us. Keeps his distance.

"I wanted to come and see you," he says. "More than anything."

"I know. Thank you. And I'm glad you chose to stay away. It's best that way."

"I'm sure." His smile doesn't reach his eyes.

I don't know where the two of us stand. Can't make sense of the chaos in my brain. The warmth I've felt towards my husband these past days has been undeniable, but I know how this will go: one day soon, the warmth will give way to silence and the cold will creep back in. I know this with every piece of myself; and yet if there's even a scrap of a chance I might be wrong, how can I turn away?

But I can't deny the joy that Will has made me feel. Perhaps it's wrong to seek a happiness that might never come, when I have a chance at it right in front of me.

Either way, I know I must make a choice. I know how lucky I am that neither Tom nor Will have turned away from me yet. I know it's what I deserve. And I know, if I stay trapped in indecision, one day soon they'll both wash their hands of me, and I'll find myself alone.

Will folds his hands behind his back, but he stands close, eyes on mine. "There's been talk," he says, "of the shooting. Gossip. A man firing at the Green Lady."

I nod. In spite of his stiltedness, there's a kind of relief to being around someone who knows everything that happened that night. Despite the truce that appeared between me and Tom these past two weeks, I was constantly aware of my secrets. They hung between us, draining the air.

Will says, "I think we ought to cancel the play."

"Is that what you want?" A part of me hopes that two weeks without my attendance at rehearsals — or Ollie's complete inability to learn his lines — might have convinced Will otherwise. Convinced him it's a bad idea to put *The Lady of Fyvie* on the stage.

But I can't be surprised when he says, "Of course that's not what I want. The play is important to me."

I nod.

"But so is your safety," he says quickly. "The moment you step onto stage dressed as the Green Lady, people will find out you're the one who's been deceiving them."

"Yes. They will. I've known that from the beginning. The shooting doesn't change anything." I'll hide myself away for a few days and let the story lose momentum. Soon there'll be another possum hunt, or someone will run off with their kitchen maid and the Green Lady will be forgotten.

But it's not the townspeople finding out that scares me. It's Tom finding out. I feel instinctively that if he were to learn what I've been doing, if I were to bring this deep shame to him, it would be the end.

'I declare myself no longer responsible for your debts and financial upkeep…'

The thought begins to break me, and I look up at Will for strength. I know how much the play means to him. I know how hard he has been working to build a name for himself again. I want to see his work performed at Astley's, and all across the colony. And I know *The Lady of Fyvie* is a stepping-stone to help him get there. If I walk away, all the work he's put into it will be for nothing.

For all the trouble it might bring me to step onto stage and reveal myself as the Green Lady, I have no intention of letting Will Browning down.

It's getting dark when I leave the Commercial. Fine rain has begun to fall, casting a yellow haze around the streetlamps. I hear a distant burst of gunfire. A single pop, not the nightly emptying of weapons. No one reacts. A carriage rolls and women pass in chatter. A boy jogs past with a dog at his heels.

When did we all become so desensitised to such a thing? When did the sound of gunfire become a mere inconvenience?

But the screeches that come minutes later, they're

impossible to ignore. A woman's howl, tightening my shoulders with dread.

People hurry in the direction of the scream. Others step from the taverns, squinting into the fading sunlight.

The body is lying on the road to Melbourne. People are clustered around the figure, and I shove my way to the front of the crowd.

A dark shadow of blood is growing on the man's chest. Still strapped to his shoulders is a large pack and swag. It's clear he was attempting to leave Castlemaine.

I can't pull my eyes from the body. Shot on the road out of town. Was he, like Fred Buckley, involved in this racket run by the troopers? Was he trying to escape, just like Buckley had been? Was he shot down by the police themselves?

Perhaps I'm jumping to conclusions. Seeing things that aren't there. Perhaps the man was killed in a squabble over gold. It's far from unlikely. But the alternative gnaws inside me.

I try to push away the dread that is building inside me. But when I look up to see troopers approaching, fear strikes me between the ribs. There are five of them marching towards the crowd – no, six. Among them are the two men who attended the break-in at Clara's.

Leaving, Mrs Earnshaw?

And yes; leaving, leaving, leaving. Leaving this place and never looking back. The thought swings at me with sudden, violent intensity. Though I'd not spoken a word to them before today, the troopers know who I am. Has Stone told them I caught him night fossicking? I'm painfully aware I know too much. And even more aware of how easily I could be removed from the situation.

The terror is suddenly consuming. I can't stay here another day.

I hurry to the cottage. Though the darkness is thickening, Tom is not yet home. I light the lamp and pull our trunks out from beneath the bed. I stop suddenly. One trunk or two? After everything I've done, will my husband flee with me? Do I want him to? I have no thought of either. There's every chance I'll have to find the courage to leave this place alone.

I leave Tom's trunk at the foot of the bed and toss mine open on the mattress. Pull my clothes from the cupboard. I shove them into the trunk, not even bothering to fold them.

My mind is full of Will. Will's play, Will's kiss, Will's offer of a new life. Leave Castlemaine tonight and I'll be leaving that behind forever. The thought aches. I promised him I would not let him down. But I'm too scared to stay.

"What are you doing?" I spin around to find Tom in the doorway, arms folded across his chest. "You're leaving? With who?" His voice is ice.

I shake my head hurriedly. "No. It's not like that. I… It's not safe here." I grab a stray shift from beneath the bed and shove it into the trunk. "A man was murdered on the road out of town tonight."

"I heard." Tom reaches for my arm, forcing me into stillness. "Stop, Lucy. Look at me." He turns me to face him. "What are you not telling me?"

I want him to hear everything. Fred Buckley, corrupt troopers, and the Black Forest racket. I want to tell him how it may all be connected to the dead man on the road. But I can't risk putting him in the line of the troopers' pistol fire.

Buckley's warning was clear: to keep my husband safe, he can't know any more than he already does.

"I don't want to be here anymore, Tom," I say instead. "I don't want to live in a place where men are murdered in the streets."

Something flickers in his eyes. "We can't leave."

"We can go to the other goldfields," I say desperately. "Ballarat or Bendigo. Or up to the mountains even. Perhaps you'll have more luck there. Please."

"We're not leaving." Tom runs his hand through his hair.

"Why not?"

"Because this house is all we have in the world. Run away from it and we won't have a thing to our name." He lets out his breath, as though irritated by my questioning. "Besides, I'm so damn close to that haul. Do you know how many hours of my life I've put into it?"

A cold laugh escapes me. Yes, I know every damn second of it. A thousand days of promises and wishes, and desperately hoping things will change. "You've been so close for the past three years! Do you truly believe things will be different now?"

"I have to believe it," he hisses. "Otherwise what has all this been for?"

"We failed, Tom," I say. "Why can't you just accept that?"

He shakes his head. "No."

My anger rises. "We failed. You found nothing, and we lost our daughter, and I—" I stop abruptly.

"And you *what*?" Tom presses. "What did you do? Go to another man's bed? And what else? What have you got yourself involved in that's making you so damn terrified?" He begins to pace, back and forth across the tiny space. "Do you think this man on the road was killed by the same man who shot you?"

A murmur of shock escapes me.

"I know it's a gunshot wound, Lucy," he says sharply. "Mr Hamilton told me he took the ball out of you at Clara Snow's shop." Before I can speak, Tom says, "Did you really expect him to say nothing? I'm your husband. I have every right to know." His hands clench. "Can you imagine how it feels to have you keep something like that from me?" He pounds a fist suddenly against the wall and I back up against the bed in shock. He's carried this knowledge for a fortnight, I see now. Carried it in silence.

Somehow, that only makes me more furious.

"Yes," I hiss. "It's a gunshot wound. I was shot in the street when I was playing the ghost."

"Playing the ghost?" he repeats. "What in hell does that even mean?"

We need this, I tell myself. Need these secrets to come out. If we are to have any hope of being happy again, it's the only way.

"Hoaxing," I say. "Playing a part. Making people think they're seeing a ghost. Because that's what's people want to see."

Tom stares at me, not speaking.

I drop my voice. "I just needed to be someone else for a time. I needed an escape."

His boots thump against the floorboards as he paces. His eyes are down, as though he can't bring himself to look at me.

"The man who shot me, it was an accident. He'd just come from the possum hunt, and I caught him by surprise." I perch on the edge of the bed, knotting my fingers together.

"I told the police I didn't want the man charged. It had nothing to do with the murder tonight."

Tom stares out the window into the dark street, his back to me.

"Are you not even going to speak?" I ask finally.

"And say what? What should I say when you tell me you've been out pretending to be a dead woman because your life is so unbearable? And that you were shot in the street and you thought to hide it from me?"

"Anything!" I cry. "I don't care what you say! Anything but this silence we've been living in for the past eighteen months!"

Instead of speaking, Tom looks back at me. *Eighteen months.*

No doubt he can see how closely my behaviour is tied to Elsie's death. He turns away, jaw clenched, as though trying to keep his rage inside.

But I want his anger. I want to be confronted. I want to know what's inside his head.

"It was Will Browning," I say, rounding on him to look him in the eye. "From the theatre. He's the man I went to Melbourne with. We spoke of making a life together—"

I stop talking suddenly because I see my words have had the desired effect. I see the anger flaring in Tom's eyes, see the tremor in his locked jaw.

I brace myself for his fury. Never once has he struck me, but never before have I given him a reason like this. He takes a step backwards. I come at him, shoving hard against his chest.

He grabs my wrists, holding me at a distance. "What are you doing?" he demands through gritted teeth.

"I'm trying to get a rise out of you. I want to see that you're angry."

He laughs icily. And he strides past me, through the back door of the cottage. I race after him onto the grass behind the house.

"If you know what's good for you, you'll stay away from me, Lucy," he says, marching back and forth with his hands behind his head.

"No." I want these threats. I want this rage. "I want to see you have some damn emotion inside you."

Tom stops pacing. "What are you talking about?"

I glare at him, aware that tears are rushing down my cheeks. I have no idea how long I've been crying. "It was as though losing Elsie didn't even affect you."

He stares back at me; lips parted, but silent.

"You just went on as though nothing had happened. The day after we buried her, you were back out at the claim. Carrying on as though everything was normal. And you just stopped speaking of her. As though she'd never existed."

"I thought…" Tom's voice is strangled. "I thought that was the best way to get through it."

"If she'd been a son? Would you have felt different?"

He makes a noise in his throat but doesn't speak for a long time. Wind flies across the yard, blowing his ragged hair across his cheek. "I was trying to hold myself together for you," he says finally. His voice is low and taut. "Because I thought that was what you needed. Do you really think I wasn't falling apart?" He stares out into the darkness, refusing to look my way. "I took her crib to the fire while you were asleep so you didn't have to see it. I went up to Pennyweight Flat alone to choose where she was to be buried. And you think I wasn't falling apart?" That faint waver in his voice, am I imagining it? It sends fresh tears down my cheeks.

I wipe my eyes with the back of my hand, feeling grief tear open inside me again. "I didn't want you to hold yourself together, Tom. I wanted you to fall apart with me. I wanted to see that Elsie's death broke you as much as it did me."

He rubs a hand over his face. "I can't believe you would doubt that." His voice is thin and cold, and as strained as I have ever heard it. Deliberately hollow, as though even now, he has no emotion to give. Or at least none he's willing to let me see.

And so perhaps, even now, I do doubt it. It's easier to keep telling myself that Tom is the cold, emotionless man I convinced myself he was. Because if he really is this achingly decent man who buried his grief so he might carry mine, what kind of person does that make me? It's more than I can bear to think about.

"That's what you've been thinking all this time?" he asks. "That my daughter's death meant nothing to me?"

I don't answer. I know I don't need to.

And how is it that we are only speaking of these things now? How might things have been different if we had found a way to be open with each other in those days of burning cradles and burial sites? How might it have been if we'd done those things together?

But we didn't. We've lived through almost a year and a half of coldness, and now the walls we've built around ourselves are so high we can't find a way over them.

I glance at Tom, who is leaning against the outside of the cottage, the moon lighting one side of his face. If our daughter had lived, I know she would have grown up to look like her father. I saw it in Elsie's mop of sandy hair, in her broad cheeks, her vivid deep-sea-blue eyes.

I wipe my tears and step back into the cottage. Look down at the packed trunk I've laid across the bed. We're not leaving, that much I understand. At least, we're not leaving together.

"Put your clothes away, Lucy," Tom says from the doorway. "We're not going anywhere. This house is all we have in the world. We're not just walking away from it."

"But—"

"You're not going anywhere," he barks again. "I forbid it."

He walks from the bedroom without another word.

Something yanks me from a broken sleep. I sit up, trying to find my bearings in the dark. The other side of the bed is empty, but I can hear Tom snoring softly in a kitchen chair. After all we discussed a few hours ago, I'm surprised either of us have managed to find sleep.

There it is; the creak and click of the gate. Footsteps approaching the house.

I slip out of bed, grabbing my shawl from the end of the bed and tiptoeing to the front door. It's madness, of course, creeping about like this when a man has just been murdered. But whoever is coming to our door, I feel instinctively it's my misdeeds that have brought them here. Constable Stone ensuring I'm keeping my mouth shut. Or perhaps even Will. I don't want Tom entangled in my messes any further than he has to be.

My first guess turns out to be correct. Stone is hovering on the doorstep, fist raised, as though he were about to knock. I step outside, pulling the door closed behind me.

"It's not a good time for a woman to be out at night, Mrs Earnshaw," he says.

"I'm not letting you inside," I hiss. "So if you wish to speak to me, we speak out here." I fold my arms across my chest. "I promised you my silence. And I told you I'm not going to come forward about the shooting. So I think it's time you stayed away from my house."

Stone's mouth opens, as though he's taken aback by my boldness. I'm a little shocked by it too. "I'm not afraid of you," I tell him. "Not anymore. I know you're not the one pulling the strings." I've said too much, of course.

His eyes flash. "Whatever you think you know, you would do well to keep your mouth shut. You understand me?" His voice is thin; half-warning, half-threat, and it sends a shiver through me.

I manage a nod.

"Where's your husband?" Stone asks.

"This has nothing to do with him," I say. "Leave him out of it."

Before Stone can reply, the front door cracks against the wall and Tom blusters through it. "Get away from her, Stone," he hisses.

Stone takes a step back and Tom ushers me back inside. I don't want his protection. I don't feel as though I deserve it. I got myself into this mess and I don't want to drag my husband into it any further. I've already hurt him enough. Constable Stone and the troopers are my problem.

But Tom seems intent on getting involved.

"Stay the hell away from my house," I hear him say through the closed door.

I can't hear Stone's response, but I know his words, at least, can't hurt me anymore. I've told Tom everything. Laid the whole truth out for it to destroy me.

After a few moments, he steps back inside. I'm hovering just inside the door, arms wrapped around myself. "Are you all right?" he asks.

"I'm fine." I go to the window and peek through the curtains. See the dark figure of the constable disappearing down the street. "Stone has been paying me visits since the night I saw him fossicking," I say. "But I don't know why he came here tonight. Maybe he thinks I hold him responsible for the murder of the man on the road. Perhaps he's worried I might tell someone."

Tom frowns. "And do you? Hold him responsible?"

"I don't know. I don't think he's a killer." Stone is nothing but a pawn to the officers; I know this now. But of course, I cannot tell Tom.

"Do you think the murder is connected to the thefts on the diggings?" he asks.

"Maybe."

I reach for the matchbox and light the lamp. I guess it still a few hours from dawn, but I'm not going to sleep any more tonight. I sink into a chair at the table.

"In the morning," I say, "I can… leave you if you wish. You deserve to be free of me."

Tom sits. Folds his hands on the table in front of him. He stares into the flame flickering inside the lamp. "Is that what you want?"

After a moment, I shake my head.

Tom slides his chair around the table so it's close to mine. A fragile peace has settled over us, and a part of me is afraid to speak in case I upturn it. But I can manage no more silence.

"I'm sorry," I say. "For everything." The words don't feel like enough, not even close. But I have to start somewhere.

Tom's eyes are on his clasped hands. "So am I."

"What do you have to be sorry for?"

He draws in a breath. "I know you wanted to speak about her. About Elsie. I know that would have made things easier for you. But I couldn't. I just couldn't, Luce. I'm sorry. It was too much." He stares into the lamp for a long time, the firelight making his eyes shine. "And I'm sorry I brought us out here."

Tentatively, I slide my hand around his elbow, relieved when he doesn't pull away. "I chose to come," I remind him. "I chose to marry you."

I rest my head against the broad plane of his shoulder. It feels like a miracle that he is sitting here with me, after all I've confessed. Perhaps he and I are too broken to ever be fixed, but right now, it almost feels possible.

I feel the weight of his head against mine.

"Why are you being like this?" I ask.

"Like what?"

"Understanding."

He doesn't answer at once. "Because I've missed you, Lucy," he says finally. "So much. Besides, haven't we gone through enough?"

CHAPTER TWENTY-ONE

"The peculiar shrinking which ghost stories excite in children's and some mature minds is due to the … combination they present of the familiar and the unknown."

Northern Argus
Rockhampton
24th July 1865

I must have dozed off at the table because I'm next aware of dawn lightening the kitchen and the cold shaking me from sleep. I shift uncomfortably in my chair, aware of a dull ache in my hip.

Tom is crouching in front of the grate, holding a match to fresh pile of kindling. "Good morning," he says.

"Good morning." The cold has stretched the distance between us again, but perhaps something has shifted.

"All right?" Tom asks, and I nod. Last night's fear has

faded with the morning. While I'm still desperate to leave Castlemaine, I can see that tearing into the darkness with no money and no place to go is not the right way to do so.

As we move about the cottage in our well-trodden morning routine, there are faint smiles, eye contact. We don't make such a show of stepping aside to allow the other to pass. While the wall between us still stands tall, its foundations have been rattled.

But this is the day of Will Browning's play, and I know I have no choice but to speak of it.

"The play is tonight," I say throatily, as Tom makes for the door after breakfast. "If you're to forbid me from going, I ought to let Mr Browning know."

I stare at my feet. I don't want to put Will between us again. But I also know I owe him more than to just to walk away from the play. Especially after I threw him in the path of Tom's rage by admitting whose bed I've been visiting.

"I'm not going to forbid you from going," Tom says shortly.

"Thank you," I murmur. "I… It wouldn't be fair to the others if I didn't go, and—"

"Then go." Tom pulls on his boots and laces them without looking at me. "I'm not going to stop you."

A broadsheet is attached to the door of the theatre.
One night only – The Lady of Fyvie
An exciting new work by Mr William Browning
And there at the bottom, for everyone to ponder:
Lucy Earnshaw as the Green Lady

It doesn't matter. Not now. Tom knows it all. And somehow, that knowledge has led us to a peace I can't quite understand. I know enough to suspect this peace will not be long lasting, but at least now my secrets can't hurt me.

When I slip through the side door of the theatre, an anticipatory stillness has settled over the place. I glimpse the stage as I pass through to the dressing rooms. Long shadows lie across empty seats. A hot draught blows in, making the calico walls of the castle move.

Inside the dressing room, I find Clara sitting in front of the mirror, running a comb through her hair. Her eyes are dark with theatrical lampblack, and with her cascading curls and the hard look she gives her reflection, I am almost back to being afraid of her.

But when she sees me, she turns, and the expression on her face lightens a little. She nods to a pale green gown on a coat hanger over the door.

"Your costume. Just one of my old dresses, I'm afraid. I didn't have the time to make anything new."

My mind goes suddenly to the blood-dark folds of the Green Lady's gown. To the violent, blazing pain of a bullet in the hip. Scissors cutting the dress away from my body.

And at the thought of playing this part again, I'm suddenly alive with panic. It's only fear of the past, I tell myself. And after tonight, I never need think of the Green Lady again.

To Clara, I say, "Thank you. I'm sorry you had to go to the trouble of finding me something else."

"You're lucky I found anything. Those bastards that ransacked the shop didn't leave much for me to work with."

I sit at the dressing table beside her. "What happened with the troopers yesterday?"

She snorts. "Nothing of any use. I showed them the letters but they said there's no proof of any connection. This whole place is a bloody gentleman's club."

"You've no idea," I mumble.

She catches my eye in the mirror. "You don't have to do this, you know. Play the Green Lady again. Will will understand."

"I want to."

Clara sees through my lies, of course. How could she not? But she doesn't say more. Doesn't try to talk me out of it. She just stands behind me with a comb in hand and begins to turn me back into a ghost.

The lights are lowered and a hush settles over the audience. We have hung crude curtains to operate as wings and I wait behind them beside Edith, as Clara and Ollie take their opening positions, act through the opening scene. Will stands in the wings opposite. He holds his breath as Ollie stumbles through his lines. But I feel his eyes flickering to me.

Out I go. Out onto stage with my name on the broadsheet and guilt in my eyes. My gaze moves over the audience. I'm stunned by the size of the crowd. When our little troupe last performed, we managed to wrangle an audience of ten from outside Murphy's tavern. But almost every seat in the place is full. The Green Lady sightings have done just as I once hoped – they've drawn people in to hear her story.

With the theatre near full, the air is stifling and thick with breath. I recognise face after shadowed face; there's Meg and

Richard, their children between them. There's Leo, Clyde, faces from church, the diggings, the market. And there, standing by the door at the back of the theatre, is Tom.

My first instinct is one of panic. He's here to confront Will, surely. And yes, we deserve no better, I see that with clarity. But – I send him a silent plea – please not here, with half the settlement watching.

He is leaning against the wall with his arms folded across his chest, and as I catch his eye in desperation, his face lightens into the faintest of smiles.

He's not here for Will, I realise. He's here for me.

Tears of gratitude prick my eyes. I don't deserve for him to be here. I deserve an announcement in the papers in which he throws me aside. But despite every lie, every second of stilted silence, every time I climbed into Will Browning's bed, there is Tom.

I don't care that I'm breaking character. I smile back at him.

Then I force myself to focus. Force myself to wade through the Green Lady's lines.

I have been here longer than you know…

Lines I've spoken so often they have become second nature, but here on stage with the audience before me, and every piece of my life so uncertain, I'm grappling to find the right words.

Tom slips silently out of the theatre. I understand, of course. Understand that his being here was a knife to the ribs. I am infinitely grateful he made an appearance at all.

More so, I'm grateful he disappeared before Will stepped on stage. I'm well aware of Tom's new willingness to swing his fists.

"'Beware the man you married,'" I say to Lady Fyvie. And I hear the crowd murmur.

Yes, it was me. The Green Lady who walked the alleys of Castlemaine, who haunted the forest on the edge of the diggings. Whose blood was spilled in the lane behind the dress shop.

I push through the shame. Remind myself it will all be over soon.

Harsh whispers, growing steadily louder. Clara raises her voice slightly to make herself heard. A group of men get up from their seats and head for the door. Ollie falters mid-line. His eyes dart between Clara and me; curious, uncertain.

"Just keep going," Clara murmurs to me as she passes.

For several long moments, I'm alone on stage. Alone with the murmurs and the restless crowd. I search my memory for my next line, relieved when I manage to prise it up from the chaos inside me.

When I speak my next line, my voice is lost beneath the hum of the crowd. And just as I have rehearsed a hundred times, I turn my face from the audience, hiding them from my sight. I kneel in the back corner of the stage, my head down. Try to ignore the sound of footsteps moving between the aisles.

And then Will is on stage with me. No, this isn't right. This isn't his entrance. But he's rushing towards me, frantic, a hand around my arm yanking me to my feet.

"Get off the stage," he hisses.

And I see them; six – seven – wild-faced men charging the stairs onto the stage. Will whips me behind the curtain before the men can get a hand to me, and I rush down the passage towards the dressing room. I hear Edith behind me, demanding the men stay on their side of the curtain. Will slams the dressing room door behind us.

"What about the others?" I ask breathlessly. "You can't leave them out there."

Will turns the key in the lock. "You're the one they're after, Lucy."

Fists pound on the door. "Where is she?" an angry male voice demands. "Where's that prowler who's been playing the ghost? Scared my ma half to death, you did! She hasn't got out of bed since!"

The knot of regret tightens inside me, and I take a step towards the door. Will grabs my arm, pulling me back. "What are you doing?"

"I need to tell him I'm sorry. I never meant to hurt anyone."

His hand tightens around my wrist. "Going out there is not going to fix anything. Not while they're angry like this. It's just going to put you in danger."

More wild thuds at the door.

I squeeze my eyes closed. And I feel it all crumbling; that fantasy I created in which I could escape reality. That fantasy in which Will Browning would take me away from everything that caused me pain. There's no magic that can change the past or make me forget. It's all just trickery and illusion. Hidden wires and hollow walls.

A woman in costume trying make herself believe.

"I just wanted to escape," I cough. "Just for a little while."

Will puts a hand to my arm, turning me to face him. "From what?" His eyes meet mine, imploring. "Escape from what, Lucy? Why did you play the ghost?"

I shake my head. Because Elsie, she's not for Will's ears. Losing her was a thing Tom and I should have carried together. I want to speak of my daughter, yes, but I want to do so with her father. Not another man.

Will nods almost imperceptibly. A nod of understanding. But also one of sadness. Because he knows, I can tell, that I will never truly let him in.

He hurries to the window and pulls back the curtain. It's narrow and high, but I'm sure I can fit through. I take off the Green Lady's gown and throw on my own colourless skirts.

Will hesitates. "Perhaps I ought to come with you."

I shake my head, ignoring the knot in my throat. "No. You need to stay here. Make sure everyone else is safe." My voice catches.

He nods wordlessly. And he takes the cloth from the washstand, wiping the pale makeup of the Green Lady from my skin for the last time. His thumb brushes my cheek. At once there is everything and nothing to say.

I see it now; that magical, painless world Will led me into – that can never be reality. I've been through far too much for that. All the theatre in the world can't change what has already been.

Nor do I want it to.

Neither of us speak. This is the end; that much is clear.

People will talk of this night, of course. They will talk about me, the Green Lady of Castlemaine, and the way the people came for her. And perhaps when they do that, they will talk about Will's play too. Perhaps his name will be spoken around the colony; first as gossip, then later in theatre circles. Maybe by the crowds that file into Astley's Amphitheatre and cheer beneath that glittering chandelier.

I hope it desperately. I hope the Green Lady will help people remember his name. Hope my disgrace will give him back his career.

I kiss the edge of his lips for a long, still moment, and for a few seconds, the shouting at the door feels distant.

"Thank you," I murmur. "For everything."

He nods faintly.

I drag a stool to the window. Will offers me his hand to help me climb onto it. Ignoring the dull ache in my hip, I push on the jamb. Hot, fragrant air gusts through, blowing my loose hair back from my face.

"Be careful, Lucy," Will says finally. His fingers slide through mine as I gather my skirts and ease myself over the window frame.

I can't look back at him as I lower myself down onto the street.

CHAPTER TWENTY-TWO

I hurry to the cottage with my head down and my bonnet pulled low. The men are still inside the theatre and I'm able to slip unnoticed into the dark alleys behind the hall.

I rush towards the cottage. Try not to think of Will. Of all I've turned away from. All I've left behind.

I feel, somewhere deep, that I have made the right choice. Feel, in that same depth, my love for Tom. The desire I have to mend things between us.

Because he's the one tied inescapably to both my past and my future. He's the one I wanted most when I lay on the street with my blood running into the earth. And he's the one I'm thinking of now, as I hear shouted voices echo in the night. My need to get to him is overwhelming.

The cottage is lightless, curtains drawn over the windows.

Where is Tom? I expected him to be home. Needed him to be. He's out at one of the taverns, I tell myself. Tossing back liquor to drown the sight of me on stage in Will Browning's play.

Not far away, I can hear the angry voices of the townspeople. How long will it take them to realise I'm no longer at the theatre? How long will it take them to come after me?

I fumble in my pocket for my key and clatter the door open.

And I'm greeted with a revolver, pointing between my eyes.

A scream escapes me, the sound dying in my throat at the sight of my husband on the other end of the gun.

He lets out his breath. Lets the revolver fall. "Jesus, Luce. I thought you were someone else."

"I used my key…" I'm hardly breathing.

"I know. I'm sorry. I—" He grips my wrist and pulls me into the bedroom. Confusion and fear pour into me and I shake free of him. A single candle flickers on the nightstand, and in its rusty glow, I can see the cupboard has been emptied, its doors hanging open. Two bundled packs sit at the foot of the bed. My thoughts charge.

"What's happening?"

Tom stands with his back pressed to the closed bedroom door, fingers wrapped around the revolver. "Isn't this what you wanted? For us to leave?"

"Is this because of the men at the theatre?" I ask. "Because they haven't followed me. They—"

"What men at the theatre?"

I take a step back. Away from my husband. Away from his gun. "Tom? What's happening? You're scaring me."

He pulls back the curtain to peek outside, then turns back to me. Nods at the pack closest to the door. "Look inside."

I creep forward and unbuckle the pack. Tucked between

Tom's shirts is a large coin pouch. I pull it out. It feels firm, heavy in my hand. My breath leaves me when I see the mass of coins inside. I look up at Tom with wide eyes.

"Leo and I found a nugget today. A big one. We took it to the bank this afternoon and split the money."

"You found…" My words fade. This was all Tom wanted. So why are we hidden away in near darkness? Why does he have a revolver in his hand? No part of this makes sense.

A violent thump on the door. And then another.

"Open the damn door, Earnshaw. I know you're there."

Constable Stone.

Is he here for me? Have the troopers sent him? Do they know of all the things Fred Buckley told me? I wish for my ignorance; wish I'd let Buckley disappear into opium smoke, nothing but a ghost.

Tom's knuckles whiten around the revolver. "Don't move," he murmurs. He steps out into the kitchen, closing the bedroom door silently behind him.

Another violent knock against the front door. And the sudden splintering of glass. Stone's footsteps thump in through the window.

I peer through the keyhole. See the two men facing each other on opposite sides of the table.

"Give me the money, Earnshaw. You and I had an arrangement."

Tom's voice is steel. "This was not part of it."

I have no time or space to make sense of these words. Because I see the pistol in Stone's hand, barrel to barrel with my husband's weapon. And just as there's no space for thinking, there's also no space for chance.

I tiptoe to the bed. Take the candlestick, a heavy makeshift weapon. I blow at the flame and the light vanishes, leaving me in a darkness thick with sound.

I edge towards the door on silent feet, skirting the inky shape of the pack full of coins. I understand, in all my confusion, that it's this Stone has come for. But nothing makes sense on either side of that knowledge.

"Get the hell out of here, Stone," Tom is saying.

"Do you really want to push me? You know I could have you in the cells for all you've done."

And maybe it's the horror of finding out what these words really mean that has me blowing through the bedroom door and swinging the candlestick into the back of Stone's head. He crumples forward against the table, then slides onto the floor. I hear a murmur of shock, and I can't tell if it comes from Tom or me.

I stare at my husband through the darkness, hand trembling around the weight of the candleholder. "What arrangement?"

He bends to pick up Stone's weapon. "Get your pack, Lucy. We need to leave."

I'm frozen in place. "What arrangement?"

Tom moves through the shadows towards me, and instinctively, I shuffle back, gripping the candleholder.

"We can't stay in the house," he says impatiently. "We have to get away from Stone while he's down." He glances at the motionless body. "Unless he's…"

Dread squeezes my chest. A thin line of blood snakes down past Stone's ear — but have I truly struck him hard enough to kill him? I reach a trembling hand down and touch his neck. Sigh with relief when I feel a steady pulse beneath my fingers. I have not become a killer.

"Get your pack," Tom says again. "I'll tell you everything. But not here."

My fear is fraying the edges of reality and I'm not sure how to react. Fear of Stone and the angry townspeople; and yes, perhaps, my fear of Tom. I shake that thought away before it comes too close. I can't fear my husband because where would that leave me?

But if I am not to fear him, I need answers. An explanation. And I need them now.

"I'm not going anywhere. Not until you tell me what's going on."

Tom glances desperately at the door, then at the constable's motionless body. Finally, he looks back at me. Rubs his eyes. "I've been working with Stone."

"Working with him? What do you mean?"

"Night fossicking. Thieving."

I stare at him. No, this isn't right. The pieces don't sit where they're supposed to. My husband isn't a thief. And when I caught Stone fossicking at Forest Creek, he was alone. Tom was home in bed.

No. The cottage was empty when I returned. I believed Tom had left the house to look for me. Had he been out there with Stone? Did we pass each other unseen while I was playing the ghost?

My stomach knots.

The night of Fred Buckley's burial; the night claims were raided at Moonlight Flat. I'd slept so deeply then I'd not have noticed if Tom slipped out of bed and…

I feel suddenly unmoored as the pieces fall into place. And they make sense, I realise. They make perfect, horrifying sense. Stone's visits to our cottage. Visits I believed centred around my witnessing his theft. They were not about me at all. He had come to speak to Tom.

Did Clyde suspect his involvement? Was that why they fought that day? Tom's anxiety over the thefts, I see with sickening clarity, was not because he feared his claim would be robbed. It was because he feared he might be caught.

Or perhaps he feared I would find out the truth.

I think of the look of pity Stone gave me when he came to the cottage after the shooting. Was it pity over all I didn't know?

My stomach turns over and over, and I take a step backwards, my spine pressing hard against the wall. My fingers grapple behind me, searching in vain for something to cling to. I stare up at my husband, so many questions knotting in my mind.

His eyes find mine. "Say something, Lucy."

But before I can find words, Stone's boot scrapes against the floorboards. Tom inhales sharply and grabs my hand. "We need to leave."

As he throws open the front door, a storm of angry voices flies into the hut. It's that drunken, wild chaos that engulfs this place on the nights of the possum hunts, or when someone strikes it rich and pulls the whole town into their celebrations. But tonight, I'm all too aware the chaos is my doing. Those men have marched from the theatre and whipped the streets up into madness. No doubt told everyone in earshot who was behind the Green Lady.

"A man at the theatre," I splutter. "His mother... I frightened her... playing the ghost. The men want me punished."

A groan comes from Stone, his fingers scratching the floorboards. Tom darts into the bedroom and grabs the coin pouch from the top of the pack. Then he snatches my hand again and pulls me out into the yard.

He leads me towards the tall wooden fence at the back of our property. "Reach for the top," he hisses. "I'll lift you over."

But before I can move, I hear Stone calling Tom's name. Inside the cottage, chairs scrape against the floorboards. The glass of the lamp shatters and the bedroom door thumps against the wall.

Tom pulls me down to hide behind the woodpile. Silently, he brings the revolver out of his pocket. He cocks the trigger and the click echoes in the darkness.

The back door opens with a creak and I press a hand over my mouth to silence my ragged breathing. I hear Stone's footsteps sighing against the dry grass. In the faint moonlight, Tom's knuckles tighten around the revolver.

I see now that I have underestimated Stone. He may be a pawn, but that has made him desperate. And I know the kind of madness desperation can drag you towards.

I feel my body tremble as Stone's footsteps cross the yard. Hear my pulse thundering in my ears. It's a fear of the mob. It's a fear of Stone. And it's a fear of the things my husband has done. And why.

The footsteps disappear. I hear the front door click closed.

Tom lets out his breath. "I think he's gone."

But the thought brings me no relief. Because Constable Stone has left our cottage with blood snaking down his neck. Is he going to the other troopers? Will he tell them of my attack? At best, the assault of a police officer will lead me to the cells. At worst, to the hangman.

Tom stands from behind the woodpile and peeks tentatively into the house. He looks back at me and nods. I stand, catching his arm before he steps back inside. I pull on his wrist, forcing him to look at me. "You were working with him. Why?"

He scrubs a hand over his moonlit face, and for a moment, I think he will refuse to speak. Then he says, "He caught me thieving from a tent one night. A few weeks after Elsie died. He told me he'd not arrest me if I gave him a cut of what I'd stolen."

I try to swallow, but my mouth is dry. "A few weeks after Elsie died? You've been doing this all this time?"

He nods faintly. "After that one time, Stone wanted more. He told me I was valuable to him. I knew which claims were unguarded. Which men were camped out there with their pistols loaded. I told him I wasn't interested. That that one time he'd caught me had been a mistake. But he said he'd arrest me if I didn't help him."

I let out my breath. All those nights I believed Tom out protecting his claim against thieves. All those nights I was sneaking around guarding my secrets, he had been keeping secrets himself. Not guarding his claim against thieves. Thieving to fill Stone's pockets.

"Stone found me on my way to the theatre tonight," says Tom. "Said he heard I found a nugget. Guess Leo couldn't keep his mouth shut. I told Stone I hadn't found a thing. He let me go, and I thought he believed me. But then he turned up at the cottage."

"Wanting money."

He nods. "He claimed we had a deal. I'd give him a cut and he'd keep me out of the lockup. But I'd only agreed to give him a cut of stolen goods. Nothing I found myself."

"Why?" I ask shakily. "That first time. Why did you do it, Tom? You're not a thief. You've never been that kind of man."

He sighs heavily. "I was desperate, Luce. I brought us out here and promised you the world, and couldn't find more than scraps. And every day I'd think of our child, and how I'd given her a home she couldn't survive in. Just once, I wanted to bring you something more than gold dust. Just once. I know it could never make up for what we lost, but…"

I swallow hard. Let my tears slide off my chin.

Tentatively, he touches my hand. "I'm sorry, Lucy. More than you could know. I'm sorry for all of it."

But what I feel is not anger. It's relief. Relief that I was not the only one so marooned by loss that I would throw my life upside down. Relief that Tom mourned our daughter as deeply as I did. Relief that I was not the only one to break.

I throw my arms around his neck, holding him close. I don't want to let go. Because this is how it ought to have been from the moment we buried our child on Pennyweight Flat; us together, leaning on one another. Because apart, we foundered and flailed and tore ourselves to pieces.

I brush my lips lightly against his; a tentative, testing thing. Tom's fingers dig into my hair to prevent me from pulling away. His kiss is fierce, possessive, and my body comes alive at the memory. Somehow, through his crimes, I have found my husband again.

"We'll go inside and get the packs," he says, his lips close to mine. "Then we'll get out this way. Over the fence. Where the mob won't find you. And then we're going to leave this place. Tonight."

But as I cling to him, fingers digging hard into his arms, that fleeting relief I felt slips away. Because I think of Fred Buckley, a living ghost in opium smoke. I think of the empty box we gathered around at the cemetery on Campbell's Hill. And I think of the body found on the road, with all his worldly goods tied to his back. Tom may be coerced by Constable Stone, but Stone's strings are being pulled from far above. By men who do not allow those caught in their net to slink away carrying their secrets.

And here we are, planning to leave Castlemaine with a pack full of gold.

I pull back, gripping Tom's forearms.

"You've no idea what you've gotten yourself into."

CHAPTER TWENTY-THREE

"This isn't just about Stone," I say. I'm pacing, pacing, dry grass crunching beneath my boots. Forgotten laundry flutters in the hot wind.

"What are you talking about?"

"He's being forced into this. The officers are forcing him to go out thieving and give them a cut of everything he takes. Everything *you* take. It's not just Stone that's corrupt, Tom. It's half the damn police in this town. Or all of them. I don't know. I—" I gulp down my breath as my words threaten to run away. "The officers are running the racket. There are other men just like you. Men they arrested for petty crimes who are being forced to do their bidding. Stone is under their control, just like you are."

Tom's lips part. "How do you know this?"

I blurt out everything; about finding Fred Buckley in the opium den, and all he told me about the troopers' racket. I see Tom's jaw tighten. See the look of faint disbelief in his eyes.

"The man who was murdered last night…" he begins.

"I think was being coerced by the police, just like you and Buckley. He had his pack on his back. He was clearly trying to leave. To escape the troopers."

"Men leave this place all the time. He was probably leaving for other goldfields—"

"So late at night?" I demand.

Tom falls silent. "Men like me and Buckley," he says finally, "we're just penniless diggers. Why would the troopers go to such lengths to stop us from leaving?"

"You said yourself – you're valuable to them. You know what's happening on the diggings. You know who's out guarding their claims. Besides," I swallow hard, "you know the police here are corrupt. They're not just going to let you walk away. Who knows who you might tell?"

I think about the officer at Clara's shop who knew my name. Did he know me because I'm Tom's wife? Is that why Stone recognised me so easily when I was playing the ghost? Have they been watching us? My stomach rolls at the thought.

"We have to assume the police know Stone is coercing you," I say. "And Stone knew you found gold today. So we have to assume the other troopers know that too."

"And you think they'll know I'm planning to escape tonight?"

"Maybe. I don't think it's a risk we can take."

Tom closes his eyes for a moment. His jaw ticks, shoulders rigid with tension. He puts his hands behind his head and begins to pace across the yard. Kicks at a log that's rolled loose from the woodpile and curses under his breath. "You ought to have gone with him. Browning. You ought to have taken what he was offering you."

His words strike me. "No." I see that more clearly than I ever have. That life of theatre and breakfast rooms and roast pigeon on gold-rimmed plates, that is not what I want. I want to escape in the night with my criminal of a husband. "No. I love you."

I stand on tiptoe and reach my arms around his neck. He holds me at the waist and presses his head to my shoulder. "Neither of us have done very well, have we."

I allow myself the briefest laugh. "No." My words are muffled by his hair. "We've not done very well at all."

Fists pound the front door, making me swallow down my smile. My chest tightens.

Tom takes the revolver from his pocket and strides into the house. Men's voices are flooding in through the broken window. Too angry, too jumbled to make out their words. But their meaning is all too clear. They want the Green Lady punished.

"Get the hell away from my house," Tom bellows through the locked door.

I fumble in the darkness for the matchbox, broken glass crunching under my boots. "The window." The words escape on my breath. The men outside have found the broken pane. One of them leaps up, cat-like, his boots crunching against the window frame. Tom shoves him backwards. Fires a warning shot over the man's shoulder.

I drop the matchbox and push in front of Tom. "I'm sorry," I plead. "I never meant to do anyone harm." My stomach rolls at the size of the crowd. The handful of men who came after me at the theatre has become a heaving throng of faces; some laughing, some jeering, some flashing with anger like the man trying to climb through the window.

The son of the woman I frightened in the alley.

He gives a cold laugh. "Sorry?" He looks between the other men. "She's sorry, she says."

"Let me see your mother," I say, desperate. Desperate for him to leave, to take this crowd with him, to get the hell away from our window before Tom puts a bullet in his chest.

"You ain't getting nowhere near my mother," the man snaps. "But I'm sure the rest of town would enjoy a public shaming. They do like a spectacle."

What his shaming will entail, I can't imagine. But I see that, if the town's eyes are on me – if the *troopers'* eyes are on me – perhaps they will not be on my husband. Perhaps he can escape. Perhaps—

Tom scoops me into him with one steely arm, the revolver pointed between the man's eyes. "Leave," he says firmly.

"You can get away," I argue. "The troopers—"

"Don't be mad." His voice leaves no room for argument.

But I say, "I deserve it, Tom. All of it."

"You can't go out there." His voice is low. "You can't let anyone see you. Especially not the troopers. If Stone told them you struck him…"

He doesn't need to finish. The cells or the hangman. Then the town will really have their spectacle.

Tom's arm tightens around me for a moment, then he turns to the mob. "Get the hell out of here." He gestures with the revolver. "Believe me, I've nothing to lose by using this." I hear his voice strain on the last words. And I look up to catch a glimpse of dark blue uniforms through the broken glass.

Police.

Are they here to prevent Tom from leaving? Or to punish me for my attack on Constable Stone? Either way, it doesn't matter. We can't let them find us.

Tom and I rush through the back door. I hear broken glass crunch as the men from the theatre haul themselves through the window, but I don't turn to look. We scramble for the fence, trampling the vegetable plot beneath our feet.

I hear the troopers calling Tom's name. And we run.

CHAPTER TWENTY-FOUR

We are in a back alley, another alley, and then out onto
the main street. I stop running, knowing it will draw attention.
Head down, my hand gripping Tom's, we walk; past the
dispensary, past the bank. Directionless, but too afraid to stop
moving. At any moment we could turn a corner and find one
of the troopers, or one of the men from the theatre.

Instinctively, wordlessly, we find the darkest, least-
inhabited streets and alleys. I'm walking the same route I took
when I played the ghost.

We pass the road that leads out of town to the north. The
urge to take it, to leave Castlemaine behind us, is almost
overwhelming. But the troopers were waiting for Buckley on
the road out of town. They were waiting for the man who was
killed yesterday. And if they've heard about Tom's success in
the claim today, there is every chance they'll be waiting for
him too.

"We'll go out to the diggings," Tom says, his voice close
to my ear. "Hide ourselves in the bush outside the claims."

I think of that dark mile of road that leads to Forest Creek, lonely at this time of night. I'm afraid to walk it with so many people after us. But stay in Castlemaine and we're rats in a trap.

Tom puts a hand to my shoulder, ushering me back down the street we've just come from. We'll make our way to the edge of town, and out towards the diggings.

As we reach the end of the street, I see them, flashes of blue – two troopers striding in our direction. Instinctively, I run. Run with no thought of where I'm going. And it's not until I pass the boarding house that I realise Tom is no longer behind me.

I whirl around, panicked. Hiss his name. There are men behind me now, a dark shadow of uncountable bodies. The old woman's son is at the front of the throng. He and another man grab me; one at each of my arms.

They drag me back towards town and I swallow my screams. Fight my urge to call for Tom. I can't draw attention. Not to him. And not to myself. I can't let the troopers find us.

The men drag me into Murphy's Hotel. I glimpse the alley where the Green Lady was first sighted, sparking Will to write his play. And I think fleetingly of the men gathering there the night of the ball, seeing a ghost in the fluttering curtains.

Murphy's is crowded. Men shove up against the bar, their drunken voices a tangle of sound. The air is thick with pipe smoke, the floorboards strewn with earth.

"Here she is," shouts the man, his grip vice-like on my arm. "Your Green Lady."

At once, all eyes are on me. I scan the crowd, desperate

for an ally.

A barrage of voices is at me, words I can barely make out. Some are angry, some are wild. Other men just laugh, enjoying this spectacle of the Green Lady's demise.

My captor uses his foot to drag a stool towards him. "Stand up here," he hisses. "Let them see you."

"I'm sorry. No. Please." But there's little I can do as they lift me onto the stool. The wound in my hip groans in protest.

"You're soft in the head, Lucy Earnshaw," shouts one man, and I think he may be right.

From high on the stool, I see Clara slipping into the tavern. At the sight of me, trapped in the jeering crowd, her mouth opens in horror. She tries to push her way towards me, but the men shove her back violently. I see an older man shout at her with venom in his eyes, but his words are lost beneath the noise of a crowd turning wild. She mouths something to me, something I can't make out, then she darts back out the door again, leaving me alone with the mob.

She will get help, I tell myself, but the thought brings me little peace. Because if she brings help, it will be in the form of the troopers, and I'll be thrown in the cells for my assault on Constable Stone.

I see sudden movement in the corner of my eye and I pitch forward as something strikes me above the ear. Glass explodes against the wall, and in the same second, I feel the burn of it. One of the men catches me before I tumble off the stool. I feel a thin trail of blood run down my cheek.

"That's enough, Bobby," I hear someone call across the tavern. "You've had your fun. Let her go."

The man, Bobby, snorts, and shoves me off the stool. I pitch forward onto my knees, pain rattling through me.

Hands pull at my hair, yanking my head back. Drinks are poured over me, soaking my clothes and hair. I feel thrown objects strike me, unseen as I cover my head to shield myself. I let out a cry as someone kicks at my arms.

I'm an outlet for them, I realise suddenly. Their despair, their exhaustion, their frustration; each of these men is like my husband – so desperate for the earth to give up that treasure that might change their lives. And just like Tom, none of them have found it. Instead, they've been stolen from, been betrayed by their troopers and been haunted by a woman who had nowhere else to stow her grief. In a twisted way, as my heart hammers with fear, I understand their anger. This is not rage at me. It's rage at this brutal, blazing life they chose because they thought it would lead to happiness. It's rage at their empty claims and their aching bodies and their children buried on Pennyweight Flat. I'm just a place to put that anger. And this childish game I played, in an attempt to escape it all; I see now that perhaps I might just die for it.

I smell the smoke first. Acrid and tarnished, wafting under the doors of the tavern.

Is my frightened mind just imagining it?

No, because now people are starting to talk. Starting to flood to the windows. Starting to grow bored of me.

I stay for a moment on my hands and knees. Unplaceable pain pulses through my body and sounds are distorted in my ears. Can I make it to the door without anyone noticing? Doubtful.

But then someone is pulling me to my feet.

"This way," Clara says, dragging me with her as she races for the door. Her presence bolsters my courage, and I rush out of the tavern on shaky legs.

Outside, the air is thick and smoky. I rub my stinging eyes and feel the blood smear along my cheek.

"A fire…" I begin.

"Yes," says Clara. "I know."

And I see it then. See, through the curtain of smoke, that it's Clara's shop the flames are pouring out of.

I can't hold back a shout of despair. Of wild, consuming anger. "The bastards!" I cry. "Who…? What happened?"

"It doesn't matter. Those dogs in the tavern are distracted now. You're safe."

And the possibility swings at me. I snatch her arm, wide-eyed, hoping desperately that I'm wrong.

Those dogs in the tavern are distracted now.

This fire in her shop; it was all her doing. And she has done it for me.

A spectacle of her own creation.

"Clara, no. How could you?"

"You were in danger, Lucy. Who knows how far those men were going to go?"

"The shop was your dream."

"The shop was a target," she says bitterly. "If I'm going to make something of myself, I need to go somewhere no one knows my past. Somewhere no one knows the things I had to do to get here." She stares ahead, the firelight making her dark eyes glitter. I feel the heat against my cheek. "It's no stretch to believe someone would want to burn this place to the ground. I'll collect the insurance money and try again in Melbourne. Somewhere I won't draw quite so much attention."

I don't speak, because what can be said? It's far too late to change her mind.

The doors to Murphy's Hotel have been thrown open, and people are spilling into the street, most with glasses still in hand. Horses are rattling down the road, pulling the fire pump behind them. A group of children runs excitedly beside the cart.

Clara gives my wrist a squeeze. "Go back to your cottage. Hide yourself away for a while. The mob will forget about you soon enough."

But of course, I can't go back. Can't hide away. I need to find Tom. And somehow, we need to leave Castlemaine.

There they are in their neat blue uniforms; the town's troopers, some marching towards the burning building, others working the fire pump. And I see that Clara has done more than distract the men from their ghost hunt. She has also drawn the attention of the police. Perhaps the roads out of town are not being guarded tonight.

Clara watches as a mannequin in the window is swallowed by flames. A roar comes from the front of the shop sending sparks shooting above the roof line. In the copper light of the fire, I see a tear slide down her cheek. She pushes it away quickly.

"Well," she says, too brightly, "now I've just to convince them I'm heartbroken about my loss. It's a good thing I'm a fine actress." We both pretend there is no waver in her voice.

I enfold her hand in mine. "I have to leave Castlemaine," I tell her. "Tonight."

"What? Why? Because of Will? And Tom?"

"No." Tom will be waiting for me at the diggings, I tell myself. Waiting by the claim for me to find him. And then we'll disappear into the bush like we planned. And maybe, with the troopers gathered at the fire pump, maybe we'll have a chance to escape. "Best you don't know the reason," I tell Clara, thinking of Fred Buckley's warning.

I pull her into my arms. Hold her tightly. Hope I convey the ocean of gratitude I feel towards her. I take a step back, meeting her eyes. I have no thought of whether I will see her again. No thought of what shape my life will take once I run towards the diggings. But the life Tom and I have made here needs to be destroyed.

"Be safe," says Clara. And away I rush, into the dark, sweaty and smoke-stained and bleeding.

CHAPTER TWENTY-FIVE

Tom is not at the claim.

I should have known he wouldn't be here; if Stone were to come searching for him, this is one of the first places he would look.

I stand for a moment beside the shaft, staring down into the inky earth. I imagine Tom pulling a nugget from the mud, imagine it glittering within the cradle.

Not far away, the night is lit with campfires, and the laughter of the men around them feels strangely calming after the chaos in town. I can still see the silver column of smoke rising from Clara's shop.

In spite of the heat, the sight of it chills me. Makes me desperate to find Tom, and to leave these diggings behind. When I leave this place, it will be for the unknown. But that doesn't make me want to stay.

I start to walk, ignoring the groans and aches of my battered body. I feel, instinctively, that I know where to find my husband.

The cemetery is almost lightless. A thin moonglow struggles through the trees, catching the motionless stares of the wooden dolls guarding the graves. I shiver in the silence. I have never been here at night before.

But I am not alone. Tom is crouched beside that tiny, unmarked circle of stones I have come to know all too well. His eyes are cast downward, but he has a distant look about him. I can't tell if his thoughts are in the present or the past.

For a moment, I just stand there and watch him. A ghost in the moonlight. But as I shift my weight, the ground beneath me crackles, and he turns. Rushes towards me.

"Where have you been? I thought you ran ahead, and when you weren't at the house, I thought maybe you might come here—" He stops, eyes pulling towards the dried blood on my cheek. At the liquor-scented hair clumped against my neck. "You've been hurt."

I shake my head. "It's nothing." What happened to me doesn't matter. Not anymore. "The troopers. They're in town. A fire…" I can't bring myself to say more. Clara's sacrifice stings too much.

"All of them?" Tom asks.

"I don't know. But we have to take a chance. If we keep away from the roads…" The journey ahead is overwhelming. A night of picking our way through the darkness, hoping we remain unseen.

Tom puts his hands to my shoulders, follows their curves with his fingers. "When the sun comes up, we'll find the Melbourne road. It's always busy. Someone will take us into town."

The confidence in his voice, whether forced or not, goes some way to easing my fears.

"And then?" I ask.

"And then, whatever we want, Luce."

I don't let that future take shape in my mind. Not yet. When we're out of this settlement, when the buildings of Melbourne are cutting the sky, then I'll let myself think of what might come next. Right now, it feels too far away.

I take Tom's hand, and in our clumsy, wordless way, we walk back to Elsie's grave. I kneel beside it and run a hand over the smooth, weather-worn stones. Tom crouches beside me.

"When was the last time you were here?" I ask.

"I don't come here," he says. "Ever. Not since I stopped coming with you." He clears his throat. "I don't think of her as being here. I can't. It's not how I want to remember her."

I wrap both my arms around one of his and rest my cheek against his broad shoulder.

I don't want to think of Elsie as being here either, not anymore. We are to leave this place forever, and I need to believe we will carry our daughter with us.

As I kneel there pressed against Tom, I wonder what Elsie would think of us; her foolish, flawed parents. Neither of us have handled our grief with grace, but perhaps if we learn to lean on each other, we might find our way back to decency.

Just as I must believe we can make it through that dark forest and emerge onto the Melbourne road at dawn, I must believe we can forgive and move forward.

"Are we terrible people?" I ask.

"Yes," says Tom. "The most dreadful. The very worst." But there's a smile on his lips and light in his eyes. I kiss my fingers and touch Elsie's grave. Tears blur my vision, but they're not entirely tears of grief. There's hope in there too, and things I can't quite find a name for. And then we stand together and walk into the dark, in the hope it might lead us to a place far less haunted.

HISTORICAL NOTE

The legend of Springheeled Jack entered English folklore in the 1830s. According to stories, he was a terrifying entity with clawed hands and glowing eyes, and the ability to leap to enormous heights. Sightings of the creature, which were later proven to be the work of ghost hoaxers, were recorded across London, the Midlands, and as far north as Scotland. Springheeled Jack featured in several Penny Dreadful stories (also known as Penny Bloods) from the mid-19th century onwards.

But it took some time for the practice of ghost hoaxing to reach the Australian colonies. "Playing the ghost" became popular on the goldfields of Victoria from the late 1860s, and continued into the early 20th century. As it was important for the story that playing the ghost was as yet a little-known pastime, Lucy and co – ghost-hoaxing in Castlemaine of 1857 – are somewhat ahead of their time.

The goldfields, thanks to its vast mix of cultures and superstitions – and the extraordinarily high death rate – provided a fertile breeding ground for belief in the supernatural. The spiritualism movement gained momentum across the colony, while ghost hoaxing was hugely popular in the "golden triangle" of Ballarat, Bendigo and Castlemaine. As the years progressed, ghost hoaxers would dress themselves in increasingly elaborate costumes, often involving highly toxic phosphorescent paint. While some hoaxers simply slipped away unpunished, others faced fines, jail time, or beatings at the hands of the public. A number of ghost hoaxers were even sent into the care of the nearby Ararat Lunatic Asylum.

Theatre was another important part of life on the diggings, with few acts more memorable than Lola Montez's Spider Dance, performed across the goldfields of both California and Victoria. Appearing on stage in risqué knee-length skirts, Lola's act involved repeatedly touching her legs as though trying to get a spider out from within her skirts – incensing half the audience and enchanting the other. Today, theatres still stand on the sites of both Astley's Amphitheatre in Melbourne and Castlemaine's Theatre Royal, although there is little remaining of either original building. Astley's Amphitheatre was rebuilt in 1886 as the iconic Princess Theatre – and is now home to one of Australia's most enduring ghost stories…

ABOUT THE AUTHOR

Johanna Craven is an Australian-born author, composer, pianist and terrible folk fiddler. She currently divides her time between London and Melbourne. Her more questionable hobbies include ghost hunting, meditative dance and pretending to be a competitor on *The Amazing Race* when travelling abroad.

Find out more at www.johannacraven.com